— REPENTANCES —

REPENTANCES

Annette Meyers

Five Star • Waterville, Maine

First Edition
First Printing: March 2004

Published in 2004 in conjunction with
Tekno Books and Ed Gorman.

Set in 11 pt. Plantin

Printed in the United States on permanent paper.

Library of Congress Cataloging-in-Publication Data

Meyers, Annette.
    Repentances / Annette Meyers.—1st ed.
      p. cm.
    ISBN 1-4104-0187-1 (hc : alk. paper)
    1. Refugees, Jewish—Fiction.   2. New York (N.Y.)—
Fiction.   3. Jewish families—Fiction.   I. Title.
PS3563.E889R46 2004
  813'.54—dc22   2004041150

For Rita

— Acknowledgements —

For graciously letting me pick their brains,
I thank former curator John Podracky,
and former assistant curator, Dominick Palermo,
New York City Police Museum.
And Carol Bushell,
retired Associate Director of Alumni, Cooper Union.
And Marcia Lesser,
psychotherapist and friend.

Special thanks to my friends
Sandra Scoppettone and Camilla Trinchieri
for their editorial input and encouragement.

And to Marty
whose enthusiasm and love keep
me writing.

— Author's Note —

As an oil painting ages, its paint may become increasingly transparent, and sometimes the ghost of another painting or drawing that was painted over will reappear. When these occur, they are called "repentances," an English translation of the Italian "pentimento."

— 1 —

New York—1936

Zweikel

Everyone hangs out at Auster's on Second Avenue. Zweikel is no exception. The candy store is a good place to do business. Like a bookie, which he isn't, he doesn't have an office. Nevertheless, he is treated with respect because he provides a service. And his wife, Stella the Gentile, has a good job as a nurse in the Willard Parker Hospital on Sixteenth Street. Zweikel's poor mama, of blessed memory, would have died a thousand deaths if she'd known about Stella, but she would have been proud of her son's success in his own business.

For a fee, Zweikel arranges to bring families over from the old country. Lately, thanks to the turmoil in Europe, business is so good he buys Stella a real pearl necklace with a diamond clasp, and for himself, a large diamond tie pin, which he is fond of stroking.

He learned the law business from Ikey Zimmerman, a distant cousin who took pity on Zweikel's widowed mother and gave Zweikel a job, mostly delivering documents to Immigration and picking up steamship tickets. A sideline was looking for clients. For each one he found, he received a bonus of twenty-five dollars. Zweikel was particularly adept at this because he was small, slight, unobtrusive, and poorly dressed. His shoes were down at the heels. But he paid attention.

Zimmerman rented a tiny space in Weiss's drugstore near the telephone for five dollars a month. He conducted business from an old card table on which a small, hand-lettered sign said: Immigration Services. I. Zimmerman, Attorney.

You could say that Zweikel caught the business as you would a cold because after Zimmerman died, Zweikel painted out Zimmerman's name on the sign, sat down at the flimsy card table, and became M. Zweikel, Attorney.

Like a butterfly from a runty caterpillar, Zweikel, the attorney, blossoms. He's turned into a natty dresser. Always a jacket, a nice starched shirt, a silk tie, shoes polished, a clean handkerchief in his pocket. He smokes the best cigars and tips generously.

The Depression has hurt his business a little, only because he had to lower his prices, and so now he is offering a discount on more than two children.

Take the case of the Ebanholz woman and the child. He'd offered an extra discount for the two. One thousand total, plus passage. Half now, half when they were on the ship. He has all but the last five hundred dollars in his pocket, and Ebanholz is to give Stella the final payment today. The ship left from Bremerhaven yesterday.

He'll be glad to see the last of Nathan Ebanholz. Stella has a fever for him. Not that it hasn't happened before. But this time, although Zweikel is neither particularly intelligent or even sly, he senses it is different. She works with Ebanholz at the hospital. Zweikel is sure he's shtupping her, and this Ebanholz, what is he? Nothing but a poor slob. Not like Zweikel with a successful business. Of course, Zweikel is barely five feet even with his hat on, and Ebanholz is as big and as broad as a Cossack.

Auster puts another egg cream in front of him, wipes up

the pale chocolate puddle, and takes away the empty glass.

Zweikel knows Stella has other men. She is a lot of woman. Over a head taller than he, she wears her blond hair braided around her head like a crown. On top of this she pins her real crown, a high white-pleated cap. She has no hips or ass at all, but high round breasts with huge nipples that push against the fabric of her white uniform, luring men like flies to honey.

She's been married before, or so she says. There is a child, a girl, whom she boards out with a Polish couple who have six of their own.

Yes, she attracts men. They take one look at those nipples pressing on the fabric and they can't keep away. But Stella likes, as she always tells him, only circumcised men, which means Jews. His cigar has gone out.

"Zweikel! There he is. Zweikel!" Yankel Berman is jumping like a jumping jack near the door, trying to get Zweikel's attention.

Soon Berman is pushing his way through the crowd of people, towing behind him a confused-looking young man in a yarmulke and ill-fitting clothing.

Business, Zweikel thinks.

"Zweikel!" Pointing Zweikel out to the young man in the yarmulke, he says, "Jakey, this is a great man, let me tell you."

Yankel Berman is a fat baker, with three chins. He sweats even in the winter. He's dripping with it now and Zweikel wonders if he sweats into the bread.

"This is my cousin, Jakey Schimm from Brooklyn," Berman says. "He's got a job for you. He wants you should bring over his wife and five children."

Zweikel cocks his head. Brooklyn. A wife, five children. He smacks his lips and orders another egg cream. And

11

feeling generous of spirit, he treats Berman and his cousin to their own.

"Zweikel knows everything, let me tell you," Berman says, snuffling his egg cream. "He brought over Sarah and her mother, may she move in with her son in Chicago, last year. Listen, Zweikel. Tell him, Jakey."

Jakey opens his mouth to speak, but nothing comes out. He is a man of small stature, not much taller than Zweikel himself, pale, with skin so thin you can see the little blue veins in his cheeks.

"So tell me, Jakey." Zweikel is inspecting Schimm's overcoat. Good quality. "Your family is presently in Lublin?" Zweikel prompts. Lublin is where Berman comes from. He drops the dead cigar in the empty egg cream glass.

"Jakey has a little trouble with his English, but he can stitch a seam you wouldn't believe. They come from all over for him to tailor."

Zweikel congratulates himself. He takes a stub of a pencil and a small pad from his pocket. He touches the blunt point of the pencil to his tongue, then poises over the pad. "So, where in Lublin?"

"N-n-n-no, n-n-n-no." Schimm is a stutterer.

"So then where?"

"N-n-n-near B-B-B-Brzesco."

"I'm telling you," Berman says, clapping his cousin on the back, "Zweikel is a magician. He can do anything. He's the best."

"A wife, five children. How old?"

"T-t-t-twenty-s-s-s-seven."

"Not the wife, the children."

Berman looks embarrassed. He smiles apologetically. "He's nervous. Don't be nervous, Jakey."

"What does he got to be nervous about?" Zweikel says,

but he is proud that people are nervous in front of him. It shows respect. After all, he doesn't take just anybody as a client, although Stella doesn't understand why not. He draws the line on Communists. And anarchists. That is it. They are too hard to get through Immigration. Anarchists are crazy. You never know what they'll do. And the Communists talk too much. They can talk your ear off about workers' rights.

"F-f-four, f-f-five, s-s-s-six, s-s-s-seven." Schimm's eyes are moist behind his glasses.

"That's four only."

"Twins, he's got," Berman says, tweaking his cousin's cheek. "I'm telling you . . ."

"Healthy?"

"Of course, healthy. What then?" Berman has taken over, having obviously lost his patience.

"Two thousand five hundred it'll have to be. Fifteen hundred in cash after we shake on it."

"Don't worry, Zweikel, he can pay."

"Give me the address, why don't you?" Zweikel growls. He could have charged more. He sees that. "And the names. If you want, I should get things started. It's not so good in Europe right now."

"Y-y-yes, y-y-y-yes." The cousin's head is bobbing up and down like he's davening or something.

"It's terrible these days," Berman says. "Only last week in Brzesco, near where Jakey's wife and children are, the anti-Semites set fire to a house and burned up an old lady, a woman, and a child."

"I need a deposit of five hundred from you," Zweikel says. His fingers are itching. "What's the address?"

"Gimme da pencil, Zweikel. Jakey will write it for you. It's easier."

Zweikel hands over the pencil. "Okay already."

"So, Berman, how is the bread business?" Bookie Sam Meltzer comes over to talk while Schimm writes, painstakingly shaping each letter, his nose grazing the pad.

"Come on, come on, Jakey. You don't have to make a Rembrandt. Here." Berman snatches the pencil and pad from his cousin and hands it to Zweikel. "Give him the money, Jakey."

Jakey reaches into his coat, unbuttons his shirt, pulls a string, and up comes a small pouch. Hunching in on himself, he counts off five hundred dollars in wrinkled fifties as Bookie Sam, Zweikel, and Berman watch. Impatient, Berman pulls the bills from Jakey's hand and pushes them at Zweikel. "Here, Zweikel, get started."

Zweikel counts the money, lining up the heads one on top of the other. He folds the wad once and puts it in his pocket. "So now we're in business." He looks down at the names and the address on the pad. Gut, Zakliczyn. It's the exact same place that Ebanholz comes from. Near Brzesco. From where Zweikel's bringing over Ebanholz's wife and child. A chill comes over him.

"So, okay?" Berman says.

"So, okay." Zweikel clears his throat. "So, Schimm, maybe you know a distant relative of mine from Zakliczyn, near Brzesco?"

"M-m-maybe."

"By the name of Ebanholz."

Schimm's already pale skin turns pasty. "You-you n-n-know him?"

Zweikel pats the pocket where he put the fifties. "A distant relative. I lost touch. What about it?"

"It's a tragedy, let me tell you," Berman says. "This Ebanholz doesn't even know yet about his family because

14

no one knows where he is. Everything burned up in the house with them. Jakey put an advertisement in the *Forwards* today."

"N-N-Nat-t-than E-E-Ebanholz."

If Zweikel had been alone, he would have torn his hair from his head, which is a good thing because his hair is already thinning. He waits for them to leave, then he pays for the egg creams and threads his way out of the candy store. He needs something a whole lot stronger than an egg cream.

— 2 —

Zweikel

Zweikel walks west to Houston where he finds a wop tavern. Dark and dirty. No one knows him here. He drinks his whisky straight down and orders another. The whisky goes right to his head.

"Burned up. Ei, ei. A tragedy." And on the day he is to get the final payment. "Nothing but ashes." Zweikel doesn't know he's mumbling.

The man on the next stool is talking guinea to him, telling him a long story. Zweikel keeps nodding, understanding maybe a word here, a word there. He can handle Eytalians but not Irish. Finally, Zweikel shakes hands with the man, pays for the whiskys, and leaves the tavern.

It is bitter cold and the wind cuts through him. He holds tight to his hat as he makes his way home. He has to talk to Stella. Ebanholz's money is theirs. It's only right. They shouldn't have to give it back just because the woman got herself and the kid killed. It isn't Zweikel's fault.

He groans, struggling with the wind. Ei, so now he's thinking like Stella. It's not good. He has competitors. It will get out that Zweikel's cheated Ebanholz and no one will use his services ever again.

Zweikel stops to let the traffic pass. Ebanholz is coming to the house with the final payment. Taking out his gold pocket watch, Zweikel stares at the time. Stella will be getting ready to go to work. She likes working the night shift, she says. He begins to walk faster. Maybe he can catch Ebanholz before he goes upstairs. He'll take him for a drink, like a friend. Put his arm around him, break the news. And then tell him he doesn't have to pay the final five hundred dollars. Of course, what he's already paid in, Zweikel will keep, for he's acted in good faith.

Sweating, but lightheaded, Zweikel walks up Second Avenue to Fifth Street, where he and Stella have two small rooms and a kitchen on the third floor of a tenement building in better shape than most because the Polack who owns it lives in the ground floor apartment.

He waits for a short time in the vestibule, hoping to see Ebanholz, but something stirs in him and he becomes impatient. He longs to plunge his face into those huge-nippled breasts. There is time for him to have her before she goes to work. She will never refuse him. Forgetting entirely about Ebanholz, he starts up the stairs. Their neighbors are all Polacks and the building reeks of cabbage. When he gets to the third floor, he can hear Stella singing with the Victrola music. It's "Remember," one of Berlin's songs. "Jews make nice music," she always says.

But he sees at once he is too late. Stella is in the bathroom, running the water and singing, and five crisp hundred-dollar bills are lying under the sugar bowl on the kitchen table. An ashtray full of cigarette butts is nearby.

"Is that you, Marvin?" She always calls him Marvin. She doesn't like the Jew names, she says.

"Yes." He hangs up his coat in the narrow closet near the door. In the bedroom, he can see from here the bed is rumpled, the blanket on the floor. Cigarettes and semen are the pervasive odors. Stella's white uniform, freshly laundered, waits on a hanger hooked to the top of the bedroom door.

"I see Ebanholz has been here," he says, over the sound

of running water and the Victrola.

The water sound stops, but she chooses not to notice his sarcasm, or maybe he hasn't made it sharp enough. She comes out of the bathroom totally naked, brushing by him in the bedroom door.

"Not now, Marvin," she says in response to the quick grab he makes, his face glancing the soft pillows of her breasts. She pushes him away and sits on the edge of the bed, and begins slowly rolling on her white lisle stockings, to just above the knee. She fastens them with the elastic. Then the fancy white silk bloomers he bought for her on Orchard Street last week. It's like the strip tease only the other way. She takes no notice of his erection.

Slipping the white uniform over her head, she buttons her nipples away from him. She never wears brassieres like other women. And she never starches her uniforms.

Zweikel sighs. He sits down at the kitchen table and puts his head in his hands. "Ebanholz's wife and kid are dead."

She stops in the bedroom doorway, hands on her hips. "So?"

He looks up at her. "What do you mean, 'So?' You knew already?"

"There was a notice in the *News*. I called the number." She sits across from him and slides her feet into the white shoes and waits. He gets on his knees and laces them for her. It is one of their rituals. Then he kisses her ankles, working up her shins. She pushes him away with her free foot and he falls backward, on his ass.

He scrambles to his knees. "You knew already and you didn't tell me?"

"I only found out yesterday."

"But the five hundred dollars. You didn't tell him?"

"Why should I tell him? He'll know soon enough."

"We can't keep his money. They died two weeks ago, maybe more. We'll have to give him back the final payment."

"We'll do no such thing. We give nothing back. We acted in good faith. They didn't." She gets to her feet and wraps her head in a scarf, puts on her coat.

"But they are dead."

"I am not interested in hard luck stories."

"But my reputation. No one will trust me if word gets around what happened." He's forgotten he's still on his knees.

She opens the door and turns back to him. "War is coming. You will be needed regardless. The money is ours."

— 3 —

Nathan

Nathan Ebanholz has a good job, but he works the evening shift, and when he finishes sometimes he has too much energy to go home. He knows he won't sleep. At these times he takes the subway to Brighton Beach and walks. Walks the boardwalk, takes off his shoes and socks and rolls up his pants, maybe, and walks, squeezing the sand through his toes. He walks to the edge of the water and talks to Miri and the child across the ocean. As if they can hear him.

Now Miri and Rayzela are on this very same ocean on their way to him. They'll be here soon.

Today it is cold and the early light is corrupted by black-edged clouds. A storm is coming and Nathan hopes it won't come anywhere near the ship that is bringing his family to him.

A sharp wind blusters in off the ocean, chopping white breakers. The sand is gray, starved for the sun. His foot touches something half-buried in the sand. A Coke bottle. He digs it out and pitches it spinning into the churning surf.

He is half a man without Miri. And the child. He has never seen her, except in the snapshot Miri sent him last year. Ah, he has not always been such a lucky man.

Only four years earlier, while Nathan was at the university in Lodz, studying medicine, Miri got pregnant and he ran out of money. Everything happened at once. At the university they tell him there are already too many Jew doctors and they give his place to a fine Polish Catholic.

Miri and he make a plan. Miri will stay in Zakliczyn. She has an elderly aunt in Brzesco who will take her in after the baby is born. Nathan will go to America where his older sister Anna lives in Brooklyn. He'll stay with Anna and work to bring Miri and the baby over. After all, Nathan has an education and it will be respected in America.

Or so he had thought.

But by the time Nathan arrives in New York, Anna has taken a job as a housekeeper in New Jersey, and has moved away, and there is little work to be had because times are bad and his English isn't good enough. He's been fortunate to get a job as an orderly on the night shift at the Willard Parker Hospital.

It's here he meets Stella.

Even now, in this cold, he feels his sex stir and swell. Stella has that effect on him.

The first night he is at the hospital she finds him stacking the clean linen and rubs herself against him. Smelling of summer and lilacs, she whispers to him unmentionable things in Polish. He's been in America six months without a woman.

Stella closes the door to the linen closet and unbuttons her uniform, releasing breasts that are almost all nipple. They do it there, standing up, then on the floor. She puts her mouth on him and he is lost, enslaved.

Only short, despairing spells of guilt make him try to stop, which just serves to enrage her, and she punishes him with work until he's ready to drop. He knows she is Jezebel and can get him fired, if she wants. And Nathan needs the job, the money. And Stella. His need for her is an obsession. As a fever, it will run its course, and when he has enough money, Miri will come with the child. He can think of little else.

Stella makes demands of him. Jewish men, she says, are her addiction. She takes particular pleasure in doing it in her husband's bed. Zweikel, she calls him, always by his last name.

"Zweikel is okay," she says. Naked, except for high heels, she models for Nathan the pearl necklace with the diamond clasp that Zweikel has given her. Back and forth she walks, nipples taunting him. She has a yellow thatch, and her thighs are full and dimpled. There are stretch marks across her belly.

He fucks her in her pearls and her high heels. It's what she wants. It's what he wants.

Afterward, he lies in Zweikel's bed, sated, and thinks about Miri. Each time he is with Stella he kills Miri a little. Tears burn his eyes. He dresses quickly. Stella watches him through slitted lids while she smokes her cigarette.

"So, you are determined to bring them over?"

She blows smoke rings through pursing lips. He can feel her lips on him. He closes his eyes and swallows hard.

"Zweikel can do it. That's what he does."

He stares at her. Is she playing her games with him? Why has she never told him this?

"You wait," she says. "Zweikel will be home soon."

Nathan is suspicious, but she seems to have taken pity on him. "Why didn't you tell me this before?"

She gets up and stands close to him. She is his height in her backless heels. "You can make your arrangements with Zweikel separately," she says. "And then there's my commission . . ." She lets the words settle on him. Her eyes are a sharp, brittle blue. The burning tip of the cigarette comes close to his beard. She inhales and releases the smoke through her nostrils. "Oh, yes," she says, "you and me, we have our understanding, don't we?"

He watches as she puts on her uniform, her nipples pressing against the white cloth. She rolls up her white stockings and fastens them with a band across her voluptuous thighs.

When Zweikel's key goes into the lock and the door opens, he finds Stella and Nathan Ebanholz having a glass of tea.

Nathan sees at once that Zweikel may be an ugly runt of a man, but he is no fool. Right away, Zweikel has sized up the situation.

"See, Zweikel, I'm wearing my pearls," Stella says. "They are good luck. Nathan wants you to bring over his family." She rises and gets a glass, heats the water, and pours it over the tea bag.

Zweikel hangs his coat from a hook and sits in her seat. He takes out his little notepad, touches pencil stub to tongue, and writes what Nathan tells him.

"It's as good as done, Ebanholz," he says. "Of course, that is after I get your deposit."

Stella brings his glass of tea, and he strokes her ass, letting his hand rest on one of the small flat mounds, all the time looking at Nathan as if to say, you may fuck her but she is mine.

"Come," Stella says. "We have to go to work."

Nathan watches Zweikel, who is slurping his tea noisily through a sugar cube locked between discolored teeth. "How much?"

"A bargain for sure . . . because you're a friend of Stella's." Zweikel finishes off his tea and takes out a cigar from his inside pocket, unwraps it, and bites off the end, spitting it into his tea glass.

Stella rolls her eyes at Nathan. "So, come on, Zweikel. Give him the price so we can go."

Paying no attention to her, Zweikel strikes a match and lights his cigar, drawing long breaths to get it started. The pungent smell of expensive tobacco fills the small room. Zweikel takes the cigar from his mouth. Through the smoke he says, "One thousand for two. My price is usually fifteen hundred, but I give you a break. Five hundred to get it started. Five hundred when I get the tickets and they're on the way. I guarantee nothing at Ellis if they're sick." He takes another puff on the cigar. "Are they consumptive? If they are, they'll never get through."

"They are healthy, thank God." Nathan rises. "It's a lot of money." If he gives Zweikel the money, he will have nothing left. But he has the job, and if he doesn't bring them over soon, Stella will drive him mad.

The rain comes, hurtling down on him, and he runs for the boardwalk. Under the moderately protective planks, he stands on one foot at a time, brushing off the sand as best he can, restoring socks and shoes.

On the train, which smells of salami and pickles, he dozes among people going to work in the sweatshops in lower Manhattan.

He feels himself a lucky man.

It is past nine when Nathan gets to the Bronx, to Crotona Park East, where he boards with Abe Kravitz and his wife and their four children. It is only three small rooms, but because Abe is a blocker of straw hats who works days, and the three older children are in school, Nathan can sleep in the crowded bedroom.

On Sunday, he sleeps, if he can with all the noise, on the sofa, which is too short for him and gives him a stitch in his back.

Already he's arranged for a place when Miri and Rayzela

arrive in two weeks. On the fifth floor an apartment in the same line as Kravitz is vacant.

Nathan climbs the three flights listening to the familiar sounds of children: laughing, whining, crying. Mamas yelling in Yiddish, Italian, broken English. The marble stairs are scooped where generations past have climbed as he does now.

Opening the door, Nathan smells coffee. Fannie Kravitz, in a blue cotton dress covered with tiny red and white flowers, is emptying coffee grounds into the sink, washing them down the drain. "Ah, Nathan," she says, then changing her voice, "Go away from there." She smacks a dish towel against the backside of the year-old boy who is probing in the garbage, a glint in his eye. The other three children, two more boys and a girl, are in school.

Nathan hangs his wet coat on the hook behind the kitchen door. "Is there coffee?"

"Of course there's coffee. I always have coffee for you."

Her cotton stockings are rolled around her thick ankles, her flesh spilling from stylish cut-out shoes too small for her peasant feet. "How about an egg maybe? Some toast?" She drops a pat of butter in the frying pan and strikes a match and lights the gas.

He sits down at the bruised porcelain-topped table. "Okay. Sure."

"Heshy, get outa there!" Fannie grabs the boy and plunks him down on the floor.

"No!" Heshy screams, purple like a beet. When his mouth opens again, Fannie thrusts a chunk of bagel into it. Distracted, Heshy's screams stop, temporarily replaced by sucking noises.

"Oh, I almost forgot," Fannie says, breaking an egg into the hot butter. She puts two pieces of bread into the toaster. "A letter came for you. From Brzesco, looks like. It's on the chifforobe in the bedroom."

Nathan goes to get the letter, noting his bed is ready for him. He turns the letter over and over in his hands as he comes back to the kitchen. He doesn't recognize the handwriting.

"Eat, Nathan, while it's hot." Fannie puts the fried egg and toast on a plate and sets it in front of him. She fills his cup with coffee and one for herself, dries her hands on her apron and sits with him as she always does.

He slices open the letter with a table knife, then butters his toast. He slips the sheer paper from the envelope. "It must be to say they are on their way."

The letter is in Yiddish from a Kalman Rabinowitz of Brzesco, who introduces himself as a distant cousin of Miri's great aunt.

Nathan reads the words twice, three times, over and over. "No, no."

"Nathan, what's the matter?" Her boarder's face is white like he's seen a ghost. To ward off evil, Fannie puts two fingers in front of her lips and blows on them three times.

"No." Nathan gets up, sits again, hard. He hits the side of his head with his hand. "No, no. It can't be."

"Nathan, tell me. What is it?"

"Nothing. It's nothing." He crumples the letter and throws it down, grabs his coat from the back of the door, shouts, "Lies!" The door slams behind him.

Heshy begins to howl.

Fannie is shaken. Nathan didn't even eat his breakfast. She hesitates only a brief moment, then smooths out the letter on the table. "Guttinhimmel." The letter says that Miriam and the child are dead, killed in a fire set by a gang of young Polacks.

— 4 —

Nathan

Nathan has never learned to hide his rage and now it shoots from him like quills from an angry porcupine. He walks. Day ends and people scurry homeward. Night rolls over him and he hardly notices.

Stella had known. She and that dwarf husband of hers. They had to have known. Yet they took his money and told him Miri and the child were on their way.

He crosses the street oblivious to the shrieking brakes and the shouting, "Wassamatta you crazy?"

The cold pinches his nose, the lobes of his ears.

Wassamatta you crazy? Yes. He leans against the lamp post. The circle of light on the sidewalk provides him a platform, and he howls, giving his anguish a voice.

"Mister, you sick or somethin'?" A tiny woman, hair hidden by a babushka, peers up at him with the face of his old grandma. Her accent is thick, but not Eastern European. Irish, maybe. "You got a hospital near here if you sick or somethin.' " She shifts her heavy bag to her other hand.

"No, no. S'all right, missus." He rubs his eyes with his fists, then looks around. He's in familiar territory. Second Avenue. "You want I should help you carry your bundle?"

She hesitates for only a moment. Grease stains through her brown paper bag. She holds the bag out to him.

Nathan looks down at her, but doesn't take the bag.

Instead, he picks up the old lady, package and all. "Where to, mamalla?"

Her initial open-mouthed surprise turns inside out and the old lady gives a girlish chortle. "Across Second. There." She is pointing to a tenement building on the corner, partially obscured by the elevated train platform.

A train screeches and rumbles above them, its light silhouetting the disembodied, bobbing heads of the night travelers. In less than a minute the train, with its flickering lights, is gone.

Nathan navigates the slippery, cobbled street with his giggling parcel and sets her down in front of her building.

"You're a good boy," the old lady says, patting his hand. "God will bless you."

That's right. God will bless him. Because it's a mistake. He is sure of it. Mistakes happen all the time. He feels in his pockets for the letter and then remembers he crumpled it and threw it down on the Kravitzes' table. It has to be a mistake. Otherwise, Stella would have told him yesterday when he brought the final payment. She would have known already if they were on the ship or not. The last remnant of his anger, already muted by his encounter with the old woman, is flushed away by the surge of hope.

Nathan adjusts his cap and walks down the hill to the hospital. It's his day off. She'll be surprised to see him. And he will have the truth from her. They're alive. He knows it. Wouldn't he know inside himself if they were dead?

The hospital rises in front of him like a forbidding fortress, its glazed lights trembling against the dark sky. Although the Willard Parker Hospital for Contagious Diseases is a children's hospital, meant to be a place of healing, the bars on the windows and the isolation rooms work to keep the children within fearful, and therefore, victims.

This is not medicine as he'd dreamed it.

He hears the shouting before he enters the lobby. A man's voice, loud. Drunk and abusive. Women's voices. Other men. A snarl of people, including nurses, orderlies, and blue uniforms. In the dimly lit lobby, Nathan sees two policemen trying to subdue a wild man. The fumes emanating from the man sear the eyes, the lining of the nose. Turpentine, yes. Turpentine and whisky.

The man is bearded, tall, but with not much flesh on him, and his clothes are paint-stained and crusted. With the strength of a demon, he throws the police aside, but, strangely, doesn't run, though he can. He stands his ground and shouts, "You have no right to keep me from her."

They are on him in a second as he screams, "I'm taking her outa here!"

"Be reasonable," a nurse says and is rewarded with a fierce blow to the jaw. She sails backward, crashes. An orderly drops to his knees to help her.

Nathan knows both the nurse and the orderly, as they'll know him, if they see him. He fades back, into the shadows. Better not to be part of this, he thinks.

"Come on, buddy. Let's go, let's go," one of the cops says in one-hundred-percent Irish. He has hold of the wild man's arm with the other cop taking the other arm. But the man's fists strike again, and this time he's answered with a sharp crack on the head from a nightstick.

No one takes notice of Nathan as he drifts past the fracas. At the foot of the stairs he finds a cap of faded blue wool, streaked with colored paint. His thoughts on Stella, and Miri, Nathan tucks the cap under his arm and climbs the stairs to the fourth floor, where Stella is head night nurse.

And all the time he can still hear the faint echo of voices

from below, and around him, the dull sounds children make when they're desperately ill. Muffled moans, mewling cries like lost kittens, gasps and choking from those who can't breathe.

He has never gotten used to it, never gotten used to children dying, so many of them alone. Tears stream into his beard. His child lives. He knows it. A father knows these things.

The fourth floor is quiet, the lights dimmed. He pushes open the swinging door marked CONTAGION: ONLY AUTHORIZED PERSONNEL, and walks to the nurses' station. The ward lies only a few feet farther down the corridor. There is no one around.

Nathan knows that behind the nurses' station is a small square room with a desk, a medical supply cabinet, and a narrow bed. He and Stella have used that bed well for the past three years. Now it's over. Miri will come with . . . He throws open the door.

She is asleep on the bed, her shoes sitting empty on the floor, her uniform unbuttoned. She lies on her back, mouth open. Her cap, which she has not bothered to remove, seems part of her blond coronet. A soft snore and a whistle breath come from her.

He stands looking down at her. She would never lie to him. He feels the heat of her. She's like ripe fruit. He squeezes her nipple and it grows hard. Waking, she murmurs to him, "Nathan. You couldn't stay away." She holds out her arms.

He unbuttons his pants and falls on her like a man possessed, knowing he's wrong. They will be here soon, though, and it will be different.

Afterward, he watches her accomplish the miracle of replacing her outer skin, becoming a nurse once more. She is smiling a satisfied smile and stretching like a cat. "We make music together," she says. She runs her hands over her breasts and down her thighs.

God help him, he feels himself stir. He wants her again. But he can't do this. She plays him like a fiddle. "Where are my wife and the child?"

Her eyes skid away from him. "On their way, of course."

"How do you know?" He comes close and takes her by the chin, forces her face to him.

"We know. Zweikel has his agents." She makes as if to straighten her cap, escaping his hands.

Then he knows she is lying. It comes to him like a thunderbolt from heaven. He grabs her shoulder and spins her around, catching the shard of fear in her eyes before her quick cover of a smile. "Bitch! You're lying to me. You knew all the time."

She tries to push him away, snapping at him, "We only just found out."

"You knew and you took my money." He lets go of her, horrified, his hands burning where they touched her. God is punishing him. Choking, he sinks down on the cot where he's just performed sacrilege over his dead wife and child, and hides his face in his hands.

"Nathan," she says. "Listen to me. This is the way the world is. You take what you can get. It's better they're gone. They would have held you back." She unbuttons her uniform, freeing her breasts. She peels his hands from his face and pulls him to her. "I'm glad they're dead. Now you're upset, but some day you'll understand—"

When he lifts his eyes, she is laughing, her mouth magnified a thousand times, the teeth as large as horse teeth. "Shut up! Shut up!" He jumps to his feet; his hands find her throat, squeezing, squeezing. Her eyes bulge and curdle;

her face turns blue. She sticks her tongue out at him and goes limp, pulling him down on her, his hands still on her throat.

He gets to his knees. Stella lies sprawled, grotesque in death, her white cap tilted rakishly over her forehead, her nipples stark, obscene, pointing at him. What has he done?

A strange, soft sigh behind him breaks into his fugue. He turns. In the doorway stands a child with a halo of white-gold hair. She is clutching the paint-stained cap and is beckoning to him.

— 5 —

Nathan

Dense curtains of rain turn the city into a gigantic waterfall, drenching streets, buildings, trees, and anyone unlucky enough to be outdoors. Then the faucet shuts off and sleet comes down like millions of sharp knives. Relentless, it drives the apple and the pencil vendors indoors, at least temporarily.

No one takes notice of the bearded man on the wooden bench who dozes, wakes with a start to check the schedule on the blackboard, dozes again. His possessions are lumped in a white laundry sack, which he holds in his arms as if it's a living creature, fondling it, murmuring to it. He looks like just another one of the slightly mad refugees New York is receiving, albeit with some reluctance.

"Treee-en-tonnn! Treee-en-tonnn train now receiving passengers at gate five. Gate five. Stopping at Newark—"

The bearded man stirs uneasily, as if forcing himself back from a peaceful place.

"Treee-en-tonnn! All aboard."

The man rises, fixes his sack over his shoulder with some care. Only Old Bob, the Negro handyman with his mop and bucket, who has stopped for a smoke, gives him a second look. And that, because for a moment Old Bob thinks he sees something move in the bag. He rubs his eyes, his field of vision limited by the beginnings of cataracts. The bearded man is gone before Old Bob looks again. Never mind, he says to himself. It isn't his business anyway. Oftentimes, folks take pets, cats and dogs, on the train with them. Or maybe it's just his old eyes. He parks his cigarette in the corner of his mouth, thrusts his mop into the pail, and pulls it through the ringer. He'd better get a move on before the daily traffic starts. The mop slaps against the floor, and Old Bob makes a wide, wet circle on the marble floor and begins to fill it in.

The train is cold and Nathan is alone in the car. He places his sack gently on one seat and sits down beside it. A smoldering heat like the aftermath of a fire radiates from the bag.

Miri is dead, but his baby is saved. He loosens the drawstring neck of the bag and rolls it back only until the child is revealed. The child's eyes are glazed with fever. Her platinum curls are matted, and she smells of vomit. She wears only a flimsy flannel gown.

Better to keep her in the sack, Nathan thinks. He shrugs out of his jacket and buttons it around the sack, holding her close. Never, never will he let her go again.

Fat mail bags and thick stacks of newspapers tied with twine are tossed on board. The train begins to move. They travel through a long tunnel into a bleak overcast dawn. Swampy brushland surrounds them until they pull into the Newark terminal. Here some of the mail bags are deposited, as well as bundles of newspapers. A number of riders board, men going to business and a woman with two little girls in fine velvet coats and hats.

"Papa?" The breath is like a feather on his beard. His bundle stiffens in his arms.

"Papa's here," he whispers in Yiddish, then in English.

Blue eyes stare up at him. He brushes wet strands of hair

from her forehead and kisses the fiery brow. "Papa loves you."

The child shudders a great sigh and snuggles against him.

Nathan is infused with a strange joy. The engine's thumping rhythm mixes with Rayzela's heartbeats and brings him peace.

He drifts back more than three years. He is traveling to Vienna again, watching as the Polish farms and countryside remain and he flies by toward his new life in America.

"Tickets, please. All tickets."

Nathan wakes in terror. A uniformed man is bending over him. Police. The child stirs, catching his fear, and begins to cry.

"There, there, little one, nothing to be afraid of." The conductor smiles.

Breathing deeply to slow his panic, Nathan pats his coat, in which the child is wrapped, and finds the ticket. The child's forehead suddenly beads with perspiration. The sack around her is sodden. The fever has broken.

"Ah, Clayton Lake," the conductor says. "You have folks there?"

Nathan nods, unwilling to give further information, which Americans seem to demand and give in plenitude.

"Four more stops."

"Rayzela." He speaks softly, smoothing her hair. "We will soon be home. You'll see."

The child stares up at him without fear. When he kisses away the salty dampness on her forehead, his beard caresses her. Her lids droop. She is in a deep sleep and doesn't hear the train whistle as it passes through a grove of pine trees and across the meandering lake. Fog floats over the lake in white wisps and shrouds the village as the train creeps into the station.

Nathan comes down the steps carefully holding the sleeping child, hidden once more in the sack, and looks around. A mail bag lands near his feet with a thump, then comes a bundle of newspapers. No one else gets off the train, but two people are being helped on board by the conductor. The station master waves. The conductor calls, "All aboard."

Catching the cord on the mailbag, the station master drags it into the small stone station house. He goes out once more and brings in the bundle of newspapers. The engine snorts and shushes, filling the air with soot. The train gives a fierce whistle, motor chugging, as it moves off across Clayton Lake and is swallowed up in the mist.

The squat, stone station house sits on the fog like a houseboat on a deserted stretch of sea. Nathan follows the station master into the small waiting room. Two oak benches, their varnish discolored to a sickly yellow, are unoccupied. The station master sets the mail bag in a corner and goes into his cage, first slipping a newspaper from the stack on the floor. "You want me to call a taxi for you?"

Nathan shakes his head. Balancing the white sack against his chest, he thrusts one arm, then the other into his coat and awkwardly buttons it around the sack. He nods to the station master and walks through the station and out the other side, setting off on foot.

Back inside his cage, the station master shrugs. The bearded man clutching his belongings in that bag had looked confused when he stepped off the train, but maybe the station master is mistaken. The man seems to know where he's going. He opens his *Herald Tribune* to the sports page.

It is body-piercing cold accompanied by a fine, icy drizzle. Behind him, the train gives a shrill whistle. The chugging fades away. As Nathan walks the footpath around the lake, a stillness settles over him and the child. All he hears is the crunch as his soles meet, first path, then pavement. The business street, called Main Street, of Clayton Lake is just over the bridge. Nathan takes bigger strides.

He passes the gray cedar-shingled Clayton Lake Hotel, which faces the lake. His body has merged with that of the child, keeping them both warm. The town is wakening. A milk delivery truck drives by and stops in front of the hotel. Ahead of him, a swarthy young man unlocks a store with a display of shoes for men, women, and children in the window. Violetti's Fine Shoes, it says.

Nathan turns right where Main Street runs into Jefferson. A diner on the corner wafts the smell of bacon and fried eggs. Already there are people, men mostly, sitting at the counter.

Jefferson Street is wide and tree-lined, although you can't see much of it for the fog. But he knows the street because he has been here once before and remembers every direction clearly.

He walks past the U.S. Post Office, a red brick building with white trim, and the Loew's Movie Theatre with its white columns, the city hall, the Carnegie Library, a stone Presbyterian church, a Catholic church, also stone, with its neatly-kept cemetery. The weathered gravestones peek at him through thick chunks of fog.

He feels no cold, for the child is hot again, and the fever burns through his shirt into his chest. She moans, restless, her limbs pushing at the confines of the sack and his coat.

"Darling, Rayzela," Nathan whispers. Maybe he should have waited and not rushed off as he did. But it will turn out all right, he knows that. Anna had cared for him as a child after Mama had the stroke.

Dead leaves lie squirrelly in damp gutters. A car travels slowly toward him, its headlights piercing the haze. Just beyond the cemetery, Nathan crosses over the broad street. Here, there are beautiful homes with wide verandas holding porch swings and wooden furniture. Stone walks lead to spacious front doors. Nathan knows every house has turrets and balconies, like a castle, although these cannot be seen for the fog.

He passes no one on the street. Just ahead of him a car backs out of a driveway and drives off in the opposite direction.

Thick shrubs and huge old shade trees, barren of leaves, surround the house at No. 37 Jefferson Street. An expansive holly tree with dark green foliage guards the front steps. The sign next to the front door says, DAVID BLACKWELL, M.D.

For the first time, Nathan falters. His arms tighten around his small burden, not visible to the casual observer, of which there is none. He had best go around to the back door. Rayzela moves against him, moaning, as if she is having a bad dream. Her small body burns with fever.

A short, pebbled drive runs alongside the house to the rear, leading to a garage, where Nathan knows the car, a gray Ford, is kept. Only the door is open and the garage is empty.

He sits down on the back steps, weary, his legs trembling. Why could he not have saved Miri? His mind is fuzzy. Pressing the child to him, he feels if she were to die, too, he will not want to live.

The back door is windowed, covered by a lace curtain. Near the door is a metal mud scraper. Three bottles of milk, their long necks yellow with cream, stand waiting.

Nathan gets to his feet, clumsy with his extra weight, and comes up the steps. If he can just sit down someplace warm and rest, he'll be fine. He puts his hand on the door knob and it turns without any effort from him.

— 6 —

David

Anna's English isn't so good and she's always found it hard to read this particular newspaper, so it is something of a miracle that the one day she picks up the *Times*, is the day David's advertisement runs.

Housekeeper wanted for country doctor.
Room and board with small stipend.

She responds immediately, writing with painstaking care, her background, and David Blackwell sends her a train ticket to come for an interview.

David Blackwell is a stocky man, broad shouldered, with huge but gentle hands and soft gray eyes that give away a caring nature. His hair is a thick, almost white, crop over a high forehead.

He has expected someone older, for he is a widower approaching fifty, so he is unprepared for the vibrant young woman with the brilliant red hair. Words fail him, and she ends up interviewing herself. That she speaks accented English and is Jewish doesn't bother him. He sees she is strong and determined. He offers her the position and she accepts.

Martha had been ill for years with diabetes, and it had damaged her kidneys irreparably, but while she was alive she'd run the household and his practice, making appointments and

39

taking care of billing. He is lost without her.

Anna Ebanholz, with her red hair and creamy skin, her bubbling laughter, brings him a curious delight. He listens for her footstep on the stair, her singing in the kitchen, and feels a great longing.

Quickly, they fall into a routine. By mid-afternoon, after the last patient is seen, David goes off to make house calls while Anna cleans the waiting room, the surgery, and sterilizes the instruments. Then she prepares dinner: soup, kasha with varnishkas, maybe a pot roast or a chicken fricassee with onions. Anna cooks as her mother did, and David Blackwell doesn't seem to mind. In fact, she's never known such a man. He never complains and thanks her all the time.

They work together all day and eat dinner together when David comes home from his calls. Her initial awe and discomfort settles into companionable silence, in spite of his continuous attempts to draw her out.

David is an educated man, and a gentile. Anna has never before had such a close relationship with a gentile. Self-conscious about her accent and her poor English, Anna is humbled by his plain acceptance of her as she is.

Spring begins to drift toward summer, and the days grow longer. The screen door is installed and the winter door removed and stored in the garage. Late in the afternoon, after dinner is prepared, Anna has taken to sitting on the back steps, a library book in her lap, Ernest Hemingway her shepherd this day.

But beguiled by the language of the birds, bemused by the family of squirrels that scamper and chatter up and down the trees in the yard, her thoughts wander.

David's eyes are the grayest of grays and when they

rest on her, as they often do, the hairs on the back of her neck shiver.

Sweet is the quiet, sweet is the smell of the grass, newly mowed. Greens, the most vivid shades surround her, trees abundant with foliage; the deep blue of the sky above her is like butter to her soul. Her limbs and heart are light.

Anna sets the book aside and hugs her knees, burying her face in her skirt. The lilac bushes that Martha Blackwell had planted many years ago are in full bloom and bathe her reserve with their heady perfume.

Yesterday, in the kitchen, David reached over her head to get a glass from the cabinet and his arm brushed the side of her face. A shock, as from a worn electric plug, made her gasp.

He said in almost a whisper, "I'm sorry," and touched her shoulder, causing aftershocks.

She'd thrust her hands up to the wrists in cold water to hide the commotion going on within her.

Clayton Lake had been, in prehistoric days, under water. While the earth is loamy, topsoil must be brought in from elsewhere. David Blackwell's narrow driveway, therefore, is white-gray sand, salted with yellow gravel. Nestled along the back stairs, where Anna sits, are blackberry bushes, beginning to berry.

She will serve them in a bowl with sugar and cream, and David will look at her with those soft gray eyes, and say, "Thank you, Anna," never knowing how her fingers itch to smooth his hair from his forehead, to run along the line of his lips.

★ ★ ★ ★ ★

Her senses confuse her. He is a goy, he is much older than she. She must pull herself together or she'll have to leave. Return to the city. She doesn't want to do that. Nathan will be happy to see her come back, but soon enough Miri and the child will arrive and Anna will be Tante Anna, the maiden aunt. No, she is better here. Here, she can breathe. The city is like a tight band across her chest.

He has beautiful hands, huge, but with fine, elegant fingers, flecked with whitish gold hairs. She wants to take his hand and bring it to her cheek, her breast.

Four months after Anna begins working for David, Edgar Hall, the pastor of the First Presbyterian Church, and Bill Sanderson, president of the Clayton Lake National Bank, both of whom have gone through school with David, come calling.

"It doesn't look right for a single man and woman to live together without benefit of matrimony," Edgar says.

"The whole town is upset," Bill adds. "You have to send her away."

"Or marry her, which we understand would not be appropriate," Edgar says.

David protests that there was nothing between him and Anna, but he isn't telling the truth. He's already in love with her.

He's been up all night with young John Milling, who'd fallen out of a tree and cracked his skull. The boy dies just when David thinks he's seen him through the worst. He hates to lose a patient, particularly such a young one with his whole life ahead of him. He's never managed to build the shell around himself as other doctors, and he takes the Milling boy's death hard.

It's still dark when he comes home. Failure devastates him. He doesn't turn on the light and so doesn't see her at first. She is standing on the stairs, an apparition, in her white nightgown, her hair down in a long braid.

He looks up at her. "I lost him."

"David," she says.

Just *David*, and he knows.

— 7 —

Anna

"Ei, Nathan!" Anna steps back. "You scared me half to death." Recovering, she takes his arm and brings him into the house. "What are you doing here?" The child begins to cry, weak bleating sobs, drawing Anna's eyes to his bundle. "What is this? My God, Nathan, this child is burning up." He unbuttons his coat and she takes the child from him, cradling her, but the crying grows more piteous. "Nathan, talk to me."

"Mama! Mama!" the child cries, pushing at Anna with her fists.

"Anna, Miri is dead. Rayzela—they almost killed her, too."

Anna peels the white sack from the struggling child, frowning. "How could this happen?"

The child, tears clinging to her cheeks and lashes, stops crying. Her arms, freed from confinement, move stiffly. She looks around, dazed, frightened, until she finds Nathan. With a small gasping sob, she reaches for him.

Nathan takes her from Anna and holds her. She moves her head back and forth under his beard, her thin arms pushing at his chest.

Anna gets a small bottle of aspirin from a cabinet and shakes out one pill, breaks it in half, and mashes one of the halves into some water. "Open, Rayzela," Anna says in Yiddish. The child stares at her. "Open your mouth, Rayzela

44

darling, show me your tongue," she says again, not even noticing she's speaking in English.

The child cringes, terror in her eyes. She looks to Nathan, who kisses her forehead. "Take the medicine, zeesilla."

Rayzela opens her mouth, still fearful, and Anna manages to put some of the aspirin paste on her tongue with a wooden tongue depressor. "See, that wasn't so bad." Anna holds a glass of water to the child's dry lips. "You see how red her tongue is, Nathan? The doctor will be home soon. He'll know what to do."

Nathan's legs begin to shake on him again. He pulls out a chair and sits down. They are in a large kitchen, as luxurious as something from the movies. It even has a Frigidaire and a big white enamel gas stove, on which a percolator begins to perk coffee. The table is set for two for breakfast. Anna's red hair is in a braid down her back. She wears a chenille bathrobe over a long flannel nightgown. Pale freckles float against luminous skin. It comes to Nathan slowly. Of course. This is a doctor's house.

"It is not what you think," Anna says. "We are married."

"Married." His mind is numb. "Married?"

She shakes his arm to bring back his attention. "Ei, ei, Nathan, Rayzela is very sick. We must bring the fever down. You stay here and eat something. When was the last time you ate?" She doesn't wait for an answer, but takes the child from him. Rayzela begins to scream, squirming weakly in Anna's arms.

The cries cut Nathan deeply, but he knows in his heart he will be no good to her if he gets sick. He pours himself a cup of coffee, goes to the back door, and brings in the fresh milk. Coffee with sugar and cream. A piece of toast with butter. He is a new man. But Rayzela's continued sobs torture him.

Upstairs somewhere he hears, over the screams of his child, the sound of water running. He follows the sounds, rushing up the carpeted stairs. "Anna? Anna?"

"Here, Nathan."

He passes a large bedroom. Anna's robe lies on the bed. Two smaller bedrooms look uninhabited. The door at the end of the hall is open, but where is Anna? His knees buckle under him and his hand grasps the wall to steady himself. Kneeling at the tub is Stella in her white uniform. He has not saved Rayzela after all.

"Rayzela is very sick, Nathan," Anna says, breaking the spell.

Nathan puts his hands to his face and weeps.

"Of course, they can stay, Anna. They're your family. Here now, dry your eyes and let's have a look at them."

Anna's waited till he's had breakfast to tell him, fearful of his response. And yet, he is such a kind man, somehow she knows he won't fail her.

The night after the visit from his friends, David asks Anna to be his wife. In spite of their age difference, she cries and accepts. That she loves him and he loves her, he has not one moment of doubt.

He's never met her brother Nathan and often wonders if she's ashamed that she married a Christian. Now, as he follows her up the stairs, he lets himself hope that he will have a family. He's the only child of two only children. Martha had no siblings and they could have no children because of her condition.

"Nathan is not well himself, David," Anna whispers. "I don't know what happened to Miri. I didn't even know she and the child were here. There must have been a terrible accident. He talks of a fire."

David knocks on the door to the small bedroom and opens it. The man he sees is young, bearded, his beard the color of Anna's hair. The eyes staring at David are ablaze, set deep. The room smells of rubbing alcohol.

The child is perhaps three, not much older. It is hard to tell for she is skin and bones. A bottle of alcohol and cotton strips lie on a towel on the floor. Nathan is sitting on the bed, the child resting in his arms. The child's face is scaly and flushed. She is covered with a towel and a blanket. When Nathan sees David, he clasps the child to him with an urgency that feeds the child's obvious fear of separation.

"Nathan," Anna says. "Let David look at Rayzela. He will know what to do."

The child's face contorts. Her eyes become fearful. "No, no, no! Mama, Mama."

"Shshshs, Rayzela." Nathan kisses the scaly forehead, lays her down on the bed, and steps back. "She's frightened," he says. "She doesn't know where she is and she doesn't know you."

Anna holds Nathan's hand in hers, and the two watch David take his stethoscope from his pocket. To Anna, the rash on the child's chest seems fainter now and is beginning to peel—somewhat like a sunburn. When the child sees the stethoscope, she begins to howl.

Nathan places his hand on her head. "Sha, sha, tyrinka."

The child stops crying, keeping her eyes on Nathan as if trying to memorize him.

David sees at once the faint strawberry tongue and the scaly peeling of the skin. The child's pulse is rapid, but as he examines her, she breaks into a heavy sweat. "Scarlatina," he says. "The last of it, I would say." He covers the child with the towel and then the blanket.

"Scarlatina!" Tears run down Nathan's face. He pulls his hand from Anna's. "In Poland children die from scarlatina."

"Children die of scarlatina here also, but I think she's out of danger now, if we can keep the fever down. And you've done a good job of it. But she still may be contagious. This means we all must wash up very carefully after we touch her and we must not mix her eating utensils or her clothing with ours."

"David, Nathan was at the university in Lodz. He was going to be a doctor, too."

"Good, so it's decided," David says. "You will stay here with us. I can use an assistant. And now I will wash up and change my clothes. I have patients to see." He looks around at his new family. The child will live. And Nathan will heal. And David has only to look at Anna to see how happy he's made her.

That is all he wants.

— 8 —

David

David has never known, never imagined the unfathomable happiness of having a child in the house. His parents had been reserved, proper Methodists. One does what one must, his mother always said. Duty. He'd followed his father into medicine, dutifully. And he'd married the daughter of his parents' close friend, the minister. Which is not to say it wasn't a good marriage. It was built on respect and trust.

This utterly foreign emotion he is now experiencing is splendidly excruciating, almost like the birthing process. He sees his life before Anna as a flat, arid plain.

She lies down beside him, careful not to jostle him. Her scent is honeyed, sweet and lush. He gathers her to him, inhaling her, still amazed that the mere thought of her can kindle such passion.

"The child?" he says.

"Sleeping. I made tea for Nathan." Her tongue grazes his lips. "My love." She opens herself to him.

It's still dark when David hears Anna in the kitchen, the familiarity of filling the coffee pot. He gets up and washes. His suit and shirt are freshly pressed and waiting for him. He's never known such peace. She is a gift from God, an angel come to wake him from a lifelong sleep. He wonders how long he will have her, then shakes away the thought.

They'd spent a wary night, David, Nathan, and Anna, watching over the sleeping child. Like the Wise Men, David muses, as he buttons his shirt, sitting vigil over the child, the Jewish child. Well, maybe two wise men and one very wise woman. And the child in this case is a girl.

Dressed, he takes his stethoscope from his leather bag, hooks it round his neck, and walks down the hall to the guest bedroom. He hears Nathan's murmuring voice. Yiddish. Close to German, which David understands, but not close enough.

The door is ajar. Even sitting, Nathan is a presence, thick of shoulder and limb. A plowman, David thinks. Brother and sister are unlike physically but for the thick brick-red hair. His features are broad and Hebraic, like the actor Paul Muni.

David's patient is awake, eyes a startling green, unblinking, glued to Nathan as he sits on the bed facing her, murmuring in Yiddish. She doesn't smile or reach out. Undernourished and dehydrated, she's almost lost under the blanket. What little strength she has is consumed fighting the disease.

But her lack of reaction troubles him. She just watches. Nathan is demonstrative and emotional. He's her father. Why isn't the child responding even in a small way? Has the fever damaged her brain?

Nathan, face drawn, eyes heavy-lidded, gives him a hesitant smile. "My baby, she's going to be all right, I think."

The child breaks off her gaze from Nathan, turns toward David. Abject fear blurs her tiny face. She burrows into the blanket.

"Rayzela, Rayzela, tyrinka. Papa is here." Nathan speaks in Yiddish, turning the covers back. "See? Nothing to be frightened about."

The child studies Nathan's face, his lips, as if she's unable to hear him. It worries David. Scarlatina can leave its victims deaf.

David touches Nathan's arm. "The sooner she learns English, the better."

"Oh, I'm sorry. English, Rayzela. We are in America. We must speak English."

The child blinks and stares at David. Tears bunch on her pale lashes.

Finally, David thinks.

Nathan says in his accented English, "My Rayzela, she is not used to new people and she doesn't understand English yet." He kisses Rayzela's forehead and puts a pillow under her head. "Rayzela, this is your uncle David. He made you well."

Uncle David, David thinks. He likes the sound of *Uncle David*. When Nathan smiles, as he does now, the peasant look to him disappears. There is a magnetism, like his Anna, but rawer. And intelligence. He seems older than the twenty-five years Anna says he is.

"We must test her hearing."

"Why?" But Nathan understands and tears slide into his beard. Rayzela whimpers and ducks into the blanket.

"Here, here, now," David says. He whistles.

Rayzela's eyes peer from the covers. David is relieved. "This is no time for tears." He stands at the foot of the bed and smiles at her. "Nathan, you saw. It's okay."

Nathan dries his eyes. "Is she healed, David?"

"Let's listen." David adjusts the earpieces of his stethoscope. The child disappears under the blanket.

"No, Rayzela, this is Uncle David. He loves you. He won't ever hurt you, will you, Uncle David?"

"Never," David says, his throat catching on his words.

Nathan says, "Let me put the—how do you say in English?"

"Resonator."

"Resonator." He holds the disk out to the child. "See Rayzela, this is called resonator." He warms it between his palms, then sets it against her narrow chest. "Uncle David is listening to see how you are."

The child, tense, holds onto Nathan's arms.

"Her lungs are good," David says, listening.

"So she is okay?"

"It seems so, but high fevers can affect the brain. And she has not spoken so much as a word. At least we know her hearing is all right." He takes her hand. "The pulse is fast." He tucks both hands back under the covers. "I read about a case last year where the child recovered, but her speech and memory did not and she had to relearn . . ."

"But I think Rayzela, she's only frightened now. I don't think she remembers how we came here."

"Yes, of course. We have to consider everything that's happened to her, Nathan."

"Nay-ten?"

The men look at each other, overjoyed. The child spoke. Nathan covers her face with kisses. "My good Rayzela."

"Rayzela," David says. "We must give you an American name, now that you're in America. What do you think, Nathan?"

The child frowns, opens her lips as if to say more, but no words come.

"Something with an R," Nathan says. "Rayzela is named for Anna's and my mother, may she rest in peace."

Uncle David's fingers glance against her crusty cheek. "We'll put some salve on this and you'll feel better." He smiles. "A name beginning with R? How about Rose? Nathan, what do you think?"

Nathan rolls it over his tongue. "Rose. Yes. I like it. What do you think, Rayz—Rosie? Do you like your new name?"

She closes her eyes, shrinking as her strength wanes. "Mama," she whispers. "Want Mama."

"God in heaven." Nathan wipes tears from his eyes with a striped handkerchief.

She'd spoken in English. Clear as a bell. How quickly children learn, David thinks, in passing, more concerned about father and child. "Now, now, Nathan, don't take it so hard. We have to expect this. The child misses her mother and it's only natural. What she needs now is nourishment."

She watches them, hollow-eyed. "Nay-ten. Mama. Papa."

"Papa is here, baby, right here." Nathan picks her up and clasps her to him. He looks at David, his eyes full of pain.

She shakes her head back and forth. "Nay-ten. Mama."

"Kiss your Papa, baby," Nathan says, covering her face with kisses. "We are all that's left."

The child curls fingers in Nathan's beard and falls asleep against his breast.

— 9 —

Anna

Anna leaves the house early and takes the train to New York. She hasn't shared her concerns with David, cannot bring herself to spoil his apparent joy with his inherited family. So she tells him she's going to Macy's to buy the accouterments that go with child rearing, showing him the list she's made. The youth bed with side panels. And clothing for Rayzela—and for Nathan.

But Anna has another reason for the trip. She knows her brother well. Something is terribly wrong.

"Where are your belongings?" she'd asked.

"Belongings?" His eyes evaded hers.

"Yes. Did you give up your room with the Kravitzes?"

"Yes, Anna. Don't ask so many questions. There was a fire. Miri—may she rest in peace—died. I thank God I saved Rayzela." Still, he didn't look at her. "If you don't want us here, say so, and we'll go."

"Nathan, David and I are happy you are here with us and hope you will stay. But you had a good job in the city. What about your job?"

"There was trouble at the hospital. I couldn't stay. Then the fire came—"

She turns it over and over in her head. The local newspaper is a weekly and doesn't cover New York news. The *Herald*

Tribune didn't mention a terrible fire, but it covers world news, and a fire in the Bronx would not be considered news.

Of course, after all this time to bring Miri here and then lose her is a tragedy, but Nathan is so evasive. He'd written only a few weeks ago that they were coming to America, that he had made the arrangements. And Anna had written him that she would help and Nathan should tell her what they needed. Then she had heard nothing more from him until three mornings ago when she opened the back door and found him and the child.

And there is Rayzela herself. A child of three should be talking already. And she hides behind her eyes, staring, as if she can't understand what they say. Yet, David tested her, and her hearing is fine.

Rayzela lost her mother; the shock may have made her mute, David says. But with love and care, her voice speech will come back.

Anna takes the "D" train to the Bronx and gets off at East 174th Street. It's mid-morning and the trains aren't crowded as they will be later. The wind whips across the open platform, making billowing flags of skirts and coats, teasing hats to flight. She holds onto hers, which is fastened to her thick hair with a long hatpin.

Walking carefully down the steps from the elevated, Anna is aware that in her black coat and its fox collar, in her tall, brimless black velvet hat with its large pearl clip, she stands out either as a stranger or someone who is—God forbid—paying a shiva call, or going to a funeral.

The sun is very bright; the sky the palest of winter blues, cloudless. Crotona Park is a very nice neighborhood, and the building where Fannie and Abe Kravitz live is directly across from the park. It's a place hospitable to young families with children.

Everywhere you look are babies in carriages, in arms. Others, barely walking, are wrapped in many layers of clothing, holding on to mothers' skirts. Anna thinks about this new generation, all American born. They'll create their own world here and it will be stronger, healthier, and no one will be hungry or afraid . . .

So, she tells herself, you are a dreamer, too, like Nathan.

A stoop-shouldered peddler with a pushcart is walking slowly, crying, "I cash clothes! I cash clothes." He stops in front of the building where Abe and Fannie Kravitz live, and hollers again. This time someone hollers back for him to wait.

Anna sighs. There is something nervous and alive here that Clayton Lake is missing.

She knows Fannie Kravitz by sight and knows also, at this hour, where she will find her. On such a day, even in winter, women bundle up themselves and their children and go to the park. The sunlight and the fresh air are good for children, and the park bench society of the mothers is a necessity of life.

They have so much in common. They are, for the most part, immigrants from Russia or Poland. Their English is broken, chopped up and reconstructed. They have young children; their husbands work long hours in "the shop," the garment industry, as cluckmachers, piece-workers, or machine operators. They talk primarily about their children and how to make ends meet with little money. They rarely discuss their marriages, though some are not easy, and a problem marriage is always the wife's failure.

Yiddish is the key to fitting into this society; it's the lingua franca of this section of the Bronx.

Eyes follow Anna as she comes into the park and down the path. She knows she doesn't look like a greenhorn; she never had. Her trade had been dressmaker and her gift was the ability to copy what she saw in the movies or the magazines and adapt it to herself.

Fannie Kravitz is sitting on the third bench with another woman, while on the flattened grass nearby, two little boys in bright snowsuits and knitted caps play kick ball with a large rubber ball. Two strollers stand askew at the side of the path.

The women's conversation, interspersed liberally with beseechings and warnings to the young ones, have to do with luckshun pudding and its ingredients, which differ radically depending on which area in which country you come from.

Head swathed in a woolen babushka, Fannie's pleasant face reflects no recognition of Anna. They met only once, when Anna found Nathan the room and made the arrangements with Fannie.

"Mrs. Kravitz?" Anna stops in front of the bench.

Fannie looks up at her, eyes scrunched. The other woman stares at Anna with a mixture of envy and flagrant curiosity.

"I'm Anna . . . Ebanholz, Nathan's sister." She touches her wedding ring, hidden by the black leather glove. It's easier to say Ebanholz than Blackwell here.

"Oh, yes?" Fannie struggles to her feet. She sends a significant look to her companion. The other woman frowns as if trying to read from Fannie's gesture who Anna is.

"Can we talk?"

"Heshy! Come on!" Fannie calls to the children. One looks up but goes back to the game as if she's never spoken. "Heshy!" This time Heshy doesn't even look up. "Americanisher kinder," Fannie announces. Of course, America is to blame for a willful child. She marches over to

57

the boys and grabs Heshy's hand.

"No! No! No!" Heshy screams, twisting to free himself, but Fannie holds tight. "Ball! Ball! Ball!"

Fannie picks up the wriggling child, who by now is howling, sending waves of fury into the air, his face an unpleasant crimson. She thrusts him into the stroller and ties the strap. The other child stops and stares, clutching the large ball tightly to his chest.

"See what happens, Moishela, when you don't listen to Mama," the other woman tells her son.

This makes Heshy scream all the more and struggle against his bonds as Fannie pushes the stroller out of the park, with Anna following.

When they enter the vestibule, where Fannie leaves the stroller, Anna notices at once there is no evidence of a fire, no smell of smoke or cinders. She follows Fannie, who carries a sobbing Heshy, up the three flights of stairs, murmuring in Yiddish about the nice lady who came to see him and how he should behave. Heshy stops crying and stares at Anna over Fannie's shoulder, his thumb in his mouth.

In the small, crowded apartment, Fannie takes off Heshy's cap and jacket and sets him into the high chair. He looks surprised and takes only a moment to acclimate himself.

"Spoon!" Heshy screams.

Fannie hands him a spoon and he begins to bang on the tray of the high chair.

Over the din, Fannie says, "Come in, sit down, let me take your coat. Is Nathan all right? A week he's been gone now."

She hangs her coat from a hook near the door, then offers to take Anna's. Anna shakes her head.

"He's with me in New Jersey."

"Ei, yei," Fannie says, making a tsking sound of tongue

to teeth. She fills the kettle with water and sets it on the stove. Striking a match, she holds it to the open gas jet and the flame makes a smart pop. "I told the landlord he wouldn't need the apartment after all, but he lost his deposit. He can stay here."

"How did the fire start?" Anna watches as Fannie opens a can of peas and drains the liquid into a pan on the stove, lights the gas. Reaching into a bag on the counter, Fannie takes out two carrots, scrapes them, and cuts them up, throwing them into the saucepan.

Heshy's thumping continues. "But I got him some money back anyway so he doesn't have to pay me for this week." She fills the percolator with water and measures in Bokar coffee from the A&P bag. "Stop that, Heshy. Be a good boy."

"The fire, Mrs. Kravitz?"

She shrugs. "Who knows? Anti-Semites, the letter said."

"Anti-Semites?" Anna shudders. "Even here we're not safe from them."

Fannie looks up. "True, but it is very bad over there right now."

"There?" Did Fannie say something about a letter? "Did you say a letter?"

The thumping begins to alternate with short screeches. Anna's head is throbbing.

"Stop already, Heshy." Fannie puts a piece of zwieback in his hand, then nods to Anna. "From Poland it came. It said they all perished." She holds two fingers in front of her mouth and makes spitting noises.

"They?" The kitchen, the child, Fannie, begin to spin.

"Here, sit. Sit. He didn't tell you?" Fannie moves a kitchen chair to Anna and Anna sinks into it. Vaguely, from a distance, she hears the thumping slow and then stop. The soft plop-plop of the percolator takes over. The smell of coffee fills the small kitchen.

"I don't understand," Anna says.

Fannie dries her hands on a dish towel and opens a drawer. She takes a letter from the drawer and hands it to Anna.

"But the child lived—" The letter burns in Anna's trembling hand. Cinders fill her nostrils, then dissipate.

"No. No one. See for yourself."

Anna opens the letter and reads. So they never even left Poland. She folds the letter and puts it in her bag. "From now on, Nathan will be staying with me in New Jersey, Mrs. Kravitz." She chooses the words carefully.

"Oy, now I will have to find a new boarder. He is such a mensch, your brother. Where will I find anyone like him? And what about his job? He has such a good job."

"Of course, you'll keep any money you get back from the deposit."

Fannie smiles. "So you want to pack him up?"

Anna nods.

With a fork, Fannie mashes the boiling vegetables into a paste and tastes it. "Just right. Heshy, see what I have for you." She puts it in a small plate, sets the plate on the tray of the high chair, and guides Heshy's hand with the spoon to it. Heshy gives it a dubious look.

"The top drawer is his," Fannie tells Anna. "Come, I'll show you."

Heshy stares in disbelief as his mother leaves the room. He begins to howl and thump the tray.

They pack Nathan's few belongings into a small, battered suitcase. On top of the bureau is a photograph of Miri and Rayzela, which Miri had sent for Hanukkah. Anna puts it into the suitcase under the shabby underwear.

60

"Tell him we are all thinking about him," Fannie says, walking Anna to the door. From the kitchen comes an ominous silence.

"Thank you."

As Anna closes the door, she hears Fannie yell, "Heshy! No! Bad boy!"

Balancing the suitcase and her handbag, Anna steadies herself on the wall as she walks slowly down the narrow stairs. The letter keeps repeating itself in her mind. Until finally, at the foot of the steps, she stops to catch her breath, and the thoughts she's been avoiding come at her like evil crows.

If Miri and Rayzela are dead, who is the child?

— 10 —

Anna

At the Thirty-fourth Street stop, Anna gets out, a sleep-walker, carrying Nathan's battered valise. She goes through Macy's Department Store with her list, knowing this is a waste of money for they must find the child's parents and take her back to them as soon as possible.

But she continues to shop. A crib that will become a youth bed, mattress, sheets, and pillows, to be delivered. In the children's clothing department, underwear, socks, flannel pajamas, and dresses. A snowsuit in red. Shoes she'll get in Clayton Lake, at Violetti's, where they can be properly fitted.

In the men's department, she buys underwear and socks for Nathan. Three shirts, a pair of corduroy trousers. She packs them into Nathan's small valise.

She takes the elevator to the toy department and buys a beautiful doll with flaxen hair, a teddy bear, a ball, and an afterthought, a box of crayons.

With her bundles, she walks the short distance to Pennsylvania Station and finds a Red Cap to help her. It's three o'clock. Her train is at four. She feels she's been deathly ill and this is her first excursion. Her knees quake. And now she realizes she has not eaten since breakfast.

Leaving her packages and the suitcase with the Red Cap, she goes into a coffee shop. A few people are sitting scattered at a long counter. She chooses the last seat at the far end, where no one else sits.

"What'll ya have, lady?" The counterman wipes down the counter and gives her a napkin.

"Coffee and a Danish."

"Cheese or prune?"

"Cheese."

The coffee and Danish arrive at once, with a speed that is endemic to railroad and bus stations in this country. She cuts the Danish in quarters and eats slowly.

A man in work clothes sits down at the counter two seats away and lights a cigarette. He takes *The Daily News*, folded, from the pocket of his coat and opens it on the counter top. "They still haven't found the kid," he says. The counterman puts a cup of coffee in front of him.

"Naw. Whoever took her probably killed that nurse."

"Maybe. Maybe it was two different things. The kid was real sick; maybe she died and someone got rid of her."

"She coulda seen who done it."

"A kid that sick? How could she get outta one of those hospital beds with the bars by herself?"

"Listen, my kid is younger and can get out of the crib by hisself."

"I heard that the nurse was a tramp and that the husband mighta done it."

"Could be. But what about the kid? More coffee, lady?"

Anna is unnerved. She's been lost in their conversation. "No, thank you."

He drops her check near her plate. "Listen, the kid didn't have it so good either."

She lays the money and a tip on the counter and leaves. In the waiting room she locates the Red Cap and her packages.

"Ready?" he asks.

"Yes." She follows him to the train, where he helps her get settled. In a short time, the train pulls out of Penn Station and she is on her way home.

A tiny spark of panic flutters in her breast. What has Nathan done? Is he crazy? Who does the child belong to?

The man next to her is reading *The Daily News*. If Nathan has stolen a child, he can go to the electric chair like Bruno Hauptmann. She shivers. The man gives her a strange look and she realizes she's been trying to read the front of his paper. She turns away. This won't do. She's acting crazy herself.

She must go home and confront Nathan.

The man finishes the sports pages, folds the paper, and shoves it at her. "You want it, take it."

She stares at him, appalled. He gets up and drops it on the seat. "I'm getting off anyway."

She waits till he gets off, then picks up the paper and folds it back to the front page. Her eyes go from frightening headline to frightening headline, and then, on page five, Rayzela's picture stares out at her. Only her name is not Rayzela at all. Her name is Jenny Topinski.

The headline says:

WHERE IS LITTLE JENNY?
SICK CHILD STILL MISSING.

She disappeared from the Willard Parker Hospital the same night a nurse was murdered.

God help us, Anna despairs. She reads on, horrified, unable to stop. The father, a painter, was the first suspect, but it turns out he tried to break into the hospital earlier and appears to have spent the night in jail. She finds no mention of the mother at all until the last paragraph. The mother lies near death in Bronx Hospital. Dying of what? Anna thinks. Sorrow?

The train squeezes round a curve and the lights go out.

Anna can't breathe. A tight band moves across her chest. She sits in the dark. They must give the child back. When the lights come on, she tears out the page of the newspaper and folds it into her handbag.

She wants to block everything from her mind, but much as she pushes it away, the thought intrudes with a ferocity that terrifies her.

In his anguish, Nathan has stolen a child.

— 11 —

Zweikel

Zweikel misses her smell most of all. In the beginning, it greets him at the door like a temptress, beguiling him into thinking she is still alive. It lingers in the sheets. It sings to him from the closet. When he opens the bureau drawer, it whispers her name. But too soon it dissipates, and now he is barely able to capture her essence, even in his mind.

He wakes each morning certain that it is all a terrible dream, that he will hear her key in the lock and the coffee pot being filled.

He sits shiva for her, covers the mirrors, as strange as it sounds. How she'd have laughed if she saw him sitting on a crate in his house slippers for a whole week. He buries her next to the empty plot that will be his space in the ground, so that he'll lie between her and his mother.

Dina Malkowitz from next door brings him food every day and sits with him. And surprisingly, some of the people from Auster's, and the pharmacist Weiss brings a bottle of schnapps. And then it's over. Stella is gone. She is never coming home.

Her clothes lie in the drawer as if she's coming back any moment. He hasn't touched them, three weeks already. He opens the drawer. Bloomers, stockings, garter belts. He buries his face in her bloomers and weeps. When he dresses, he wears her bloomers next to his skin.

The police question him over and over about the child who is missing. They seem to think that Stella tried to stop the kidnapping and got herself killed.

At first, he's not able to look at the newspapers. Every day there is her picture, the one he took of her with the Kodak where she looks like Jean Harlow. He'd tacked it to the wall near his table at the drugstore and someone had stolen it.

Now Stella stares out at him from every newsstand. They are treating her like a saint. And Zweikel pours over the stories. He himself appears in every one and with a picture they took of him coming from the Medical Examiner's office where he had to identify her. He looks like his own long dead father, he should rest in peace. *Bereaved husband, Marvin Zweikel,* it says under his picture.

"Hey, you in there?" The voice comes accompanied by pounding on the door. "Mr. Zweikel?" More pounding.

"Okay, okay, hold your horses. I'm coming. You don't hafta break the door down." He shuffles over to the door, opens it. "Oh, it's you again."

The two detectives come in, so big and broad they diminish the small room. They are all Irish, these guys. Catholics. He knows first-hand from Catholics in Krakow. A gang of them killed his brother Solly. Some mornings just before he wakes he's Mendy again on the cobblestoned streets, coming from cheder carrying his books. The boys chase him. Twice he's beaten badly and his books spread with mud. Then Solly made him wait so they could go together. "Run, Mendy, run," Solly screamed, when the boys fell on them. And Mendy ran, and they killed Solly, these Catholics.

He looks at the detectives, wary. What do they care about Jews? He's careful with them.

At first, they thought he might have done it, but no one has ever seen him at the hospital. It turns out no one there even knew Stella was married.

And just at the time it happened he had a fight with the drunken Polack who owns the building about the heat. If he wasn't so miserable, Zweikel would find it funny. The anti-Semite gives him an alibi.

"Why would I do it? Why? She was my life," he keeps telling them, but they threaten to beat it out of him. He wets himself and cries like a baby, unable to stop.

The Polack is at first too drunk to tell them anything so Zweikel spends all day at the station house. When they let him go, he staggers home, takes her bottle of gin from the back of the kitchen cabinet, and gets drunk.

That's how he finds the pictures. They are in a small tin box behind the gin. A young Stella, not more than sixteen maybe. Already full breasted. Nearly nude pictures of her in different poses that make him hard for her as if she's still alive. Then, at the bottom of the stack, the child: a little girl of maybe two, with pale curls, wearing a ruffled dress. The child she boarded out. The child he never even asked the name of. What did she tell him? She wants the child to be a Catholic. He turns the photograph over and she's written on it, Irene, 1934.

Irene.

Somewhere in his gin-fed stupor Zweikel is struck with the idea that this is the child who is missing. She must have kept the child in the hospital. That way she could see her every day. He buys a small frame from Woolworth's and moves Fredric March's picture to the back, replacing it with that of the child.

Whoever killed Stella stole his child. His child.

"Mr. Zweikel—" The older one, Kelly, has taken some papers from his inside pocket.

The detective's voice brings Zweikel back to the present.

He'd forgotten all about them. They are looking at him as if waiting for his answer. What was the question? "I'm sorry," he says, "I'm not feeling so good." Sweat clusters on his forehead and upper lip. The words, he suddenly realizes, have come out in Yiddish.

"Sit yourself, Mr. Zweikel," the younger one—what's his name—responds. In Yiddish.

A Jew is a policeman? Zweikel can't believe it. He pulls out a kitchen chair and sits down.

Kelly says, "We have a list here of people who worked at the hospital with your wife. We'd like you to look it over. Maybe you know a name."

"Maybe she mentioned someone," the younger one says, this time in English.

The list is a copy. The carbon has smudged onto the copy, and some of the letters have been typed over more than once. Names and addresses. The whole thing makes his eyes swim.

"Take it one at a time, Mr. Zweikel," the younger one says. "We know this is hard for you."

Morrisey. His name is Morrisey. What kind of a Jewish name is that, Zweikel thinks, but he doesn't say it out loud. There's something seriously wrong with Morrisey's wife. Zweikel's overheard him talking to what sounded like a doctor on the phone when they kept him at the station house.

Zweikel looks at the list again, letting his eyes travel down the page. A few of the names have checkmarks in front of them. "What means the checkmark?"

Kelly says, "They didn't come to work after your wife was killed."

"So it could be one of them?"

"Could be, but maybe not. The records aren't perfect.

Some of these people may have moved away some time ago or gone to other jobs."

It's only when he gets to the H's that Zweikel realizes that Ebanholz is not listed under "E." In fact, he is not listed at all, anywhere.

"Looking for someone?" Morrisey asks, giving him the eye.

"No. No. I just thought maybe I would recognize a first name." He goes back over the list. There. He stops when he sees Holz, Eban, with a checkmark next to him. Ebanholz. Zweikel is jubilant. God in Heaven has reached down and touched him. Ebanholz killed Stella and went off with Zweikel's child. Irene. It's a punishment because they lied to Ebanholz and took his money. Zweikel bursts into tears. Great wet blobs drop on the paper with the list of names and addresses.

"There, there, man, don't take it so hard," Kelly says, gruffly.

Morrisey takes the smudged list from him, but not before Zweikel puts to memory Ebanholz's address in the Bronx. 2255 Crotona Park East. Care of Kravitz. It's a tiny hesitation, but Morrisey notices.

"You recognized a name, didn't you?" Morrisey says. He holds the list in his hand, studying the names, hoping one will jump out from the others.

"No. I don't know them." Zweikel shrugs. "She never talked about the hospital—not to me."

After a while, they leave him. He hears them arguing out in the hall. That Morrisey wants to watch him. Kelly brushes it off.

Zweikel waits until the footsteps fade away. Waits some more. He'll find Ebanholz and get his daughter back. He knows what he has to do.

— 12 —

Anna

David is out on a call when Luke Applegate brings Anna and her packages home from the station in his taxicab.

"Somethin' sure smells good," he says, opening the back door and setting the packages inside.

Anna gives him two dollars, and agrees. In fact, what she smells is her mother's—blessed be her name—roasting chicken, lush with garlic and schmaltz.

Nathan is standing in the kitchen, oven door open, basting the chicken. He smiles at her as if nothing is wrong. Sitting on the floor playing with some blocks David keeps in the waiting room to distract children from the fact they are in a doctor's office, is the child. Her small face peers out from under a gray hood made by one of David's sweaters, which she wears like a nightdress.

After a moment's hesitation, she gives Anna a cautious smile, withdrawn immediately when she sees Luke loom up behind Anna.

"Luke, this is my brother, come to stay with us. And this is—" She stops and looks at Nathan.

"Pleased to make your acquaintance," Nathan says. He shakes hands with Luke. "This is my daughter, Rosie." He bends and picks up the child, who hides her face in his shirt. "She's not good with strangers."

"That's all right. I know. I have two of my own. I'll be

going now, Miz Blackwell. Give the doc my best, you hear. Nice meeting you."

Anna walks him to the door and switches on the back porch light.

Luke says, "She's a pretty little thing. With those eyes, she must look like her mama."

"My brother lost his wife recently, Luke."

"I'm real sorry to hear that. Poor little tyke. Lucky to have you and the doc so close."

After he leaves, Anna turns off the light in the back foyer and stands in the dark for some time.

"Anna?" Nathan's calling her. "Are you all right?"

She comes into the kitchen, into the light and warmth. If she closes her eyes, she will be transported back to Zakliczyn to her mother's kitchen.

"Anna?" Nathan holds the child, rocking her. "Is anything wrong?"

He speaks Yiddish and she responds in Yiddish, the words rushing from her lips like a torrent. "Wrong?" Her voice rises. "Everything is wrong, Nathan." She opens her purse and removes the clipping, slams it down on the kitchen table so that the napkin holder, salt and pepper shakers, and sugar bowl jump. The child snuggles deeper into Nathan's arms, whimpering. "Nathan, what in God's name have you done?" She sits down at the table, her face in her hands.

Nathan peruses the clipping, evading her eyes. "What do you mean? What does this have to do with me?"

Despairing, Anna says, "Look at the face of the missing child, Nathan, and look at the child you're holding. Do you not see they are the same?"

"No! This is my Rayzela."

"Nathan, your Rayzela died with Miri in the fire. They never got to America."

"No!"

The child begins to cry.

"What do you mean, no? I have the letter right here." Anna takes the letter from her purse. "Fannie Kravitz gave it to me. Read it, or let me read it to you."

"No. It's a lie." Clinging to the child, Nathan backs away from her as if she's his enemy, as if she will destroy him.

"You must give her back. The whole of New York is looking for her. They will put you in prison, deport you. Electrocute you. You don't know about the Lindbergh baby—and what about the nurse who was—"

"You are wrong, Anna." He wheels about and goes up the stairs with the child.

Anna sighs. David will be home soon and she doesn't want him to hear any of this. Not yet. Maybe not ever. She hangs up her coat and sets the table.

On the stove, potatoes begin to rattle in a boiling pot of water. She checks them with a long fork, and finding they are just short of tender, drains the water and places them around the roasting chicken, so they are coated with fat drippings from the pan. She hears Nathan singing upstairs. He's gone mad.

Gathering up the bundles and the meager suitcase, Anna climbs the stairs. "Nathan, I brought clothing for you and—"

"Rosie," Nathan says. He is sitting in the old rocking chair they moved into the spare room. "See what Tante Anna has for you." He sets the child on the floor and begins tearing open the packages and showing her. "Oh, Anna, so beautiful. See, Rosie. Rosie?"

"Why Rosie?" Anna says.

"David thought she should have an American name."

"Ros-ie," Rosie murmurs, staring at the paper and

string. She makes no move to touch anything, not even the red snowsuit.

"So she is talking," Anna says, relieved that Nathan hasn't caused any lasting damage to the child.

Nathan gives Anna a nervous smile. "Come, Rosie darling, Papa will get you dressed up nice to show Uncle David."

Anna watches Nathan pick through the garments, holding them up for Rosie to see, trying to get her interest. "I brought some things for you. In the suitcase."

"No shoes for Rosie?"

The child is watchful; she shows no emotion.

"Shoes we'll get here so they fit right." Anna is sick with herself. She's going along with his craziness. But it will soon be finished. The child must be returned. Somehow. She can't risk the chance of getting David into trouble. Still, look how attached Nathan is to the child.

Rosie, in a blue dress, sits on the floor rubbing the soft cloth between her fingers, making small noises in her throat.

"Isn't she wonderful, Anna? My beautiful little girl."

"Nathan," Anna says in Yiddish in a harsh whisper, "Did you kill that woman?"

"What woman?" He frowns, eyes on the child.

"That nurse. Stella something."

"What nurse? I don't know any Stella."

"Nathan! You will drive me crazy." She lowers her voice. "The hospital where you worked, where you stole the child—" She tries to capture his eyes, but they shy away from her.

"Anna, you are crazy, for sure."

"Crazy, Nathan? I'm not the crazy person here. You

have got to stop this and take her back."

He begins collecting the string and the wrapping paper. "It's all a mistake, Anna."

"Is it, Nathan? Tell me how it's a mistake."

The sound of a car coming up the drive stops them. The door slams downstairs. "My kitchen has a delicious smell," David calls. "Hello? Where's my wonderful family?"

"David—" Anna says. "I don't want him to know." She calls, "Up here, David."

"There's nothing to know."

"Oh, really? My foolish brother." She watches the child, who has not changed her position on the floor. Rosie sits in a stupor, seemingly oblivious to the heated exchange between sister and brother. A thought comes to Anna. Of course. The child doesn't understand Yiddish, and they have been arguing in Yiddish. "Jenny!" Anna says.

The child shudders. She turns and stares at Anna, terror in her eyes. "Jenny," Anna says again. She hears David's footsteps on the stairs.

"No!" The child screams, holds her arms out to Nathan.

Nathan picks her up, hugging her, tears in his eyes. "Please, Anna," he pleads. To the child he says, "You are my Rosie, no? And I am your Papa. Tell Tante Anna I am your Papa."

"What's your name, baby?" Anna says.

David comes into the room, beaming at them, dark circles under tired eyes. "Rosie! How's my little niece Rosie?"

"What's your name, darling?" Nathan says, looking meaningfully at his sister. "Tell everyone your new American name."

The child looks at Anna intently, then David, and finally Nathan, calculating. Anna sees it and is afraid.

"Papa," the child says, pointing to Nathan. Then pointing to herself, she says, "Rosie."

— 13 —

Zweikel

The woman wears a hat so close to her head her hair isn't visible. Her black coat has a fox tail collar, the fox head biting the tail. Zweikel has his eye on her since he first sees her get on the train at Fourteenth Street. When she sits down across from him, he knows at once she is following him.

The police have spies everywhere. They think he killed Stella, choked the life out of her, but he would never have done that. No matter what she did.

His stubby fingers caress the neck of his shirt under which the fine lumps of Stella's pearls lie next to his skin. He found them in the sugar bowl when he came home from the police station the first time, and in his misery, he clasped them round his neck.

His eyes burn and his head hurts; pain like a dentist's drill stabs the nape of his neck. He hasn't been to his office in the drugstore since it happened. There are greenhorns pending, and things are bad in Europe.

The train on its platform above the streets screeches from station to station. He shakes his finger at the woman opposite him. "Don't think I don't know about you."

She pretends to be shocked, but he knows better. He's very smart about these things. He knows a Cossack when he sees one. It's a man dressed like a woman, Zweikel decides then and there. Maybe if he looks close he can see her beard.

"I know all about you," Zweikel says, "Don't you worry."

"Are you speaking to me?" The woman clutches her purse and gives him the evil eye.

Zweikel shudders, holds two fingers near his mouth, and spits through them.

It works. She gets off the train at the Grand Concourse and a Cossack in his blue uniform takes her place. So, he thinks, they are coming out in the open now.

Rumble, screech, watch yourself, Zweikel, the train shrieks as it goes hurtling through the Bronx.

He watches the policeman with hooded eyes. They think he isn't smart enough to see them give each other a sign when she got off and he got on.

The Cossack in blue gets up and goes into the next car.

The back of Zweikel's neck aches, and his eyes water. He rubs them with his palms. When he looks again, Nathan Ebanholz is there in front of him. "Murderer!" Zweikel screams, going for his throat.

But Ebanholz turns into a swarthy wop, who gives him a push, and Zweikel falls back hard against the seat. "Wassamatta, you crazy?"

He hears loud whispers in Yiddish, and knows they are all against him. Slumping in his seat, he begins to feel around in his pockets. Where is that address? Where has he put it? His frantic search turns into a twitching, jerking dance as the Elevated roars through the Bronx. Looking out, he sees a man almost close enough to touch in the window of a building. The man points at him and laughs.

Zweikel stands still finally, going through his pockets. A button pops loose from his coat and drops spinning to the oilcloth floor. The collar of his shirt askew, his hat tilted at a strange angle, Zweikel slowly begins to perceive a stone under his right heel. He sits down, unlaces his shoe, and holds it up to his face, peering inside.

"Guttinhimmel," a woman says.

But he hardly hears. He's found the slip of paper with the Kravitz address rolled into a ball. He wets his thumb and forefinger and rolls it open. 174th Street. The next stop is his.

He gets off quickly as soon as the door starts to open, pushing people out of his way, not noticing he is wearing only one shoe, grasping the other in his hand. The cold on the platform informs him, and he stops, jams foot into shoe without bothering to fit it right or tie it. Then he scampers down the stairs to the street, hunched over so no one will see him and follow.

The street, lined with small stores, slopes unexpectedly, and Zweikel loses his balance, falling hard to the sidewalk. He breaks his fall with his palms, scraping them on the cement. He looks at his wounded hands and begins to snivel.

Two ugly old women, one with a wart between her eyebrows as big as a nose itself, stand over him, clucking like two nosy hens. "Geddaway from me, you babbas." He wipes his runny nose on his sleeve and scrambles to his feet.

"Mishugga," one of the old ladies pronounces.

Nathan Ebanholz is standing in the candy store looking out the door. Zweikel growls and goes for him, his hat flying.

Gone.

"Geddaway from here, you crazy." The man in the candy store lunges at him with a stick.

Zweikel holds his torn hands up in front of him and backs away. This man is fat and balding. So maybe Ebanholz is a dybbuk, able to turn himself into different people. Zweikel curses him, raising both arms, lowering them, and pointing at him. So maybe it isn't even Ebanholz and his mind is playing tricks on him. Better he should find Kravitz. Then he'll know for sure.

A park comes up on his left. Crotona Park. The greeners aren't stopping anymore on the East Side. They're going directly to the Bronx, and Brooklyn. How many has he arranged for over these last years? He's lost track. Better he should concentrate on the numbers of the buildings. Not this one, not this one. It's getting dark. Everywhere he looks, he sees faces staring at him from windows. People brush past him on the sidewalk, newspapers folded under arms.

There it is. A good building with a small lobby. He walks up the low steps, slinking past a woman clutching a big bag of groceries. Stops. "You know maybe Kravitz?"

The woman looks at him, canny little dark eyes over fat cheeks. "Fannie and Abe? You want them?" She speaks in Yiddish to the shabby little man with the untied shoe.

And he responds in Yiddish, "Yes, yes. So what apartment?"

"You a relative?"

Again with the questions. Is she one of *them?* "N—yes. A cousin, just come from . . . the old country."

"No wonder," the woman says, as if that explains everything. "Go up. Fannie never said she was expecting family. 3B. But Abe doesn't come home till later. He works at Gimbel's." She's standing firmly in his way, taking her time. She'll probably take her time up the stairs, too, and he'll have to follow her.

"How can I go up if you block me?" He pushes her, and she, surprised by the unexpected attack, drops her bag of groceries. The thump and crash follow him as he runs up the narrow stairs.

"You greenhorns better watch yourselves!" the woman yells. "You're in America now."

What does he care? He stops on three, gasping, clutching the railing. His breath makes strange noises as it comes from his mouth. If he doesn't watch himself he'll die before he finds Ebanholz and kills him.

Footsteps on the stairs behind him make him move. Stumbling over his shoelaces, he slams into 3B, with a loud thump.

"Just a minute," a woman yells. "No! Heshy, no!"

Zweikel picks himself up and knocks. A shuffling sound comes from behind the door, then the door opens.

Fannie Kravitz sees a small man in ragged clothing, hair disheveled, no hat. His heavy-lidded brown eyes burn with madness, staring out from black circles. His beard is dark, uneven sprouts. "Oy Gutt," she gasps, backing away, hand over her heaving breast. Too late, she tries to close the door but he is in already. "Don't hurt me." She begins to shake and cry.

From somewhere in the apartment, a child gives piercing shrieks.

"It's her! She's here!" Of course. Boarded out here. Why hasn't he thought of it? Kravitz. Of course. "Where is she?"

Zweikel pushes Fannie. "Take me to her."

Fannie sobs, "No one is here but me and Heshy." The older children, thanks be to God, are at a birthday party downstairs.

Zweikel shrieks, "Heshy? Heshy?" He butts Fannie aside and follows the cries of the child. A barley soup fills his nostrils with longing. Transfixed. His mother's kitchen. His mother is long dead. What is he doing here? In a high chair, a red-faced child with dark hair screams and bangs on the tray.

Fannie runs to Heshy and lifts him from the chair. His diaper catches on the tray and stays there.

"It's a boy." Zweikel speaks in Yiddish.

"Of course Heshy's a boy," she answers in Yiddish, calming slightly. "You got something wrong with your eyes? You push your way in here like the landlord. What do you want from me?"

Zweikel's gut burns. He feels poisoned. "My Stella. He killed her and stole our girl." He begins to cry.

"Who?" Fannie relaxes. "Are you sick or something?" She puts Heshy back into the high chair, slipping him right into his diaper. Heshy stares at the weeping stranger, fascinated.

Fannie ladles soup into a bowl. "Here, eat something. Abe will be home soon. You can talk to him."

Zweikel sits down at the table. The soup is thick, with golden flecks of fat and tiny bits of carrot and parsley, surrounding a chunk of potato. Zweikel picks up the spoon, fills it, and inhales the wonderful smell. He blows on the spoonful and sips noisily. "Ah," he says.

He finishes the soup while Fannie watches him, arms folded across her breast. "You were hungry. You don't have a job?"

He shrugs, wipes his mouth with the back of his hand.

"Who are you? What do you want here?"

"I'm looking for Ebanholz." He picks his teeth with his tongue, clicking and whistling. "You know where he is?"

"Nathan? It's Nathan you want? Why didn't you say so?"

She takes his plate and sets it in the sink, lets the water run over it.

"So where is he?"

Fannie dries her hands on her apron. "God only knows. His sister came and packed up his things and took them

81

away. Such a tragedy. He lost his wife and daughter, you know."

"I the same."

"So, what is Nathan to you?"

"I—he—I owe him money. How can I get it to him?"

"That's serious, Mr.—"

"Zweikel."

"Mr. Zweikel. When he gets better, I'm sure he'll get in touch with you."

"No! I can't wait. I have to give it to him now. Where does the sister live?"

"I don't know. Maybe . . . wait . . ." Fannie frowns and scratches her head. "I think . . . Jersey."

"Jersey? Where in Jersey?"

"I don't know."

"But maybe she left an address with you?"

Fannie shakes her head.

"What's the sister's name?"

"What a question? Ebanholz, of course. What then? Maybe you should leave your address in case I hear something."

Zweikel stands up, wheezing. The pain in his head is starting again. "Gimme a piece paper."

Fannie takes a folded brown bag from the counter. "Here, write on this." She gives him a short, thick black pencil and watches him wet the point on his tongue and write. He's a little crazy but who isn't these days? Maybe Nathan or his sister will let her know where they are. Money is money. The sister was dressed like a queen, but Nathan will need the money this Zweikel owes him.

The little man stops writing, drops the pencil on the table, and goes off down the hall without another word. Fannie follows him. He's a sick man, no doubt. His color is bad. The wheezing grows louder. He goes out the door clutching at his throat. A sound comes like dry rice spilling on the floor.

Zweikel gives a strangled cry. He plunges down the stairs and disappears.

Heshy screams from the kitchen, furious to be trapped in the high chair.

All over the floor in the hall—everywhere you look—are pearls. Fannie goes down on her knees and begins picking them up.

— 14 —

Anna

Rosie wets the bed that night. And again the night after that. Anna buys three diapers and a rubber pad for the mattress from Berryman's Drugs.

"Well, what have we here, Miz Blackwell?" Sid Berryman says. "You have a youngster up at the house?"

Anna has reservations about Sid Berryman, or Doc Berryman, as he is called. Although he has no accent, he's Jewish, and when Anna came to Clayton Lake, he made certain she knew it.

Once, before she and David were married, Berryman had even suggested that it didn't look right for a single woman to live alone in a house with a widower, particularly a goy.

She'd responded, tartly, that it was none of his affair, and then realized that news of her attitude would be all over the small Jewish community before nightfall. Smiling, she'd switched to Yiddish, thanking him for his concern with as much sincerity as she could feign.

A week later had come an invitation to dinner from Mrs. Berryman in the form of a phone call. Molly Berryman also speaks English without an accent. They are Americanized Jews, one of maybe a dozen families in Clayton Lake. Two lawyers, a dentist, a pharmacist, Berryman, several shopkeepers, a couple of schoolteachers, and a tailor with a cleaning store. The tailor is an English Jew and has a refined accent.

Anna had been wary of the invitation. She'd check

with Dr. Blackwell, she said.

And David had said, "Of course, you must go. It would probably be a good idea . . . you'll meet some young people . . ."

John Novinger, a lawyer, and his wife Betty had also been dinner guests, as had a pale young man about Anna's age, Dr. Albert Braudy, a nephew of Sid and Molly Berryman. Braudy, an optometrist, newly licensed, is about to open an office in Clayton Lake. His face is covered with little white pustules. The baggy suit calls attention to his narrow shoulders. His breath, sour milk.

They'd seated him next to Anna at the table. She found him repulsive. The evening was torture from the moment Doc Berryman came for her, beeping the horn in the drive.

David had laughed. "Your chariot awaits," he'd said.

All through dinner they had taken turns questioning her, or so it seemed. Over the chicken soup with knaidlach, Molly had wanted to know about where in Europe she had come from, and when Anna had responded, "Poland," they'd been surprised. They had assumed Russia, as if all the new immigrants came from Russia. She had told them about Nathan, that Miri and the baby were coming to America. They wanted to know how she came to work for David Blackwell, and she had told them.

It was Sid Berryman who said, "Perhaps it isn't such a good idea for you to live alone in the house with Dr. Blackwell. You are a young, single Jewish woman. You will want to marry." He looked at his nephew with significance.

"Are you saying that Dr. Blackwell is not a good man?" Anna considered herself an independent woman. She was affronted by their suggestion.

"Oh no, not at all." They all spoke at once. "A fine man, for a goy. A good doctor."

"Of course," Betty Novinger said, "he is much older."

"Still—" Molly Berryman said.

It was as if Anna were not there at all.

Somehow they managed to work it so that Albert would take her home.

In the car, after a silent trip to the Blackwell house, Albert had asked her to go with him to the movies the following Saturday. She told him abruptly that she could never have children. No further questions were asked and she had never heard from him again.

Anna knows the Jewish community in Clayton Lake does not approve of her marriage to David, but one day, not long afterward, she'd met Betty Novinger in the butcher shop. Betty had taken her hand and congratulated her. "I want you to know I understand. David is a good man."

Now, as she carries the packages back to the house, Anna wonders what they would think, what they would do, if they knew the truth about Nathan. She can't hold back the shudder. She must take Nathan somewhere and talk some sense into him.

All afternoon she ushers patients in to see David. At four o'clock they stop for a cup of coffee and a piece of sponge cake and then David goes out on his house calls.

Tomorrow Macy's will deliver the bed. Knowing what she knows, why has she gone ahead with the order? Why has she not cancelled it? Perhaps she still hopes against hope that the child is Nathan's and so, hers and David's as well. It is becoming clear to her that their individual, and collective, need for the child will perpetuate the lie.

The child heals slowly, physically and emotionally. She is frail, with spindly legs and arms and a poor appetite. Her hair is a curly white fluff. She no longer cries out in the night.

But there is a mother, and a father, somewhere, crazy with grief. Anna goes over and over it in her mind. She has to do something, even if Nathan won't. He is young. He will marry again, have his own children.

She makes up her mind to do it while her resolve is still strong. No one will connect it with Nathan. She'll see to that.

— 15 —

Anna

Anna is not familiar with this section of the Bronx. She gets off the Elevated at Allerton Avenue and walks down the steps. When it starts raining, her apprehension increases. She is suddenly sorry that she decided to do this today. Yet, one day longer and her determination may crumble.

David has gone to Philadelphia to a conference. He'll not miss her. And Nathan, he will not suspect anything. He is so wrapped up in the child. The child.

Her anxiety is like a fever. What, oh what, will she tell David when the child is returned? Stop, Anna, she tells herself. She cannot deal with this now. The right thing must be done. Regardless. They cannot risk being discovered.

Anna knows only that she must protect Nathan. He is all the blood she has in this world.

She stops in a candy store on Allerton, near the Institute for the Blind, to ask directions and finds she is a good distance away from the Barker Avenue neighborhood. The proprietor, half blind himself, peers at her through thick lenses and gives her directions in Yiddish.

It is cold, with a drizzly chill that gnaws to the bone. Anna pulls her hat over her ears, opens her umbrella, and walks quickly.

"Excuse me."

Anna stops short. A tall man in a hat and overcoat, an umbrella over his head, stands in front of her, blocking her way with his cane. It takes her several seconds to understand that he is not the police but a blind man. "Oh," she says, "you want the Institute."

"Yes. Can you direct me? I seem to have lost my way."

She closes her umbrella and gets under his, offering him the crook of her arm. His hand finds it. She walks him the half block to the Institute and leaves him safe, on the path leading to the door.

He finds his way efficiently to the front door and disappears inside. Anna opens her umbrella once again and goes on to Barker Avenue, shaken. For all the grief, the fear, she and Nathan are together. And they are not blind. Not in that way.

Barker Avenue is a wide street that ends at the park. Because of the weather, there are few children on the street, which is just as well. Anna finds the number she's looking for and pauses in front of the clean, modest building of five floors. From here, she can see the park, even in the rain. She walks past the building to the corner, which is an empty lot.

Behind the building is an entrance to the Elevated, stairs up to the platform. So she could have, had she known, come down directly behind the apartment house.

Across from the building is a small mountain of gray rock, bleak and forbidding in size and color.

Anna folds her umbrella and enters the narrow lobby, looking for the mailboxes. The name is Topinski. Third floor front. She climbs the stairs slowly, taking in whiffs of brisket and onions, chicken soup. Several times she feels the urge to turn back, but having come this far, she must finish or they are doomed.

The hallway is dimly lit by a bulb of low wattage inside a glass globe. Voices come at her with the cooking odors, from all sides, seeping under doors, through keyholes. Babies cry. A carriage stands empty outside one closed door, almost blocking the corridor. Anna squeezes by.

She finds the apartment and knocks, tentatively. When there is no response, she knocks again, harder. This time the door slips its catch and reveals a crack of dull light.

Still she hesitates. The door hinge creaks. A corresponding sound comes from within. Anna's teeth knead her lower lip. Do it, she tells herself. She pushes open the door and gasps, stepping back.

Broken furniture and empty liquor bottles, a glittering carpet of smashed glass. The stink, like an animal. Alcohol mixed with vomit, stale cigarettes. And urine. Turpentine and the sharp odor of oil paint.

Canvases, dozens of them, colors vivid, subjects unrecognizable, slashed to obscurity. They lean against grotesque murals on the walls. Others burst from open doorways, closets. Everything in chaos. The remnants of chairs, reduced to firewood. Springs, lumps of stuffing. Shreds of a fine damask hang awry from a cock-eyed valance, letting in dreary light from a north-facing window. Jars of brushes and used tubes of paint are rampant, dripping, some overturned, on a stained floor and threadbare rug.

Anna would have walked away then and there, washed her hands of the whole thing, but the groan stops her. Where did it come from? Furling herself, she edges her way across the living room, for this is what it had been at one time. Although she tries to push them aside, shards of glass crunch under her feet.

Smudged reddish prints of bare feet track out of the living room and she follows them, listening. He's lying on his side on the floor of the bedroom, his reddish beard matted with drool and vomit, his arms making a lover of his pillow. Snores break the silence, make her start. An empty whisky bottle lies on its side nearby.

The room holds a double bed and a large crib, one side of which has been broken away. The smashed head of a doll peeks out from under it, the painted eyes staring. A confetti of pages from picture books dusts the floor near the crib. Everything has been willfully savaged. On the bed, a grimy sheet is blotched with blood.

Anna is terrified, unable to move, or, for the moment, hear her mind shouting at her to get out of there. Then it's too late. A rough hand grasps her ankle and holds it in a vise. He laughs, not moving, not opening his eyes. Just laughs. She kicks out at him hard, not realizing he can pull her leg from under her. But she takes him by surprise. The toe of her shoe finds his chin.

"Bitch!" Raw, bloodshot eyes open, he releases her ankle and sits up, rubbing his chin. But Anna uses the seconds to her advantage. She escapes to the hall, slamming the door behind her.

Leaning on the wall, panting, she mutters aloud, "A monster, the man is a monster."

"Excuse me." A dark haired woman calls to Anna from the half-open door across the hall. She holds a struggling baby on her hip. "It's better you don't go in there. He's a lunatic."

"I just saw him, and I believe you."

The woman shifts the baby to her other hip. "Maybe you want a glass of tea. You look like you could use it." She motions Anna inside. "I'm Esther Apter. This is Beatie, who today is ten months."

The apartment is similar in layout to the other, but only in size and shape. It is full of furniture, the upholstery accented with crocheted doilies on the arms and backs. On

91

every flat surface are photographs, vases, chochkas. Neat, clean, fresh smelling.

Anna sits, still stunned, in the kitchen while Esther pours hot water over Lipton tea bags. She sets out a cup of sugar and some slices of lemon.

"You're a relative?"

"Distant." Anna's hands shake.

"From around here?"

"Ah—no. Hartford." She takes a sip of the hot tea.

"My husband has a cousin in Hartford. Shapiro is the name. An electrician. You would maybe know him—"

"What happened here? Can you tell me? Where is his wife?"

Esther clucks her tongue against her teeth. "Laura? You wouldn't believe how he treated her. I don't like to talk about other people, but he is a bad one." The baby stiffens her body, jerking away from her mother. "If you'll pardon me—" As if someone is listening, Esther's voice drops to almost a whisper. "You ask me, we should stay with our own kind."

"I don't understand."

"It comes with mixing with the goyim. You know what I mean? You can live next door to them, but you don't marry them. As my mama—may she rest in peace—always said, sooner or later they'll call you dirty Jew. And let me tell you, that Topinski took a hand to her plenty, especially with the drinking. 'Jew pig,' I heard him yelling at her the last time, and the baby screaming, and everything. It was terrible."

"The last time?"

Esther sits Beatie on the floor. Pleased, the baby looks up at her mother. Esther nods and smiles. Beatie gets on her hands and knees and begins crawling.

"First they took poor little Jenny away to the hospital with scarlet fever, then he cracked Laura's head open and broke her jaw. I thought he killed her for sure this time. I couldn't stand it no more. This time, when the screaming started, I called the police. Laura, they put her in Bronx Hospital. He beat her so bad you couldn't even recognize her when they carried her out to the ambulance."

"What happened to Jenny?"

"I guess it wasn't in the Connecticut papers. Wait. Beatie, come back." Esther rises and collects Beatie, who has disappeared into another room. She returns with a petulant child and holds Beatie on her lap until the infant reaches for the glass of tea and knocks it over, barely escaping a scalding. When a modicum of peace is restored, Esther says, "She was kidnapped." She rolls her eyes. "Or so they say."

"What do you mean?"

"At the hospital where she was—not the Bronx—someone killed a nurse and went away with poor little Jenny, and, if you ask me, I know who did it."

Anna's heart jumps. "You do?" She takes out a handkerchief and blots her face and neck.

"Yes. Topinski it had to be. Believe me, he has her hidden away somewhere. The poor little thing. He'll do to her what he did to her mama, you know what I mean?"

Anna gets up in a haze of relief. "I have to go now. You've been very kind. Thank you for the tea. I'll go see . . . Laura."

"It won't do you any good." Esther Apter sets the howling baby in the high chair, and gets on her knees to wipe up the spilled tea.

"She hasn't—?"

"No, no. Not that. At least I'm not sure. God forbid.

93

She left, went away. Disappeared. And I can't say I blame her. The super said Topinski told him that he was going to find her and bring her back."

"Went away?"

"Look, I told you he's crazy. If she did run away, it's a good thing. If he found her, he'd kill her."

"You don't think she took the child with her?"

Esther shrugs. "Maybe. But I don't think so. She was in terrible condition. Broken bones, crippled maybe even. Someone went into the hospital where the child was, killed the nurse, and stole the child. And I got a pretty good idea who."

Anna thanks the woman and leaves. Her thoughts roil. In her head the words keep repeating, "It's a good thing. It's a good thing."

A bitter wind blows up Barker Avenue from the park, making loose dirt swirl like mini-whirlpools. It's turned much too cold even for the mothers who make a fetish of fresh air. On the sidewalk a shiny silver dime lies in Anna's path. She bends and picks it up, fingering it.

God knows where the mother is. Wrong or not, how could Anna put the child Nathan calls Rosie back into the hands of that animal upstairs? Better Rosie should have love, a family. Of course, she tells herself, if the mother ever comes forward . . .

It's dark when Anna gets home. Rosie and Nathan are sitting on the floor in the living room playing cards, or rather, Nathan is playing solitaire and Rosie sucks her thumb and watches. Anna stands in the doorway. "Anna?" Nathan's eyes are fearful.

Anna bends and kisses the top of Rosie's head, touches the child's cool brow.

"What, Anna? Say it."

"There's nothing to say."

"I don't understand."

She smiles. "I was thinking I might make chocolate pudding for dinner."

— 16 —

Morrisey

Brian Morrisey's chin hits his collarbone with a jolt and he wakes. Alert. Hand on his gun. For a hair's breadth he doesn't know where he is. But the antiseptic and the uneven breathing chorus anchors him.

The girl on the bed has startling eyes. Green, they are, and now they stare out at him almost feral from multicolored rims. Her jaw is wired and her lips are stretched, cracked, and crusted, raw around the impediment. Both arms wear casts. She has not uttered a word since they brought her in, more dead than alive.

He rises and stretches, takes himself a little stroll around the bed, out to the center aisle and around again, always uncomfortably aware that her eyes follow him. He sees it all the time. Mix booze and no jobs, and they go after their women. His own people are the worst, but the Eastern Europeans are holding their own.

Still, his sleep-clotted eyes give him the illusion of Pauline herself looking back at him from white sheets, seeing him, when all the time he knows his Pauline lies one floor above, barely able to turn her head.

From the beginning, it's been Morrisey who talks to the brutalized girl. Laura is her name. Laura Topinski. While he's certain she hears him, there's been no response. He knows enough Yiddish from Pauline to make himself understood, but this one hasn't even blinked.

Morrisey has taken to stopping by after seeing Pauline. Pulling over a chair, he sets up the screen to give them privacy, then he sits until they tell him to leave. And he's back again the next day after his shift, except for the time Kelly and his wife Mary came to see Pauline and insisted he come home with them for dinner.

And what he'd done that night was come back to the hospital after dinner. He'd looked in on Pauline, and then come down the stairs onto the ward without being seen, stood at the foot of Laura's bed until she opened her eyes. For a moment he had seen something flare. Recognition? A memory? Some emotion that had frightened her, for she disappeared behind her still swollen lids almost immediately after.

But Morrisey speaks to her anyway, as if they are old friends.

So it is that tonight, after sitting with Pauline, who didn't know him, he's come down to her and started talking. "My Pauline," he blurts out, his voice thick, "she keeps slipping in and out of coma. They gave her last rites. Doc said she won't last much longer. Our boy isn't ten yet." But then he's weeping. Embarrassed, he stands, back to the bed. Dries his face with his big white handkerchief.

A sound, like the mewl of a small animal, makes him turn. Her eyes are wide open. Tears, sparse as gems, give a surreal luster to her ravaged face.

"Laura," he says. He pulls the chair closer to the bed.

The next day they remove the bandages from around Laura's head, and Pauline dies.

When Kelly checks in on the call box, they tell him Pauline's gone, and he's the one who breaks it to Morrisey.

They are in the Bronx because it turns out Topinski didn't spend the whole night in jail, after all. They've come up to talk to him, but he's taken a powder. Gone. Probably took the kid from where he's had her stashed, and jumped bail. In his gut, Kelly is sure Topinski killed that nurse. Proving it is another story.

As for the family stuff, Kelly isn't one for beating up women, but it happens. A man gets some booze in him and the wife complains and he lets her have it. They're married and that's the way it is. They have to straighten it out between them.

Of course, a killing is a killing, but Laura Topinski isn't dead. And right now she isn't being helpful. She's not talking, and there's more to it, if you ask him, than just the jaw being wired. He says as much to Morrisey. Morrisey is the new breed of cop. These kids always think they have a better handle on what's right.

Brian Morrisey immersed himself in the Topinski kidnapping from the beginning. He felt it tug at him in a strange way. The investigation led them to Laura, connected him to her, oddly, through Pauline. Like his Pauline, Laura has no family, or at least no one's come forward and there's been plenty of opportunity what with the newspaper coverage.

The woman across the hall from the Topinskis mentioned a cousin, from Hartford. If so, why hasn't the cousin contacted the police, or the hospital?

Morrisey's been mourning Pauline for weeks now. He'd let everyone else pray for miracles, but he knew there would be none.

Sitting with Laura Topinski, talking to her, has made it easier.

Ma's been keeping Billy for him. How is he going to

raise a boy with his mother dead and gone? What can he say to him? Billy, your ma and me, we made a mistake and went against the doctors. They said her heart wouldn't take it. We lost her and your brother. Morrisey feels sick to his stomach.

People, Ma's friends and some of his own from the neighborhood, have been kind, coming around, bringing Mass cards, but Morrisey feels disconnected.

He goes into his old room and sits on the bed. The room is dark. "Billy? Son?" he says. It's his old bed from when he was a kid. Everything still in place, including his Regis High School trophies.

His boy's face is a pale sphere.

"I know, I miss her, too." He bends to kiss him. "But we have each other. Always remember that. It's you and me together."

When he comes out of the bedroom, Ma is talking out Angie Doyle from downstairs. She says, "It's God's will," and closes the door.

"For Christ's sake, don't say that, Ma. How can it be God's will? Pauline never hurt a soul in her life. We should never have tried to keep the baby."

Ma crosses herself, the rosary clutched in her hand. "Never say that," she whispers. As if God can hear her.

If God could hear, Pauline would be alive.

He apologizes, tells Ma he's going out to walk it off.

He walks past St. Agnes, past Selber's candy store, where he met Pauline when they were kids, the Jews from public school and the Catholics from St. Agnes. It's late; most of the stores are closed.

Doc Pomerance is just closing the drugstore. "My condolences on your loss, Brian. She was a nice girl, a good soul."

"Thanks, Doc." He pauses, thinking. "Maybe you got a jar of Vaseline? I keep forgetting to pick one up."

"Wait here." Pomerance unlocks the door and puts on the lights. He's back in a minute with a small jar and hands it to Brian.

Brian reaches into his pocket. "What do I owe you?"

"Nothing. Not a thing." Doc Pomerance shuts off the light and locks the door. "I'll say good night to you." He tips his hat and goes off down the street.

The small jar making a bulge in his pocket, Brian's feet take him to the hospital, where everyone knows him, where he is greeted deferentially. Condolences offered and accepted.

Why is he here, he asks himself. She's not your care. But that isn't altogether true. A child has disappeared. A woman has been murdered. The mother of the child lies beaten and broken in Bronx Hospital, and the man responsible, her own husband, has vanished as well.

It's Morrisey's opinion that Topinski got liquored up, broke into the hospital, killed the nurse when she tried to stop him, grabbed his kid, and took off. If this is true, the poor kid is in for it.

If he can only get Laura Topinski to talk, remember anything, maybe he and Kelly will catch themselves a murderer and get the kid back.

He climbs the back stairs and lets himself into the ward. The screen is already set up and a chair stands next to the bed. His shoes make small clicks on the surface of the linoleum-covered floor. Muffled coughs surround him; someone is having a whole conversation with herself, out loud. He takes off his hat and coat and slips into the chair. She's waiting for him.

Now that the bruises are healing, she looks even more the child. He knows that anyone who could do that to her will not be deterred by an actual child.

Her eyes stalk him. The white casts on her arms, the wires holding her jaw together, lips stretched into a hideous smile, the paint box of bruises, all give her a circus clown look, half comic, half tragic.

"No news," Morrisey says, although he isn't sure she understands. He reaches into his inside pocket, where the jar meets his shoulder harness. Setting the small jar on the bed, he remembers what Pauline said to him the last time, when they knew she was dying. She'd been obsessed with the kidnapping, with Laura Topinski. "I keep thinking about that poor girl down there and her stolen child," she'd said, when every movement was an impossible effort.

"She will heal and we'll find the baby," he assured Pauline, with no real sense that this would happen, thinking only that Pauline would never heal.

And Pauline had clung to his hand. "My dearest, mourn me, but marry again, quickly, a good person. Billy needs a mother."

He had lain on the bed with her and held her, wasting away, bones in cloth, and tears and breath merged. He would never find another like Pauline.

Now, only two weeks after, only two days since Pauline passed, Morrisey feels this girl's need excruciating. Beaten, abandoned, alone in the world, and deprived of her child.

He unscrews the jar and scoops out a dab of Vaseline with his fingertip. She cringes when he comes closer, mewls through the wires.

"Hold still," he whispers. "I won't hurt you." Her lips are like cracked leather under his finger. A whisper of a sigh grazes his hand. He speaks to her in a soft murmur. "I will never hurt you, Laura. Never."

— 17 —

Anna

Anna turns on the light in the kitchen and fills the percolator, measuring out the coffee, while David shaves and dresses. Old Mrs. Azioni is doing poorly. Her son made the call.

Patients will begin coming even before eight-thirty, but David will be back long before that. The old woman had a stroke three months ago. Her left side is paralyzed and she can't speak. There isn't much David can do. Except, Anna knows, David's very presence has a calming effect.

Not to be able to speak, Anna thinks. This is a terrible thing. A curse.

After David leaves, Anna sits at the table drinking coffee. She's worried about Nathan. What will become of him? As for the child, there's no doubt that the father is a brute. The mother has disappeared. If they take Rosie back now, Nathan will go to prison and Rosie will be put in an orphanage. No. That is not a solution.

They—Nathan and Anna—talked it through after Anna returned from the Bronx. She'll ask no more questions. What had happened, had happened. The secret will stay between them. Though it grieves her, David must never learn the truth.

She and Nathan promised one another Rosie will have a life far removed from that she might have had. She'll be cared for, loved, educated like an American girl.

Anna and David will never have children of their own. She has seen the happiness on David's face when he looks at Rosie. From the beginning he's treated Nathan and Rosie like his own.

Rosie will have the blessing of three parents.

She listens for movement upstairs but hears nothing.

What if the mother comes forward one day? What will they do? She pushes the thought away. The mother has disappeared. The brute has disappeared. Rosie will thrive in a loving home.

But the child thus far is not thriving. She hardly speaks at all, remains instead watchful. Her eyes, green as a cat's, follow them, almost as if she's waiting for something to happen.

Yet, she reacted violently to the crib, screaming, hysterical, when she saw it. Anna, remembering the condition of the crib in the Topinski apartment, makes the connection. Nathan moved it out of the room, and Rosie finally fell asleep on the big bed.

Exhausted, Nathan and Anna sealed their pact as they sat in the kitchen, waiting for David to return from his calls.

All that remains now is how Nathan will earn a living.

What they don't know is that David has already figured it out.

It is not even five o'clock, and still dark. Anna rinses her cup and saucer and puts them on the drain rack. She must stop thinking and just accept what has happened. She goes upstairs to dress, stopping to look in on Nathan and Rosie. Nathan is sleeping on his back, his face so young, a boy's face, untouched by tragedy. It takes only a second for her to realize that Rosie is not on the bed.

A low sing-song murmur comes from behind the door.

Anna steps into the room. Rosie lies in a fetal position, crayons clutched in her fists. The paper bag from Macy's is torn, the teddy bear lies discarded. On the inside of the paper bag are vivid multicolored swirls and waves surrounding two tiny stick figures, one head larger than the other. The heads wear scribbled masses of yellow crayon hair. The faces have only eyes, no other features. No mouth. And jagged red marks streak from the eyes. The effect is grotesque.

As Anna looks deeper into the drawing, the swirls and waves form into a ghastly, gaping mouth.

— 18 —

Laura

The sound—not a sound really, but an impression—skims the edges of her torpor.

She has no history before Topinski. She'd become enmeshed in the frantic sweetness of him. He'd absorbed her, then painted over her past with the power of his madness. She'd become his obsession. Until Jenny. And now he's taken Jenny.

Jenny sitting with her on the park bench, swinging her legs in her white shoes and socks, the air so soft.

This time the sound penetrates. Jenny. Jenny's crying somewhere. She must go to her. But her body doesn't respond. She begins to count her fingers, touching each to the others. She lies on her back in a strange bed, in a strange room, listening, waiting for the pieces to come together.

The big, sad cop. Morrisey. His wife dead. He comes and sits with Laura, talks softly, tells her he needs a housekeeper, someone to care for his motherless boy. He explains it all to her, but she hardly listens. She has no place else to go. And he's a good man. He'll find Jenny.

There it is again. She elbows herself into a sitting position. Her arms in their casts are useless.

The small bedroom is imbued with Pauline's presence. The nightgown she wears was Pauline's. Pauline's toilet things remain on the dressing table so the very air carries her faint scent.

Morrisey has given Laura their bed, their room. He sleeps on the couch in the living room or in Billy's room if he doesn't come home too late.

He'd said, "You need a place to live, and Billy and I need you."

She sets her feet on the carpet and stands, feeling the stiffness like new shoes. She looks down at them, pale in the semidarkness.

The despair comes slowly, as it always does, a paint spill, red, seeping into her soul. She welcomes it, an old friend, hugs it to her breast. Topinski stole her poor Jenny, sick to death with scarlet fever, stole her from the Willard Parker Hospital, killed a nurse, and took Jenny away. Jenny will die without care. Topinski will kill her one way or the other, as he's already killed Laura.

She's hardly aware of the tears. He'd been such a sweet-faced boy, tall and shy, a farm boy from Pennsylvania, lost in the city. Laura, working as a waitress, going to school at night. He'd come into the restaurant often, for coffee, a Danish, smelling of turpentine, his nails crusted with colors.

He wanted to paint her, he said, asking her haltingly, unable to meet her eyes. They all said that, these art students, flirting with her, and she always smiled, knowing they wanted more than that. But Topinski had been different. Whenever he came to the restaurant, her heart fluttered and she'd longed to hold him. She had never smelled whisky on him as she had the others.

With her pale toes, Laura nudges the bedroom door open. She listens. It's quiet for only a moment. Despair meets anguish in the sound coming from the other bedroom, the door slightly ajar. The boy is a huddled mound on the bed, sobbing under the tent of blankets.

Her Jenny would sob so for her mother. Laura comes to the edge of the bed, her cast-encased arms reaching out to touch the quivering mound. The sound stops. Laura sits on the bed. She has not spoken since . . . cannot speak . . . . The ache is bitter now.

The boy lies still under her hand.

Awkwardly, she turns down the blanket and touches her fingertips to the small wet face, to his hair. "Shah-ma-ma." The sound of her voice a whispery breath.

When Morrisey comes home he finds Laura, her back against the headboard, holding Billy in her plastered arms, her fair halo merging with his dark hair. They are both asleep.

— 19 —

Morrisey

A surprisingly hot morning in early May. Morrisey begins his day as he frequently does, talking to the tenants of the Barker Avenue building where Laura lived with Topinski. He keeps thinking something, some small thing, will come up and lead them to Jenny. But there's nothing. Jenny seems to have disappeared without a trace.

When he gets to the precinct, he and Kelly go right back out to see about a dead body in a room on First Avenue. It looks more like a suicide; according to the neighbors, the guy tried it before. This time he made it. Cut his wrists and bled to death in the tub of the shared bathroom.

Morrisey and Kelly stop at Leary's for the complimentary corned beef that comes with a beer and then head back to the precinct to write the report.

Gerry Collins is sitting on the desk. "Billy's in the hospital, but he's okay." Collins has been keeping an eye out for Morrisey to tell him the news before he hears it from someone else. Morrisey's been through hell and back and the cops in the precinct watch out for him.

Morrisey folds like someone punched in the stomach. "God, not Billy." Nothing must happen to Billy. But something has. He smacks the side of the tall desk, lowers his head, shaking it back and forth. "I gotta get outa here."

"He's okay, I'm telling you," Collins says. "They had to take out his appendix before it busted open."

"Where?" Kelly steps in, clamping a hand on Morrisey's shoulder.

"Bronx Hospital."

"No." Not there, Morrisey thinks, not again.

"Let's go, let's go," Kelly says, steering him right out the door. "Who called it in, Gerry?"

"The housekeeper, what's her name? Laura?"

They put on the sirens to get to the Bronx. When they get to the hospital, Morrisey doesn't wait for Kelly to step on the brakes. He jumps out of the car and runs. The woman at the information desk knows him from before and directs him to the floor.

Morrisey takes the steps two at a time and runs onto the floor, distraught.

"Room 304," the nurse tells him. "He's okay but he won't wake up for a few hours. His mother is with him."

Laura sits beside Billy's bed, his hand limp in both of hers. She's talking softly to him although he can't possibly hear. She looks up when Morrisey rushes through the door. "He's going to be all right."

Morrisey stands behind Laura's chair. Billy is deathly pale, but the blanket that covers him trembles with each tiny breath. His dark eyelashes make shadows on his small face.

"Oh, God." Morrisey sinks to his knees next to the bed.

"The school called me," Laura says. "I took a cab, picked him up, and we came right here."

Her voice is pure, unaccented, sweet to his ear. Morrisey has never heard her speak. Even after the wires that held her jaw in place were removed and she was pronounced healed, she's never spoken.

Touching his son's face, Morrisey hears himself groan. He buries his face in the blanket.

"Brian."

Morrisey feels the tentative touch of her hand on his head, then all that's been suppressed ruptures. He puts his head in her lap and weeps.

"He'll sleep through the night and well into the morning," the doctor tells them. "No use your hanging around. Go home and get some rest."

"No," Laura says. "If he wakes up early and no one's here, he'll be frightened." Like my baby, my Jenny. She looks at Morrisey.

"We'll stay," Morrisey says.

Kelly carries a deep arm chair from the visitors' lounge into the room and leaves them with a gruff, "It'll be all right. Don't worry about it, I'll sign you in tomorrow."

Morrisey moves the big chair closer to Laura. "Switch with me," he says. "This is more comfortable."

She shakes her head. "I'm okay."

He sits down and the leather creaks and settles under him. "Laura, I talked to Esther Apter again today."

Her eyes have lost that feral quality they'd had in the beginning. They are green, like spring grass. "Nothing new. I'm sorry. I'll keep trying."

She rests her hand on his. Her sigh is a burden shared. "You're a good man, Brian Morrisey," she says.

Fannie

1940

Heshy is in school a full day now—such a big boy he is. Fannie just wishes he won't get into so many fights. She's always getting complaints from the teachers. . . . Americanisher kinder.

Money is short since Abie's shop laid almost everybody off. Abie is lucky, but they cut his hours back. Things aren't so good. Their last boarder, Mrs. Kraus, a poor soul from Vienna, who jumped and shook whenever there came a siren, had left for California where there was a cousin of her husband. Mr. Kraus, the husband, had been arrested just as they were leaving the country. He had insisted she go on without him, but all she did was cry and shake from the minute she arrived six months ago.

Fannie Kravitz has a big heart, but this business with Mrs. Kraus was too hard on everybody. "No more boarders," she told Abe, "and that's all there is to it."

With the children at school all day, and Ezra, already thirteen and with a job at Nedick's after school, Fannie decides to become a working girl.

She gets herself fixed up nice with a permanent and a new girdle, stockings, a green print dress with white collar and cuffs, and answers an ad for Horn and Hardart.

They give her a day of training and make her a cashier,

one-two-three, at the Automat in Times Square. She works Monday to Friday and half a day on Saturday in a nice wooden booth with a marble counter, changing money into nickels, and for this she gets breakfast and lunch and seven dollars a week. And you should see the place she works. A palace.

She's busy all day making change, chatting with customers, wishing them they should have a good day. Fannie never gets tired of watching people put nickels in the slots and opening the little windows and taking out what they want to eat. She herself loves the baked beans and the egg custard.

Finally, she begins to look at the Automat proprietarily, as if it is her business. She has regulars, like the musician with his horn case who comes in and finishes peoples' leftovers. Fannie never says anything. There's also an old actor who uses a cane—a dignified man with fine white hair. He takes hot water in a cup and makes a soup with ketchup. She looks the other way. And there are always the elegant ladies in their fur coats. And gentlemen with wonderful manners.

Near noon on this Saturday, when Fannie has only an hour left of work, she is thinking she'll buy a movie magazine to read on her way home and maybe she and Abie will go see Joan Crawford tonight at the Loew's.

As she surveys her domain, a very pretty little girl in red leggings and a matching short red coat catches her eye. The girl is standing at the dessert windows on tiptoes, trying to see in. Her curly white-blond hair is caught under a red cap that fastens under her chin. She's clapping her hands, excited.

Fannie smiles benignly. Children love her Horn and Hardart. The mother is a tall, stylish woman in a small black hat with a little veil. Her fitted black coat has a wide fur collar. She wears high-heeled shoes with a strap across the instep.

Fannie watches them. They make such a nice picture. The mother fills the tray and turns to find a table. Fannie gasps, totters, almost falls off her stool. The woman is Anna Ebanholz. She can see the plain gold band on Anna's left hand. So she is married, and with a beautiful little girl. What happened, Fannie wonders, to poor Nathan? She'll never forget that day he got the letter about his wife and child.

A man puts a quarter down on the scooped-out ledge and Fannie gives him five nickels without even thinking. She watches Anna take the dishes from the tray and sit her daughter next to her, helping her off with her coat and cap. The child is flushed, eagerly waiting for her mother to settle herself so they can eat their lunch. Fannie sighs. They look like American born, like a mother and daughter from the magazines.

Fannie memorizes every detail to tell Abie. When Moira, her relief, comes to take her place in the change booth, Anna Ebanholz and her little girl are eating lemon meringue pie, which is one of the Automat's best plates. Fannie can't resist the urge to go over and say hello.

"Miss Ebanholz! After all this time. Such a surprise," Fannie says.

Anna looks up. She takes in the smiling woman with the frizzy perm and the Horn and Hardart button on her generous bosom. She's someone Anna knows . . . from years ago . . . who is she? "I'm sorry—"

"Fannie Kravitz. You know. Your brother Nathan stayed with me in the Bronx when he first came over."

"Nathan—" the child begins.

"Oh, yes, of course," Anna says. That day she'd gone to the Bronx and heard from Fannie that Miri and the child were dead is etched in her memory.

"I see you got married, so you're not Ebanholz anymore.

113

And such a pretty little girl." Fannie asks the child, "What is your name?"

"Rosie—"

"Blackwell," Anna says. "I am Anna Blackwell now."

"Do you still live in New Jersey?"

"You know Papa?" Rosie asks.

"David is a doctor in Clayton Lake."

"Isn't that nice," Fannie says. "A doctor. And what became of your dear brother?"

"He is also a doctor. He finishes in June."

"Did he marry again?"

Anna shakes her head.

"Tsk, tsk," Fannie clucks. "So sad."

"Finish your pie, Rosie. We have to pick up our tickets."

A crash of breaking china startles them.

Although technically Fannie is finished for the day, when something not good happens in her establishment, she feels it's her duty to help. A customer dropped a tray full of food near the coffee section. "Excuse me," she tells Anna. "So nice to see you. Give my best regards to Nathan."

After Fannie deals with the mess of food and broken crockery on the floor and soothes the embarrassment of the customer, she looks again for Anna Blackwell and her daughter. But they are gone.

It is on the way home as the Elevated enters the Bronx that Fannie remembers the odd little man who owes Nathan money. Where is her head? Nathan is doing all right, but money is money. Let's see, she thinks. Almost five years have passed. Would she have kept the man's card? She never throws anything away, not even small pieces of string. You never know when you'll find a use for it.

When she gets home, she'll look. If she finds it, she'll write him a letter.

Nathan shouldn't be so hard to find. How big a place could Clayton Lake be? She'll tell the man how to find Anna—what is her married name? Blackwell. Mrs. Blackwell. Mrs. David Blackwell. A doctor's wife no less. And with such a pretty little girl. . . .

— 21 —

Anna

1941

Anna is wary as she watches Nathan coming toward them in the lobby of the Warwick. He agitates the air around him, so alive, so obviously Jewish, that the wealthy patrons of this elegant hotel almost by instinct, shift out of his field.

There is no evidence of the shattered Nathan who arrived on her doorstep with the sick child five years ago. The stolen child. Anna shivers and David puts his hand on her arm, a question in his eyes.

She brings his hand to her lips. "I was just thinking about the new life you gave us."

"The new life you gave me," he says.

Rosie, who has been on the lookout, spots Nathan and is up out of her chair. "Papa!"

Lifting her high, Nathan covers her face with kisses. "Who's Papa's best girl?"

"Me! Me! Me!"

A perfect family picture, but Anna is uneasy. Something in the set of Nathan's shoulders, the way his eyes slide away from hers, makes her think he's hiding something.

But David is shaking hands with him, so full of pride.

It's a very important occasion. When they sit down to lunch, David orders champagne, forgetting for the moment that the Germans have taken France.

"No champagne," the waiter says.

"Of course," David says. "What shall we have?"

"Martinis," Nathan suggests. "And a Shirley Temple for my baby."

"I'm not a baby any more, Papa," Rosie says sternly.

"Oh, excuse me. A Shirley Temple for this pretty lady sitting next to me."

Anna relaxes. What is she thinking, always worrying that something will go wrong. She looks around the table. Nathan is being very proper, but she sees how excited he is. And David, he is practically bursting. Nathan is like his son and Nathan has just graduated from Jefferson Medical College, the same medical school David attended. Now they will work together in David's practice, and maybe David will not have to work so hard.

Rosie, their darling Rosie, is right. She's no longer a baby. She is becoming a young lady. In September she will be in fourth grade. It has been hard on her with Nathan living most of the time in Philadelphia the last four years. She's been counting the days when she will have him home being a proper papa.

David orders for everyone: shrimp cocktail and then roast beef, and for dessert, baked Alaska. They eat, listening to Rosie chatter about her new paint box and how she's painting pictures with a brush and how Auntie Anna put labels on all the colors so she won't make a mistake again and paint a horse green.

"Excuse me," Nathan says, getting up. He pats Rosie's platinum curls.

"Papa?"

"I'll be right back."

Anna watches her brother's broad back, the way his body

moves in his graduation suit. She knows him. He is hiding something.

"We'll have coffee with dessert and one glass of milk," David tells the waiter.

"I hate milk," Rosie says.

"It's good for you," Anna says automatically.

Rosie barely covers a yawn.

"I know it's been a long day," David says. "We'll be on our way soon."

Nathan reappears in the archway to the restaurant, stops to speak to someone at a nearby table. Handshakes go around.

"He is a celebrity, our Nathan," David says.

"My Papa," Rosie says.

"Yes, your Papa is a celebrity," Anna says. And a kidnapper and maybe even a murderer. She shocks herself. What is wrong with her? She hasn't had these thoughts in years.

Nathan is jumpy. He drinks his coffee quickly, moves around in his chair as if he's looking for someone.

"So are we ready to go home?" David says, paying the bill.

"I have some things to finish up here," Nathan says, checking his wristwatch. "You go on and I'll catch the train home in the morning."

Rosie is clearly disappointed, but has an idea. "I'll stay with you, Papa."

This, Anna sees, is not what Nathan wants.

"Papa has some meetings, darling. It's best you go home with Auntie Anna and Uncle David. And I'll be there tomorrow when you get home from school."

"Meetings, Nathan?"

David says, "It's okay, Nathan. Have yourself a good time. Soon enough, we'll be on a schedule."

Nathan squirms in his chair. "Well—"

"What 'well'?" Anna says sharply.

"I was going to wait until later. I've accepted a residency in surgery from University Hospital."

Trust your instincts, Anna tells herself. This is what he's been hiding. "Nathan, David got you into medical school, paid for your education. You're supposed to come home and work with him."

"Now, Anna," David says. "It's a wonderful opportunity."

Rosie is looking from one to the other. "Aren't you coming home, Papa?"

"Of course, I'm coming home," he says. "I have three weeks to spend with my little girl before I start."

Anna checks on Rosie in the back seat as they leave the city to make sure she's asleep.

"I knew he was hiding something," Anna says. What else is he hiding, she wonders. But she knows her brother. There's a woman, and since he didn't bring her to lunch, an inappropriate woman.

"My brother," she says so softly David looks over at her to make sure she's spoken, "my brother has women."

David smiles, rests his hand on her thigh. "Don't be upset." David finds the sign for Route 70 and makes the turn. "Nathan's young, terrible things happened to him. Now he has the whole world in front of him."

"But he has responsibilities, David. Rosie needs him. You need help with the practice."

"Rosie has us," David says. "And we have each other. What more do we need?"

— 22 —

Nathan

He waits for Rosie outside the school, for the line of children two by two that the pretty third-grade teacher walks out the door. He waits for the teacher, Miss Louise Corrigan, a natural blond who puts her hair up in a modest bun when she's in school, and lets it out in a pageboy like Veronica Lake when she's not. She wears a prim, tailored blouse to hide bold breasts, but Nathan knows them, has held their ripeness in his palms and sucked their engorged nipples.

The sight of her long, lean back bending over to answer a child's question only makes him harder, and he opens the door of David's car and sits, talking sense to his erection.

Why couldn't she have been one of the many old maids who teach school?

He can hear Anna in his head, when Rosie said, "I think Miss Corrigan likes Papa."

"Oh, yes?" Anna had thrown him a look. "What makes you say that, Rosie?"

"Because she gets sweat marks under her arms when Papa talks to her."

He'd avoided being alone with Anna the rest of the afternoon, but she caught up with him when he took the garbage out.

She grabbed his arm and shook it. "It won't do, Nathan. Not here. Think of Rosie, think of David. We have a life here. And what about that poor girl? She'll be fired if anyone finds out."

"No one will find out. We go up to Asbury."

Anna had blanched. "You are sleeping with her, Nathan. My God, she's not one of your whores. You must marry her."

Nathan shook her off. "I must nothing."

Nathan comes across the street to where Louise Corrigan is sending off her pupils. When she catches sight of him, he sees Rosie is right. Louise's underarms are becoming dark with perspiration.

The children begin dispersing to waiting yellow school buses.

"We're going to Seaside, Miss Corrigan," Rosie says.

"How nice, Rose."

"Would you like to come with us, Miss Corrigan?" Nathan says, pointedly eyeing the tremble of her breasts under her blouse, the almost imperceptible mound of her bush pressing against her skirt.

Rosie jumps up and down. "Oh, yes, Miss Corrigan, say yes."

"I'm afraid I can't, Mr. Ebanholz, Rosie. It's the last week of school before summer vacation and I have to pack everything away."

"Maybe you can use some help, Miss Corrigan. I can come back later."

"I don't think so, Mr. Ebanholz, but I thank you for your kindness."

"Tomorrow is another day, Miss Corrigan."

"Yes, it is, Mr. Ebanholz. And tomorrow I will be finished with my work. Then I can look forward to a lovely evening."

"Absolutely, Miss Corrigan. Come, Rosie darling." Nathan

takes her hand and they cross the street and get into the car.

"Did you see, Papa? Did you see?"

"See what, darling?" He drives out to Route 35 and heads for Seaside.

"That Miss Corrigan had sweat marks."

"Yes, I saw, but everyone sweats when it's hot. It's the way the body cools off."

It's a beautiful, clear day, and the afternoon sun is a round yellow ball in the cloudless sky. Rosie's fingers itch for her crayons. At this hour in the afternoon few cars are on the road to the beach, and they see fewer still as they cross Pelican Island, where there's always a terrible smell. Rosie holds her nose.

"Rotting seaweed," Nathan says. "See how it clumps along the shore?"

Ahead is the bridge to Seaside. It sits low on the water, almost part of the bay. They drive onto it and the car goes garump, garump, garump all the way across. It seems to go on forever, and the bay splashes up at them and wets the bridge and the car, too. Rosie is always afraid the bridge will sink into the bay, or it will break apart just as they drive over it. She moves closer to Nathan. He's her papa and he will protect her.

Nathan knows what she is thinking. He puts his arm around her and hugs her to him. "This is the longest wooden bridge in the world," he says. "I'll bet you didn't know that."

Rosie already knows it. Uncle David told her all about the bridge and takes her and Auntie Anna to Seaside often. But she sees Papa is happy telling her, so she doesn't let on she knows.

It is not yet dinnertime, but the boardwalk is always busy in the summer. Nathan takes it all in, the music of the merry-go-round, an opposing tune from the Ferris wheel, smells of frying onions and sausage, fried potatoes, salt water taffy. And sunburn and sand and the distinctive salt water air. It's intoxicating. And beyond the boardwalk, the expanse of white sand and the ocean waves crashing against the shore.

He stands still watching the crash of the incoming surf. The very same ocean he once thought would bring Miri and—

Rosie tugs on his hand and jumps up and down. "The merry-go-round first, Papa, please."

He sets Rosie on her own horse and takes the one beside her. When her horse goes up, his goes down. She holds on tight and laughs at him, so full of joy he wishes the horses were real and they could ride off together.

After three times around, Nathan tells her he's hungry. It's the only way he can get her off the merry-go-round. He buys them sausage and onion hoagies and French fries, a root beer for Rosie and real beer for him, and they sit on a bench looking out at the ocean as the tide comes in. Intrepid bathers swim out and ride the waves till the ocean throws them onto the sand. Nathan's done it himself and knows the water is still frigid in June.

There is a peace here he rarely feels. If only it could be like this. Just him and Rosie. But he knows himself. It can't last. He is not a peaceful man.

Rosie eats only half of her sausage hoagie and Nathan finishes it. She swings her legs impatiently, ready to get on the move again. Her legs, he sees, are lengthening. She will be tall like him, like Miri—

He shakes himself, stands, and crumples up the soiled napkins and papers and gives them to Rosie. "Come, Rosie, maybe you see a trash basket so we can throw our garbage away and not dirty the boardwalk."

Rosie races off, scattering a trail of trash as she goes, and Nathan follows, smiling, picking up what she loses.

The sun is drooping now. It's almost time to go home.

And he can see Rosie senses it, but she is not willing to end it yet. She runs out ahead of him, then stops. Though he doesn't see it, he knows exactly where she's stopped. In front of the frozen custard stand. They can't leave Seaside without a frozen custard.

"What flavor?" he asks Rosie, but it's a joke between them. She always has chocolate. He starts to tell the tall, sunburned girl behind the counter.

"Well, hello, there," the girl says, but she is talking to Nathan, not Rosie. Her nose is peeling and her hair is frizzy and sunstreaked under the white cap, uncannily like a nurse's cap, the servers wear.

"Chocolate," Rosie says.

The girl takes a cone and holds it under the machine and soft ice cream comes out in a swirl and fits right into the cone. She hands the cone to Rosie.

"Where've you been, stranger?" she asks Nathan. No one else is waiting for a frozen custard.

Rosie licks the delicious concoction, her eyes on Nathan and the girl.

"Medical school in Philadelphia," he says. Mary Lou something, he thinks, searching his memory for the name. Foster. Strict parents, but she had her own car. They would have died if they'd known what Nathan and Mary Lou did in the back seat of her car. All he had to do was run his hand up her skirt, and her cunt would open, full and wet at his touch, like no woman he'd ever had. He looks her over now. Four years it's been. She's no longer a scrawny high school kid. He wonders if her cunt—

"So you're finished now?" She wipes her hands down the front of her white uniform. All the way down.

"For a while. I'll be going back in a couple of weeks."

Rosie licks her cone, watches, and listens. She sees that

this lady likes her papa as much as Miss Corrigan.

Mary Lou looks at Rosie. "Don't tell me this is your little girl all grown up?"

"Yes. Say hello to Mary Lou, Rosie."

"Hello, Mary Lou," Rosie says.

"How're your folks?"

"Moved to Florida."

"I don't see a wedding ring," Nathan says.

"It didn't work out. You should come out to the house and say hello before you leave."

"Same place?"

"Same place. I don't have to be here until twelve and I'm off at nine." Mary Lou presses the small of her back, thrusting her pelvis forward.

Rosie bites off the bottom of the cone and sucks out the last bit of custard, then finishes it off.

Nathan stirs, his attention back to Rosie. He takes her hand and wipes off the custard stains. "So maybe I'll see you," Nathan tells Mary Lou.

"You had a good time?" Anna says, as she helps Rosie out of her bath and wraps her in a big towel.

"Yes. We went on the merry-go-round and we ate sausage hoagies and I had a frozen custard, and Papa knew the lady at the frozen custard. Mary Lou. She told Papa to come and visit her."

Anna cringes. Can it be? That tramp Mary Lou Foster? Hadn't she gotten married and moved away?

She puts Rosie to bed and checks Nathan's room. He isn't there. She goes downstairs. David is sitting in the living room dozing over his medical journals. No sign of Nathan.

It's after nine. Anna looks outside. The car is not in the garage.

— 23 —

Zweikel

The morning after Zweikel is released, the Japs bomb Pearl Harbor. He might have spent the rest of his life in the institution if it were not for Dina Malkowitz, his next-door neighbor. Her old mama had died not long after Zweikel was put away.

They treated him at the hospital with electric shocks. It made patches of his hair fall out and played games with his memory. But they presented him with a gift: he no longer knows if he killed Stella or someone else did. He no longer cares. He no longer sees Nathan Ebanholz's face mocking him from other peoples' bodies. He feels nothing. No emotion. No connection.

Even Stella herself has receded in his memory so that all he can recall of her now is her smell. Sweat, antiseptic, and almonds from her Jergens Lotion.

It's the thought of Irene—the child—his and Stella's child—that he clings to, hoarding her away with him as he secreted the photograph from the attendants spying on him in the hospital.

He sits on Dina Malkowitz's couch in the dark whispering to himself. He doesn't hear her come in.

"So, you shouldn't sit here in the dark," Dina says. She is carrying a bag of groceries. "It's not healthy." She goes into the tiny kitchen. "Open the shades, why don't you? Let in a little light on the subject." Zweikel thinks she sounds funny. Forced. Is she already regretting her offer to care for him, just home from the crazy house? "Are you hungry? I bought lox and bagels. Do you want?"

Zweikel rises, weary, pulls up the shades. The sun offends him and he returns to the sofa. "I don't care."

"The Japs bombed Pearl Harbor," Dina blurts out all of a sudden, and begins to snivel.

"The Japs?" he repeats, not understanding. He gets up and stands in the doorway. "Pearl Harbor? Where is that? Jersey?"

"Pearl Harbor. They say Ha-vy-ee."

"Where is Ha-vy-ee? What does it have to do with us?"

"Everything, Mendy." She calls him by his Jewish name, as his mother did, and he doesn't say no.

"American boys were killed. On the big ships. While they were asleep. Jewish boys, too. You know Shana Kantor from the candy store? Her boy is there. She doesn't know if he's alive or dead—God forbid. So terrible." She's fussing in the little kitchen, snuffling, making up a plate of lox and bagels with scallion cream cheese. Salt and yeast, pungents of his past. He leans against the door jamb, watching her. Coffee begins to perk. Plop, plop, hitting the glass bulb in the cover of the percolator, getting darker and darker.

Zweikel returns to the couch. The worn spots are covered with towels. Staring at his clenched fists, he watches his tears spill onto them, running in little rivulets through the hairs, into the crevices. Crevices, he thinks.

Dina Malkowitz's adolescent and adult existence was devoted to caring for her invalid mother. Her mother's death left her life without meaning. Her need to care for someone folded comfortably into her obsession with Zweikel. She began visiting him at the state hospital, traveling by bus, carrying shopping bags of food—knishes, rugalach, challah, made with her own hands.

A small, round woman with doll feet in impossibly high heels, Dina has a little money from her mother's insurance policy and picks up extra working in restaurants, waiting on tables. Sometimes even, they give her food to take home.

Zweikel was a professional man. Dina has it in her mind that when he gets over his wife's death, he might look on her, Dina, with some affection and they will marry. She already calls herself his fiancée and got him released from the hospital because she offered a home for him to finish his recovery.

They say he killed his wife, but never for one minute does Dina believe it. And even if he did, she deserved it, the kurveh. Everyone in the building, including Dina, knew she brought men to the house while Zweikel was at work. When the drunken Polack recanted Zweikel's alibi and the police arrested Zweikel for the murder of his wife, Dina still didn't believe it.

Zweikel was crazy for a while then, and who could blame him? So they put him away in the crazy house.

In the afternoon they doze in their chairs like two old married people as the bright sun comes through the south-facing windows. Then Dina makes a soup chicken for dinner while the radio plays music, interrupted again and again with news of Pearl Harbor. When Roosevelt himself begins to talk, Dina stops what she's doing to listen.

Zweikel sits on the couch picking through a shoe box on his lap that holds the few pieces of his old life that Dina salvaged from his apartment before it was rented out to another family. He finds a small notepad with impossible-to-decipher notes. Dina keeps telling him how respected he was, how people came to him from all over to help bring mishpocha from the old country. Had he finished his business before they put him away? For the life of him, he can't remember anymore.

Do people owe him or does he owe?

So many thoughts come to attack him all at once he gets confused and thinks the Japs are coming for him, too. He throws the box down. His marriage certificate flies from the box and floats down near his feet.

When his thoughts stop roiling, he reaches down for the document. A crumpled, stained envelope adheres by its stamp to the back of the certificate.

Zweikel tears it away, and the stamp stays with his marriage certificate. The envelope in his hand is addressed to him in cramped greenhorn writing; the seal is still intact. The letter was never opened. A letter of complaint maybe. Something he didn't finish. His eyes prick him.

He turns the letter over. On the back is a return address in the Bronx, and the name Kravitz. Kravitz? The Bronx? Why doesn't he remember? He pushes his finger under the flap and opens the envelope.

— 24 —

Rose

1942

The sky is gray, morose with moisture. There has been no sun for days now, but Rosie knows the sun is hiding because of the war.

Papa holds her tight in his arms as they stand on the platform waiting for the train. The rough fabric of his uniform burns her cheek. Everyone looks at her Papa, so tall and handsome like Clark Gable, and people come over to shake his hand. They tell him, "Godspeed, Captain Ebanholz; good luck, Nathan; kill some Nazis for us, Nathan."

But Auntie Anna's eyes are wet with tears that not even Uncle David can cure, and as the whistle of the train seeps into their consciousness, Anna's tears overflow.

"Are you going to kill Nazis, Papa?" Rosie asks.

"No, I'm a doctor. I'm going to save people."

When the train pulls into the station, breaking the moist sac into droplets of rain, Uncle David pumps Papa's arm, gives him a hug. "I wish I were going with you," he says.

Papa puts the arm that's not holding Rosie around Auntie Anna. "Don't worry," he tells her. He kisses Rosie a hundred times and sets her down.

"Don't go away again, Papa," Rosie whispers.

"Papa has to go because his country needs doctors. Stay just the way you are, Rosie darling. I'll be home in no time."

★ ★ ★ ★ ★

It's so cold that the radio is warning people to bundle up before going out and not to stay outside long. But Auntie Anna has to go to a tower to spot planes, so she puts on a lot of sweaters and the seal coat that Uncle David bought her for her birthday. Under her chin she ties the woolen babushka. For the war effort, she's learned the difference between a Messerschmidt, a Spitfire, and a B-25.

And Rosie sits beside Uncle David in the old Buick as he makes house calls. He's switched his office schedule around so his hours start later in the morning; and then in the afternoon, when Auntie Anna is plane spotting and Rosie comes home from school, he makes house calls with Rosie at his side in the old Buick.

Rosie wears shiny black rubbers and knee socks that are always sliding down, even when Auntie Anna uses elastic. Rosie's knees are all knobs and bones poking out from under her dress, a cold expanse between hem and sock. She grows like a weed, Auntie Anna says. Four inches this year, and she is almost nine.

Mr. Chernoff has lumbago and Mrs. Chernoff makes wonderful hot chocolate.

"Come, Rosie, wait till you see our new little chicks," Mrs. Chernoff says, taking Rosie's mittened hand. The chicks come by mail just like from the Sears Roebuck catalogue.

The chicks. Their golden no-neck bodies scamper on tiny claw feet. Peep, peep, peep in high voices, all talking at once. They live in little houses with their own little stoves and chimneys. Water comes from a metal container that looks like a flower pot turned upside down on a pie plate.

Snow covers the ground around the little houses and coats the tops of the roofs where little chimneys puff white smoke into the cold air. Long icicles hang from the eaves.

One chimney isn't puffing. At first Rosie doesn't notice, but Mrs. Chernoff does, for she starts running in a funny way, clumsy in Mr. Chernoff's high bulky boots.

"Oh, God," Mrs. Chernoff cries, "Oh, God, oh, God."

Rosie's boots crunch on the crisp, glazed crust of the snow. The dog Pete, a collie mixture, sits in the driveway barking.

Does he, Rosie wonders, feel cold in his tushie? He's been running in circles, slipping and sliding, making no dent in the snow cover. Now he stops barking. Everything becomes quiet.

Mrs. Chernoff keeps looking up, checking the smokeless chimney as if she doesn't believe there isn't any smoke coming from it. The cold is silent, too. It creeps from the bottom of Rosie's feet upward, until it embraces her. Mrs. Chernoff opens the door to the little house. A small sound like a wind-sigh slips from her. Or does it come from the little chick house?

Rosie stands just behind her. The chicks are stiff pale feathers covering the floor of their house like a fluffy yellow carpet. No round, peeping little bodies. She waits for them to get up.

Mrs. Chernoff is wearing Mr. Chernoff's jacket and the blue flowers of her apron grow unevenly out from under. "Don't look, Rosie," she says. "They're frozen." She takes Rosie's hand. "They're dead."

"Light the stove, Mrs. Chernoff. Quick," Rosie says. She knows if they warm up a little, they'll come back to life. "They will," she says. "You'll see." She pulls her hand away. Holds it to her mouth. Her mitten is wet, crackles with ice.

"No, Rosie." Mrs. Chernoff is very sad. "It happens sometimes. They're gone. We can't bring them back."

Uncle David stands on the back porch, his black bag in his hand. His wool hat has ear flaps. Uncle David will make it right.

Rosie runs to him, scrambles on the ice, skins her knees. "Uncle David, please. You can save them." She takes hold of his hand and pulls him. "Please. Please."

Mrs. Chernoff says, "The stove went out. They froze. Fifty of them."

Rosie looks with scorn at Mrs. Chernoff. Doesn't she know? Uncle David will bring them back. "They're not dead, Uncle David. They're just cold." She pushes open the door to the little house. "Look, Uncle David." The chicks are dry yellow leaves that flutter in the breeze from the open door.

Uncle David studies the room for a moment, then turns away. He takes Rosie's hand.

"Nooooo." A painful, tremulous sound comes from the pit of Rosie's stomach.

"I'm sorry, Rosie," Mrs. Chernoff says.

Uncle David holds her, but she is stiff in his arms like the dead chicks. He drives home, talking to her, but she's stopped listening. At home, he takes off her galoshes and washes her bruised knees. He talks to her in his quiet voice as he paints her wounds with Mercurochrome. "Nature can be cruel, Rosie," he says. "Accidents happen. I'd like to be able to, but I can't fix everything."

"They didn't hurt anybody, Uncle David. Why did they have to die?"

"It was no one's fault," he says.

A lump in her throat, she sees herself huddled on the feathered floor, frozen. "Is it going to happen to me?"

"Never, never." He takes her on his lap. "Why would you think such a thing?"

"In Europe, the radio said, people are freezing to death."

"But we are here. No one will hurt you here. I promise." He holds her and kisses her forehead. "Anna and I will never let anything happen to you."

She closes her eyes. "Uncle David?"

"Yes?"

"The chicks. Did they have a mother?"

He is silent. She feels his heart's slow and even beating. "Of course. Everyone has a mother."

"But their mother gave them away to the catalogue people."

"That's the way it is with chickens," he says. He sees where she is going.

"My mother—"

"Your mother died in an accident, Rosie. She would never have given you away."

They sit together in the rocking chair in the dusky darkness. Rosie has still another question, but Uncle David has fallen asleep.

— 25 —

Anna

"There's a meeting." Anna keeps her back to David as she turns on the sterilizer. She is hesitant because the meeting has to do with things Jewish, though David has never said or done anything that should make her feel this way. "Tonight. After dinner."

"Yes?" He is making notes for his patient files, notes that Anna may or may not have to rewrite in a clearer hand.

She turns to face him. "At the Jewish Community Center."

"A meeting?"

"I must go. Right after dinner. It's very important."

He puts down his pen. "All right. What is it about?"

"A man from the Jewish Agency is here to talk about terrible things happening in Europe. There've been rumors . . . about . . ." The words lodge in her throat.

David gets up from his desk. "They're rounding up the Jews, is that it?"

"Worse."

"I'm going with you."

She is overwhelmed, emotional. "Oh, David, you don't understand. It's Jewish problems, not your concern."

"But it is. Anything that affects you is my concern." He holds her shoulders and kisses her forehead. "We will go together."

The Jewish Community Center is a fairly recent building,

so new that the area around it looks raw, devoid of plantings or landscaping. Brick and stone, one story with a finished basement, it sits stark on the loamy soil. From barely ten Jewish families when Anna arrived in Clayton Lake, there are now at least twenty-five or thirty, some refugees, most with young children.

Many cars and farm trucks are parked on the street surrounding and even on the grounds. And children, Rosie's age and younger, sit on the steps and mill around outside. Although it is seven-thirty, it is still daylight.

"There's Larry," Rosie says.

Rosie, too young to remain alone, has come with them, but she will stay outside with the other children.

The main meeting room runs the entire floor of the small community center. Six rows of folding chairs have been set up. At the far end of the room is a raised stage on which is a white screen on a stand. A projector rests on a table in the middle of the floor among the folding chairs. Grim-faced strangers in black suits bustle about as the members of the community arrive and sit.

Anna stays close to David, who is greeted with mild, but tolerant, curiosity.

When everyone is accounted for, the outside doors are closed, walling the children off, and the meeting begins with John Novinger, the president of the Jewish community, introducing the two men from Jewish agencies and committees.

The words are unspeakable. While the shrieks and laughter of the children playing outside drift into the room, they hear about concentration camps. Extermination. The round-ups. Shootings. Mass graves. Children for target practice. Slave labor, starvation.

The film is worse. Naked bodies, hardly more than skeletons, piled one on the other like logs. No longer terrible rumors, but actual testimony from the few who have escaped. Hitler's determination to murder every Jew in Europe.

The people sit like stones, except for hands clinging, unable to even acknowledge one another, not even husband and wife.

The lights come on. No dry eyes now.

Someone cries, anguished, "What can we do?"

"We bear witness," one of the men says, his accent distinctly Polish. "We must all bear witness. Word of what is happening must be reported. Our poor people are crying for help. Money is needed to buy some freedom, to let the world know."

"Will they come to kill us?" Rosie asks, when Anna kisses her goodnight.

Anna is shocked. How could Rosie know? The children were closed out of the meeting. But were they?

"What are you saying, darling? No one is going to kill us." Though she is not so sure of anything any more. Not after what she has seen and heard this night.

"Because we're Jewish. Larry said they were talking about killing all the Jews."

Anna thinks, why do adults always think they can keep bad things from children? We try so hard to spare them the terror, the nightmares, but the war swirls around them. How can they not know now that their world has changed, perhaps forever?

She smoothes Rosie's pale curls back from her face and brings up a lighter subject. "Larry's mama told me that Larry is going to take piano lessons from Mr. Demovich. Maybe you'd like to also? We'll buy a piano and you can surprise Nathan when he comes home. Would you like that?"

Rosie shakes her head. "No."

David comes into the room. "How about a goodnight kiss for your old uncle?"

"Will they kill Papa in Europe because he's Jewish, Uncle David?"

David looks at Anna. "Of course not, Rosie. Nathan is an American. There are bad people in the world, but our good country is going to make everything okay."

"But what if the bad people come here?" Rosie asks.

"You have nothing to worry about, my sweet girl," David says, tucking Rosie in. "It can never happen here."

Anna, in the thrall of the almost foreign sensation of her Jewishness, thinks of the assimilated German Jews who said very much the same. Her kind, decent gentile husband has no idea that anything can happen anywhere in a world where Christians are taught that the Jews killed Jesus.

Rose

One evening, as Rosie brushes her teeth, the mirrored
medicine cabinet in the bathroom begins to speak. Well,
not speaking exactly. It moans, then falls into the sink with
a shrieking crash. Or maybe it's Rosie who shrieks. She
stares into the snarled abyss the cabinet's left behind.
"Mama, Mama, Mama!"

Auntie Anna rushes down the hall and pulls Rosie from
the room. "Don't cry, baby."

*Light from the street seeps through window bars and
paints black lines on the coarse, gray blanket. The claw
branches of the tree reach for her. A ghost in the wind howls,
"Hoooo, hoooo, hoooo," just to scare her, like Olga says.*

*The claw rattles the windows. "Mama, Mama,
Mama!"*

*Voices join hers from up and down the room, from beds
with bars like hers. Contagious. Everyone is awake,
screaming. She hides under the blanket.*

*A door opens, thumping footsteps stop close by. "Oh,
it's you again. Crybaby." The blanket is jerked from her
with a force that spins her around. The giant woman in
white stands over her. "We'll have to send you back to the
little room, crybaby."*

*"Crybaby, crybaby," a chorus of cheeping voices
screams at her. "Crybaby, crybaby."*

"That's enough. Go back to sleep. Good children sleep. We have only one bad child here. The crybaby."

"Mama!" she shrieks, shivering with cold. "Please, Mama—"

"Drink this." The woman lifts her head and presses a paper cup of fluid to her clenched teeth, forces her jaw open, and pours the bitter liquid down until she swallows.

The hooting cries surround her. "Crybaby, crybaby."

"Don't cry, baby," Auntie Anna says, stroking the damp curls back from Rosie's brow. "It's all right. You're all right."

"The medicine cabinet had a loose bolt. That's why it fell out of the wall and scared you, Rosie," Uncle David says, as he takes her pulse. "Just a little fast." He sees her shiver and covers her with a second blanket.

"It was sucking me into it, Uncle David."

"That can never happen, Rosie. You are safe here with us."

Rosie closes her eyes until they think she's gone to sleep.

Uncle David tapes a newspaper over the hole in the wall and secures it with surgical tape. In the morning he will get someone to come and install a new medicine cabinet.

But Rosie knows now it's in there waiting for her.

In her own bed in the darkness, she knows if she closes her eyes she will die. She has nightmares that she is closed into a dark place, the place behind the medicine cabinet, the musty shadows of the garage. Her terror is most often mute, hers alone, and she nourishes and protects it. Other times it is vocal, and Auntie Anna kisses her tears away and Uncle David holds her tight so she knows she's safe.

Papa is in the Army now, as the song says. V-mail arrives with strange markings, looking as if someone read them before. They've been opened, sections blacked out, and resealed. Papa's address is full of long numbers and letters, but no country, city, or anything.

In the kitchen, Auntie Anna and Rosie have put up a map of Europe and they are following the war, wondering where Papa is now.

Once in a while, a picture of Papa arrives with the letter. He is a handsome stranger in a uniform, laughing, arms around other strangers in uniform.

But the other photograph, the one on the bureau of the mother and the child, is fading. Rosie searches as always for some resemblance in herself to the solemn faces in the picture. She finds none.

"It was a different world, darling," Auntie Anna says, kissing her, taking the photograph from her hand and placing it back on the bureau. "Everyone took pictures like that. Are you my girl or not?" Auntie Anna laughs her throaty laugh.

Rosie is Auntie Anna's girl, for sure. She has learned to imitate Anna's throaty laugh.

In the dead of winter, light-starved, Rosie feels afraid. Left alone for any length of time, she panics. She has trouble breathing.

A little man in a green suit watches her. She first sees him when she buys a pack of gum at the candy store, and he stares at her so hard over his beak of a nose that his eyes cross. He looks like a troll from *Peer Gynt*.

Rosie turns her back so he won't see that she's laughing at him. It's not polite, and Rosie knows it.

"God, you are such a slow poke," Nancy groans. She's waiting outside on her bike.

They are going to the library and then to the Sweete Shoppe, where the big kids hang out. Some day they will be the big kids and get to ignore the little kids, too. Rosie and Nancy do the same thing every Saturday. At two o'clock they go to the matinee. Today they are seeing Rosie's favorite, Bette Davis. Nancy likes Betty Grable better.

Nancy is going to go to Hollywood and be a movie star. They talk about their plans all the time. Rosie dreams of going to New York. She wants to live in Greenwich Village and paint, just like the artists she reads about in books.

"She has an extraordinary talent, a brilliant sense of color." She hears Mr. Albini, the art teacher, say this to Auntie Anna on Open School Night. Auntie Anna has a funny expression on her face when she hears this, and she looks even funnier sitting at Rosie's fifth grade desk. Mr. Albini wears a black patch over one eye and is 4F.

Rosie writes Papa long letters full of drawings of Auntie Anna and Uncle David, Nancy on her bicycle, Mr. Albini with his eye patch. Eventually, she will even draw the strange little man in the green suit.

She sees him often now: across the street when she leaves her house in the morning, near the school yard where they play jump-rope, at the Five & Ten where Nancy's older sister, Alberta, slips them a Tangee natural lipstick once in a while, to share.

The little man stands in front of the Five & Ten, nose squashed against the window. Rosie sees him and waves, giggling. He looks startled, turns to find who she's waving to, understands suddenly, it is he. She doesn't see him again for several days and is disappointed.

One night, near dinner time, the phone rings. Auntie Anna calls, "Can you answer that please, darling? If it's for David, he'll be home any minute."

Uncle David always calls them from his last patient's

house to tell them when he'll be home. He's already called from the Siccas' in Beech Grove.

The radio is spewing war news. Rosie turns it down. "Hello," she says, "Dr. Blackwell's office." She is greeted by static, and then a voice with an English accent like Greer Garson comes echoing at her from a great distance.

"Is this the home of Anna B—?" The rest of the question is lost.

"Auntie Anna," Rosie calls, so excited she almost drops the phone. "It's for you. Maybe it's Papa."

Anna lowers the heat under the soup and dries her hands quickly. Hand trembling, she takes the receiver from Rosie. "Hello? Hello? Who is it?" She says to Rosie, "There's too much static." Then her face softens. "Nathan. Are you all right?" She listens intently.

Rosie dances around the kitchen. "It's Papa! I want to talk!"

"Shah, Rosie. Let me hear first." Auntie Anna nods her head. "Say that again, Nathan? It's hard to hear." Auntie Anna's cheeks have two bright spots. "Oh, God, Nathan." She looks at Rosie, who is pleading for a chance to talk to her father. "Okay," Auntie Anna says, "Don't worry. Here she is. She is healthy and she is beautiful. And she is a good girl."

Love envelopes Rosie like a warm, wooly blanket. She takes the phone from Auntie Anna. "Hello!" she yells into it, and her moist breath leaves a mark on the blackness. "Hello, Papa!" A wave of static flows from the phone and she is frightened, remembering the reports from London while the bombs are dropping.

"Rosie!" Papa's voice booms through the static. "How is my wonderful girl?"

"I'm fine, Papa. I love you. Where are you calling from?"

"Paris, France," he tells her. "Where all the artists are."

"Papa, I love you so much." Rosie bites her lower lip to keep from crying. "I miss you. When are you coming home?"

"It won't—" Static breaks his voice into little pieces. "Darling—" she hears. "Your letters . . . keep writing . . . listen to Anna—she knows—" The line goes dead and Rosie, holding the receiver in a death grip, knuckles white, bursts into tears.

Auntie Anna takes the receiver from her and listens for a minute, then hangs up the phone. "He is well. We shouldn't worry." She hugs Rosie to her and kisses her forehead. "He says you sent him a letter with a drawing of a little man in a green suit. I don't remember one like that."

Rosie sniffles. "The green man? I added him at the end of one of the letters because I see him all the time." Rosie dries her eyes with Auntie Anna's hankie.

"All the time?" Auntie Anna goes back to the stove and turns up the light under the barley soup. She stirs it with a long wooden spoon. "Where? In your dreams maybe?" Her back looks funny to Rosie. Scrunched.

"No, here in Clayton Lake. He's such a funny little man," Rosie says.

"Maybe you'll point him out to me so I can see him, too," Auntie Anna says. She turns to look at Rosie, unaware that she is holding the spoon in her hand and the soup is dripping on the linoleum. When the spoon falls out of Auntie Anna's trembling hand to the floor, Rosie is shocked. Auntie Anna holds Rosie close. "We mustn't give Nathan anything to worry about, Rosie," she says.

As if Rosie would. She thinks a lot about this, though, and after she goes to bed, she hears Auntie Anna moving around the house, long after Uncle David has gone to bed.

She senses more than sees Auntie Anna look in on her in the night.

The next day the little green man is across the street when Rosie leaves for school. She goes back into the house and tells Auntie Anna.

Auntie Anna shrugs into her coat. She follows Rosie outside. "Go on now, you don't want to be late for school."

The little man stands across the street, in the open, staring.

Auntie Anna kisses Rosie and sends her off. Under the tree, the little man stirs. He drops his cigarette and grinds it into the ground with the sole of his shoe. He starts to follow Rosie, but Auntie Anna is fast. She comes behind him and grabs his arm. She says something to him in Jewish, and she is very angry. The little man cringes. There is a fierce look on Auntie Anna's face that frightens Rosie. Rosie turns and runs to school.

"Do you know the little green man?" Rosie asks Auntie Anna that night. Auntie Anna's hands are full of soap bubbles. She washes the dinner dishes; Rosie dries. Uncle David is sitting in the living room, snoozing. Auntie Anna has been very quiet since Rosie came home from school.

"Know who?" Auntie Anna looks startled.

"The green man. You know, the little man this morning. Do you know him?"

Auntie Anna doesn't answer right away. "No," she says finally.

"But you spoke to him in Jewish."

"I did. I could see he was a refugee."

"Oh."

"He's a sick man, Rosie. I don't want to frighten you, but if you see him again, you must tell me."

"Sick? Like pneumonia?" A girl in Rosie's class died last month of pneumonia.

"No. Sick in the head. He might be dangerous. You must never speak to him. Promise me." Auntie Annie is talking with stiff arms going up and down.

"Okay, but—"

"Absolutely no buts." Auntie Anna is stern.

But Auntie Anna doesn't have to worry, Rosie thinks. He won't hurt her. She's sure of this. She wants to ask him why he watches her. And maybe one day she will.

But then after all it doesn't matter. The little man in the green suit never comes again.

— 27 —

David

1944

An emaciated snub-tailed cat is on the back porch scratching at the door. It stares at David with mad, pus-encrusted eyes for only a moment before flying off and disappearing into the thick woods that surround the old house.

David smells death as soon as he opens the door. But he calls out, "Mr. Kopecki?"

There's no response, nor does he expect one. The old man was a stone mason, a stubborn cuss, insisted on living alone in the house he'd been born in. David had gotten a call from California, from Ellie, Kopecki's married daughter, asking him to stop by and see why her father isn't answering his phone.

When he reaches the top of the stairs, David is short of breath, which he attributes to the putrid smell of decay. The man has probably been dead for over twenty-four hours. He grasps the banister for a moment before he goes forward.

Downstairs, from the wall phone in the kitchen, he calls the police and Warren Potts, the undertaker. Then Ellie. He'd gone to high school with Ellie Kopecki and remembered her as plain, but with the kind of good nature that made her popular with her peers.

"No," he reassures her as she chokes back tears, "he didn't suffer. A massive stroke, took him in his sleep." He can't be sure of that without an autopsy, for which she must give her consent. She does not, and he doesn't press her. He tells her he'll have Warren, another schoolmate, call her so she can make the funeral arrangements.

He takes off his jacket, rolls up his sleeves, and scrubs his hands, arms, and face with the sliver of harsh soap next to the sink. Dries himself with his linen handkerchief. From his bag he takes a small vial of eucalyptus oil, removes the cork, and inhales its intense vapor. It will be a while before he can rid himself of the smell of decay.

After signing the death certificate, he leaves Mike Walton, the sheriff, and Warren Potts, who's just driven up in the hearse, to handle the rest. Sorrow does not torment him today. Mr. Kopecki was in his seventies. He'd lived his life for better or for worse. David believes God gives man four score and ten as a birthright. It is only when someone young cannot be saved that David feels the excruciating weight of failure.

He gets into his car and is driving along Silverton Road toward the intersection of Old Freehold Road when his left hand goes limp on the steering wheel. He's not driving fast, but hits the brake and with his right hand, pulls over to the side of the road, puts the car in neutral, and turns off the motor.

He's sweating profusely, his head finds the wheel with a sudden wump. He, outside himself, has the sensation he's leaving this world. *Anna. Anna.* He calls to her but he's beyond hearing.

Sluggish and stiff, David raises his head, passes his hand across his eyes. A slavering wolf face yowls against his window, its jaws open, sharp teeth trying to pierce the glass. Wolf face? He turns and stares into its mad eyes. It's a German shepherd, and its eyes are not mad, but excited.

Where is he? In his car, alongside the road. Sleeping, doctor? He remembers during his internship when after thirty-six hours straight he'd nodded off at the nurses' station. He'd been reprimanded with those words by the resident.

But never in his entire life has David slept like this in the car in the middle of the afternoon. He takes his pulse. It is too fast. He remembers the weakness in his left hand, and flexes the digits as if fearful they'll break. He touches the slight bump on his forehead. An aberration, is all. But he notes the faint bluish tinge around his cuticles.

He starts the car and carefully pulls back onto the road. The dog chases after, but not for very long.

Anna is at the kitchen sink when David lets himself in. He kisses the damp crinkly strands on the back of her neck, wraps his arms around her waist as she turns to him.

"What is this?" she whispers.

Her lips open for him and he slides his hands down the softness of her, easing her against him.

"Where's Rosie?" He can barely recognize his own voice.

"The library."

He breaks away and she follows him, up the stairs. He's throwing off his clothes, leaving them in a pile on the floor near the door.

Anna shuts the door and smiles at him. Her fingers work the buttons of her blouse.

His need is desperate and he recognizes how deeply he loves her and the fragility of human life. Of his own life.

They do not hear the phone ring. They do not hear Rosie answer it. She has come home and come upstairs.

She's heard them behind the closed door. She's eleven and her uncle's and aunt's lovemaking is not new to her. It is the time of day, late afternoon, that is unusual. She answers the phone and tells Mrs. Westerfield that the doctor is with a patient and will call her as soon as he's free.

David holds Anna's sensual warmth against him. "You make an old man very happy."

"Old man? I don't see an old man in this bed," she says. She sits on the edge of the bed and begins to dress.

"You are my life," he says.

"And you are mine, my darling." She is waiting for him to dress.

"Anna." He pulls on his trousers, not looking at her. "If anything should happen to me—"

"What are you saying? What is going to happen to you?"

He takes her worried face in his hands and kisses her sweet lips. "Nothing, nothing at all, but just hear me out. I am so much older than you are. I expect to live a long life making love to my beautiful young wife."

"David—"

"Shush, let me finish. I want you to know that you make me very happy, beyond anything I've ever dreamed."

"And you me," she says, holding him as he holds her.

"Now, not another word," he says.

In his office, David calls his old friend, Peter Erhlich, who is head of cardiology at Jefferson. He describes the incident, and they agree David must come to Philadelphia as soon as he can arrange his schedule.

After dinner, he sits on the veranda smoking his pipe. Rosie, cross-legged on the floor in front of him, draws his picture with colored chalk.

"You are a very good model, Uncle David," she says.

"Thank you, Rosie." He reaches down and pats her crown of fair hair. He can see, even from upside down, she has caught his features and there is no mistaking who she is drawing. Her talent is so enormous, he wishes he could take her to museums and show her the old masters.

When Anna comes out with her knitting and sits on the glider beside him, he says, "I have a meeting in Philadelphia Friday morning."

"It's not on the calendar." The glider creaks slightly as she turns to him.

"I forgot. Pete Erhlich called to remind me. See, I told you I'm getting old."

"You're not old, Uncle David," Rosie says.

"That's right, Rosie darling." Anna puts her knitting aside and her hand reaches for David's, which is reaching for hers.

Rosie is fascinated by the movement of their hands joining. Hands to hands. She rolls over her drawing paper to a clean sheet and begins.

"I'll get someone to pick me up for plane spotting," Anna says. Almost imperceptibly, she moves closer to him. Thigh by thigh.

Rosie draws.

"I wasn't going to take the car," David says. "Saving on gas. You take the car and I'll go by train." He looks down at Rosie and her drawing. "See, Anna." He takes the drawing pad from Rosie. "Like Michelangelo."

"Those are your hands, Uncle David. Yours and Auntie Anna's. Not Michael Angelo's."

"Michelangelo, all one name, was a great artist, Rosie."

"I want to be a great artist, too."

Anna shivers. She thinks, someone has walked over my

grave. "You can be a great artist tomorrow. Now it's time for bed."

"There's no school tomorrow, or Friday," Rosie says. "The teachers have a meeting, too."

David has an idea. It's providence. "You know, Anna, I think Judy Erhlich's father has some connection to the Philadelphia Museum of Art. I can call her and see if she's free on Friday. What do you think, Rosie? Would you like to come to Philadelphia with me?"

Rose

"You old scamp," Mrs. Erhlich says, giving Uncle David a big kiss. "Why don't we ever see you?" Rosie is shocked. She's never seen Uncle David kiss another lady except Auntie Anna. He calls Mrs. Erhlich Judy and he smiles and looks bashful.

"Judy," he says. He rests his hands on Rosie's shoulders. "This is our Rosie and she's been showing some real artistic talent. It's time she met the masters."

The Philadelphia Museum has a long concrete lawn with geometric designs in the concrete. Its tall columns in front remind Rosie of the pictures of the Pantheon in Greece. Inside, Rosie cranes her neck to try to see the ceiling, which reaches practically to the sky.

Mrs. Erhlich wears a red suit and a little red hat with a short veil. She points to a beautiful statue in front of a sweeping staircase. "That is a Saint-Gaudens, Rose. It's made of bronze and depicts Diana, the huntress. It used to be a weathervane on top of a building in New York that was torn down."

Rosie knows who the mythological Diana is from school, but she's never seen what she looked like. She is very beautiful and is not wearing any clothes.

Everyone says hello to Mrs. Erhlich, and a slightly built man in a dark suit comes down the stairs to greet them.

Mrs. Erhlich is very pleased to see him. He shakes hands with her.

"This is Rose, and she's an artist," Mrs. Erhlich says. "Mr. Tice is the director of the museum, Rose."

Mr. Tice shakes Rosie's hand, too. "It's always a pleasure to meet young artists," he says.

"It's Rose's first visit to a museum."

"Well, we are honored you chose us, Rose," Mr. Tice says.

"I think perhaps Rose might like the seventeenth-century Dutch room and then look at some of the school."

School? Rosie is confused. Is there a school in the museum?

"Oh, yes," Mrs. Erhlich is saying. "And we must see the Cezanne. I never tire of looking at it."

Mr. Tice nods enthusiastically. "Nor do I. We're so lucky to have it in the collection."

The Dutch School, Rosie discovers, is not a school at all, but refers to a group of artists who painted in the seventeenth century. Vermeer is one. She gets up really close to a small painting of a girl with a pearl earring and is amazed that she cannot see any brush strokes.

"I've never painted with oils," she tells Mrs. Erhlich, whose high-heeled shoes click, click, click on the marble floors.

"I'm sure you will one day," Mrs. Erhlich says.

While they are looking at the Dutch School, Mr. Tice comes into the gallery. "I'm glad I caught up with you," he says. "I didn't want you to miss this, Rose. I think you'll find it very interesting." He moves them along to stand in front of another painting.

It is of women and furniture, but as she looks closer,

Rosie sees that the large checkerboard floor tiles in the painting appear faintly through the women's dresses and the furniture. "Why did he do that?"

"His name is Pieter De Hooch. And he didn't intend for the tiles to show through," Mr. Tice tells her. "What happened was he painted the tiles first, and then he painted the figures over the tiles, covering them completely. What he didn't know was that as oil paint ages, it becomes transparent. On some paintings by other artists, you can see the ghost of a child or a dog coming through. These ghosts of a previous painting are called repentances. It's from the Italian word pentimento."

"Oil paint does that?" Rosie wants to try to paint with oils but Mr. Albini says she's not ready. Mr. Albini must know about repentances.

"Modern painters know that they have to scrape off any lines and colors that are darker than the new paint and smooth out paint or brush strokes they don't want to reappear on the finished painting."

"Repentance—" Rosie rolls it over her tongue. "Like 'I'm sorry I made a mistake like this.' " She points to the black and white tiles.

Mr. Tice is delighted. He claps his hands. "Exactly," he says.

"There's your father," Mrs. Erhlich says as they start down the stairs. She is pointing to a marble bench in the lobby where Uncle David sits waiting. He is reading one of his journals.

"That's Uncle David. My papa is in the Army."

"Oh, I'm sorry, Rose. I thought—"

"Uncle David is my second papa," Rosie says without thinking, then realizes that what she has just said is true.

155

★ ★ ★ ★ ★

As the train chugs its slow way toward home, Rosie talks and talks about Diana the huntress and the Dutch School until her mouth is dry. Uncle David just smiles at her. He looks very tired and he has blue circles under his eyes.

"So, I think you had a good time," he says, putting his arm around her.

"Oh, yes!" She rests her head against his shoulder. She loves the smell of his pipe tobacco that clings to his jacket. "Mrs. Erhlich thought you're my papa, Uncle David, and I told her I have two papas, you and Papa."

He kisses the top of her head. She sees tears in his eyes.

"You are my own dear girl," he says.

Rosie's eyelids droop, but she's too excited to sleep.

"Would you like to go to college?" Uncle David asks suddenly.

"I'm only eleven, Uncle David. I bet you forgot."

He smiles at her. "Yes, you are such a grown up young lady, I did forget. I was looking down the road, into the future. Maybe you can think about it and give me an answer anyway."

She doesn't have to think about it. She knows. Mr. Albini has told her all about the artists in Greenwich Village in New York. "I would like to go to art school, Uncle David. In New York. I want to paint pictures that people will look at in museums."

"Uncle David asked me if I want to go to college," Rosie says while Auntie Anna washes the dishes and Rosie dries. As they do every night.

"Of course you'll go to college," Auntie Anna says.

"I told him I want to go to art school and be an artist."

"You're too young to make such a serious decision,"

Auntie Anna says abruptly. She shivers as if she's standing in a draft, but the kitchen is warm and Rosie doesn't feel a draft. "You will change your mind a hundred times yet."

Rosie is adamant. "Oh, no! I will never change my mind."

Auntie Anna says nothing. She's busy scrubbing the roasting pan with Brillo.

"I saw a very strange painting in the museum."

"Oh, yes?"

"The artist painted black and white tiles and then changed his mind and painted people on top covering the tiles. But the top paint got transparent and the tiles showed through the dresses and everything."

"A mistake like that and it's still in the museum?"

Rosie starts on the silverware. "Mr. Tice said it happens with old paintings sometimes. It's called repentances."

Auntie Anna stops washing. She doesn't look around Rosie. "What did he call it when what was hidden shows through?"

"Repent—"

"Never mind," she says so quietly that Rosie almost doesn't hear her. "Never mind."

Anna

The potatoes, which Rosie has helped peel, are resting in cold water so they won't turn black before Anna can grate them for latkes. Rosie is spread out on the kitchen table, studying for a history test.

Tires crunching on the gravel, David's car comes up the drive.

"Here he is!" Rosie closes her book and puts it on the cupboard.

"Good, good," Anna says. "Go set the table, Rosie darling." She finishes grating the potatoes, adds matzoh meal and eggs. The oil begins to crackle in the frying pan. One at a time she drops the batter by the tablespoonful into the hot oil.

But David doesn't come in.

"Rosie, go see what's keeping him."

"Uncle David?" Rosie stands at the back door. Uncle David's car is in the garage just as always. Rosie puts on her coat and goes outside. "Uncle David?"

The garage is silent. The engine of the car is silent. Rosie peers in. Uncle David sits in his car in the garage. She hesitates. This is not her favorite place. There are spider webs in every corner. Mounted on the far wall are all of Uncle David's old license plates, including even the tags they've issued to save metal for the war.

Uncle David is still sitting in the car, his hands on the

steering wheel, staring straight ahead. On the seat beside him is his black bag.

Rosie taps on the window. "Uncle David?" She knows he will turn to her, his eyes full of love. Rosie darling, he will say, just as Auntie Anna always says. But he doesn't move.

He's gone away and left her.

She comes into the kitchen and watches Auntie Anna finish making the latkes, placing them to drain on a towel.

"Rosie? David?" Anna turns, spatula poised. She sees Rosie's face. "David," she says. "David." She drops the spatula on the back porch.

Rosie turns off the fire under the latkes and goes out to the garage. Auntie Anna is sitting in the passenger seat holding Uncle David's sagging body in her arms.

"I wanted to grow old with him," Anna says.

Anna stares into every mirror, entreating David's spirit to stay. Her mama—of blessed memory—covered mirrors so the spirit of the dead one would leave the earth. But Anna wants David here, beside her, his breadth against hers . . .

The knock on the back door interrupts her longing. She looks in the mirror now and sees her face, elongated with sorrow. She's taken scissors to the braid he loved. Loose, her red curls are an affront to her mourning.

The knock comes again, and she opens the door for John Novinger, David's friend. David's will, he'd said when he called.

Of course, David would have a will—he was a thorough man—but he'd never mentioned it to her.

John Novinger is tall and angular; his shoulders stoop slightly under the door frame. He still wears the dazed look and black armband for Betty, who died of breast cancer three months ago. He's a decent man, she's come to know, and she lets him take both her hands in his, feeling the warmth of his emotion.

"How are you doing?" he asks, sitting at the kitchen table, leaning his briefcase against the table leg. He nods yes to her offer of coffee.

"About the same as you," she says. "I keep thinking I hear him in the surgery, or I wait for the phone to ring when he finishes his house calls. I come downstairs to tell him . . ." She leaves the rest in her head . . . *tell him to come to bed so we can make love, so I can feel you move inside me.*

"Yes," John says. "It's the mornings that are worse." He shakes his head. "And the evenings."

She sits with him and they are silent for the moment.

"Rosie's in school?" he asks.

"Yes, I thought it was better for her to be around children her own age. She loved him so—" She swallows hard, her lips pressed together. The wall she's kept around herself, cracks. She will not cry, she must not cry. But tears come anyway and crawl down on cheeks so pale her freckles look raised.

"Oh, Anna, I know," John says. He gives her his hand-kerchief.

She dries her eyes. "I'm sorry. Maybe you should tell me what David wanted."

From his briefcase, Novinger takes out a folder and in the folder is a legal document. She can see that. She also sees a white envelope with her name on it in David's cramped hand.

Novinger hands her the envelope. "David asked me to give this to you if—"

"He knew." She turns the envelope in her hand. It is sealed. "He knew. When?"

"Last month. He saw a specialist in Philadelphia."

"Philadelphia. When he took Rosie on the train. He never said anything."

"He didn't want to change anything, Anna. He didn't want to become an invalid. You and Rosie were his life."

She stares at the envelope in her hand. "I don't know what I'm going to do, what we're going to do."

"Let me go over his will with you. You mustn't worry about the future. There will always be enough money."

She looks at him, shocked. Money has never been in her thoughts. It intrudes now.

"The house is yours, of course. It's free and clear. The mortgage was paid off years ago. The practice is your brother Nathan's, if he wants it."

"If he wants it," she repeats. "Nathan is on his way home. They couldn't find him at first."

"I know. If Nathan doesn't want it, David asked that it be sold."

"Sell David's practice? How can I do that? He loved his patients; everyone loved him. The patients all know Nathan . . ." But Anna knows Nathan and Nathan has big dreams. "We'll have to see."

"David left money, ten thousand, for Rose to go to art school in New York," Novinger says. "And an additional twenty-five thousand when she turns twenty-one."

"She's too young—"

"Now, yes, of course, but the years go by fast. We love them and then we must let them go." Novinger speaks from experience. Both of his and Betty's girls are in college, one in Wisconsin, the other in Massachusetts.

Anna presses her hand to her mouth, aches with the terrible secret she and Nathan share. If she could only . . .

Novinger misunderstands. How could he not? His eyes,

deep set and distressed, are wet. "I'm so sorry," he says. "You know you can call on me any time, Anna. I'll be there for you."

John, she thinks. How strange that Novinger, the Jew, has a Christian name and David, the Christian, has—had—a Jewish one.

After Novinger leaves, she opens David's letter. Presses the sheet of paper to her breast, trying to invoke his essence.

My darling girl, he begins. *As I write this I am full of love for you. Do not grieve for me too long. Just a little while. I want to see your beautiful smile. There are things I would have liked to live for. The end of the war. Our Rosie to graduate from high school and become the artist she wants to be. I have made arrangements with John for her schooling.*

Know, my Anna, that you made my life complete and I will always believe some higher power sent you to me when I needed you so.

You will not ever have to worry about money, and while I hope Nathan will take over my practice, if he doesn't want it, please do not hesitate to sell it.

Depend on John for advice and friendship. He is a good man, and he knows my sentiments. I leave you with only love in my poor heart.

Your David.

— 30 —

Nathan

1945

"How're you doin', Doc?" Al Goodwin, the station master, is standing on the platform when they get to the station.

"Come by and let me check your blood pressure, Al," Nathan says.

"Good to see you, Dr. Ebanholz. How pretty you look, Rosie."

Luke Applegate, the taxi man, is also on the platform waiting for the train, which should arrive any minute.

"How's your mother, Luke?" Nathan asks.

"Much better, thanks, Dr. Ebanholz. Rosie's growing up to be a pretty young lady."

Nathan smiles and nods to everyone at the station. Rosie beams. Nathan is very aware of the respect he's held in the eyes of the community. He thrives on it, though it is not the life he planned for himself.

Anna's accusation still rings in his ears. "You didn't want to come home."

It was true. He'd loved the Army, loved his captain's bars, loved the uniform, the surgery. It was a world of men, soldiers, doctors, all with the same goal, to win the war. Women were incidental.

"You were having such a good time, weren't you?

163

Admit it," Anna said. "Another way of not accepting your responsibilities."

"What responsibilities?" He'd protested, but he knew. It was always there with them. What he'd done in a moment of madness.

"Rosie needs her father."

And what Anna didn't say, he knew full well. She blamed him for David's death.

"Well, I'm here now," he said.

They stand on the platform side by side, Nathan resting his hand on Rosie's narrow shoulder, as the train gives a short toot and lumbers into the station.

"Nathan!" A woman in one of the open passenger doors is waving, eager. She calls out again. "Nathan!" Everyone on the platform looks at her with curiosity. None more so than Rosie.

A quick glance back at Rosie, her mouth open, her face frozen, tells Nathan he's handled it wrong. He should have listened to Anna; instead he told Rosie they were going to meet one of his friends from the war.

Which is a half-truth perhaps, but not a lie. Helen Levy is a nurse and he did meet her in the war. They'd been lovers, drawn together by the horror of their work, and as Jews, that which made them different from the others. He hasn't seen her in almost a year because after he was called home, the Army had sent Helen on to Germany.

It's Helen who's kept up the relationship, by mail, by phone, and he acquiesced, seeing in his mind's eye their urgent coupling, her heavy breasts teasing his lips, his hands kneading her pliant ass.

She's a small woman, on the edge of being plump, with pale skin, dark eyes, and dark hair. Above and below her tiny waist, abundance blooms in breasts, buttocks, and thighs, all accentuated by her red knitted dress. She wears black gloves and a black hat sewn with tiny seed pearls.

As she steps onto the platform, Nathan drops his hand from Rosie's shoulder and rushes to take Helen's suitcase the porter hands down.

Rosie almost dies when the woman smiles at Nathan and then kisses him on the mouth with her big red lips.

What is it with Nathan, Anna wonders, as she puts away the dinner dishes Rosie washed and dried before going to bed. What makes him choose these women? This one, this Helen, and the other one, that Stella—she shudders at the thought of her—they're two alike. And that tramp Mary Lou from before the war.

There are women who use their bodies to get what they want, and Anna is certain this Helen is one of them. She obviously wants Nathan, marriage, the prestige of being a doctor's wife. Children, perhaps.

Anna watches Helen's small, dark eyes take in the shabby house, Anna herself, and Rosie. No, Anna, the widowed sister, and Rosie, that child from the first marriage, will not fit into this one's plans. Anna is quite sure of that. What she isn't sure of is Nathan.

"I want my own home," Helen says, after Anna bids them goodnight and goes upstairs. "We'll buy some land and build; then Anna can keep this house for herself." She gets up from the couch and sits on Nathan's lap, loops her arm about his neck so that the swell of her breasts presses against him. With her other hand, she rubs his cock.

Nathan closes his eyes with a soft groan as her practiced hand does its work. "But if we build a house, Anna should come too. Rosie won't want to be separate from Anna." He feels the heat of her as she shifts herself into the right place. He takes her breasts in his hands, sets his mouth nibbling on the cloth over her nipples, as he's wanted to do since she arrived.

"Nathan, the girl—Rose—is so withdrawn. She needs friends and real parents."

He raises his head. "Rosie has plenty of friends. And she has me. And Anna. Real parents."

"Oh, Nathan, you're a man, look how she dresses. She'll never attract a boy that way." Helen wriggles against him. "Let's go upstairs." She gets off him and pulls him up, guiding his hand to the zipper of her dress.

"She's barely thirteen. I don't want her to attract boys." Unzipping Helen's dress, he plunges his hands into soft, fleshy paradise.

She leans her head back against his. "Nathan, sweetheart, we don't want her hanging around the house like a wallflower after we have our own . . ."

Anna pulls her nightgown over her head and sits on the bed in the dark. She's given Helen her room and she'll sleep in the other bed in Rosie's room. The house is old and voices travel. She can't tell if Rosie is asleep, but hopes she is. Nathan is a fool having sex with that woman while his young daughter is in the next room.

Listening to the sounds from her room, Anna crosses her legs and rocks back and forth on the bed. *Ah, David, my love, how I miss you.*

"She has a mustache," Rosie whispers, breaking into Anna's longing.

Anna swallows a laugh. Helen does have a little shadow on her upper lip. "Shsh, darling, she'll hear you. Go to sleep."

"She doesn't like us. She wants to have Papa to herself."

"What makes you think that?"

"She wants to change everything. Is Papa going to marry her?"

"I don't know, darling."

"I'll die if he does."

"No, you won't. You'll be a big girl and you'll be happy for Nathan that he found someone after all this time."

"I'm not happy. I hate her. And she hates me."

Anna sighs. "What will be, will be," she says.

When Nathan takes Helen to the train the next day, they sit in the car because it's a little early. He doesn't look at her when he says, "It isn't going to work."

"What do you mean, it isn't going to work?"

"You and me."

"But we're good together."

"In bed we're good. I don't want to build a house somewhere else. I don't want more children. I have my Rosie."

"You can't live your life for one child. She'll grow up and get married and leave you. You need me, Nathan. What kind of life do you have with that dreary woman and that awkward child? I have such plans for us."

Nathan sighs. "Stella." She sounds like Stella. He gets out of the car, goes around to her side, and helps her out. He takes her suitcase from the back and they walk to the platform.

She's furious. "Why didn't you tell me there's someone else?"

"What are you talking about? There's no one else."

The train rumbles into the station. She gets on. He hands the suitcase up to her. "Then who the hell is Stella?" she says.

Rose

1949

"Rosie!"

She holds her hands up in front of her. Five fingers on each hand. Sticks her legs straight out. Five toes on each foot. She has two arms, two legs, two eyes, one head. Just like everyone else. But she doesn't feel like everyone else. She gets up from the edge of the bed and stares into the mirror that rests on her bureau. She feels beside herself, two people, almost identical. She sits on the bed again trying to recapture the errant thread of a memory. Gone in a blink—

"Rosie!"

She's Rosie. She is sitting on the edge of her bed; the skirt of her new blue moiré dress is bunched up under her.

"Rosie, you are my posy . . ." Uncle David used to sing to her. ". . . my heart's bouquet . . ."

"Rosie! What's keeping you?"

She stands, smoothing the skirt.

It's her birthday. They, Papa and Auntie Anna, and Larry and the Finebergs, Larry's parents, are going to the Golden Grill in Pinewood because they make tomato pie there and Rosie loves tomato pie with extra cheese.

She wears a new dress, two separate pieces. Blue moiré,

with a wide skirt that comes almost to her ankles. It's the latest style. The New Look, it's called. Auntie Anna took her to Steinbach's in Asbury Park to buy it. The top is long-sleeved and fitted, ending in a little peplum; a row of rhine-stone buttons goes from throat to waist, revealing only the faint curve of her breasts. Sheer nylons and her first pumps—black suede, Cuban heels.

She thinks, if only Uncle David could see me all grown up like this. But Uncle David died and left her—left them, and nothing's been the same. Papa is grumpy and doesn't talk much, and Auntie Anna grieves and doesn't talk much. And Rosie? She hides it very deep inside her, and only once in a while will she dare to let it out.

No one, not even Rosie, mentions the money, the money Uncle David left her so she can go to art school in New York. It frightens her when she thinks about it, like looking down the cellar steps into the darkness.

Larry's parents give her a set of Evening in Paris cologne and bath powder with a big powder puff, and Auntie Anna and Papa give her pearls that belonged to Uncle David's mother.

The Golden Grill is really a tavern with a bar and tables in the front, and a restaurant in the back which you can get to either by going through the bar or a side door from the parking lot. No one goes through the bar because rowdies gather there.

Bums, Papa calls them, and his mouth sets in a thin line.

She drinks Pepsi and the fizz tingles in her nose. Larry grins at her across the table as the round metal tray is set in front of them. "Just you and me," he says, pulling at a slice. The grown-ups have never understood the lure of tomato pie and are eating spaghetti with meatballs.

"Wait till it cools," Auntie Anna warns.

But she doesn't and burns the roof of her mouth with the

hot cheese. This always happens. She has a sip of Pepsi and has to go to the bathroom, which means going through the bar. So she waits until she can't anymore.

"Be careful," Papa says. "Anna, go with her."

"No," Rosie says. "I'm not a baby. I don't need anybody—"

The bar is a miasma of cigarette smoke, redolent with whisky and beer, and Rosie hesitates for a moment, then peers into the room. It is a strange place, and yet she knows the smells. She moves forward, though cold fingers squeeze her heart.

Shadowy people stand at the bar, talking and laughing, their reflections in the mirrors all around. A waiter points her in the right direction, and she walks slowly, afraid she may stumble.

The noise . . . there's so much noise . . . People close in around her, and she cringes, breaks free, moving forward, arms akimbo.

She chokes back her scream, but it sneaks out anyway. Mama is coming through the darkness to her, holding out her arms.

Rosie cries, "Mama," and runs to her.

"A mirror, darling," Auntie Anna says. "You walked into a mirror in the dark."

Her voice is so soothing Rosie almost forgets why she has a huge bump on her forehead and a bandage on her nose. Almost, not quite. She lies on her bed and aches all over. Her head thumps and thumps. "Mama. I saw Mama," she says.

"It was dark and there were mirrors. You made a mistake and bumped into a mirror," Auntie Anna says. She looks at Nathan.

"Too much excitement for one day," Papa says. He

bends to kiss her, but she is so bruised he must be careful.

Rosie closes her eyes. She wants to see Mama again. *Come back, Mama,* she pleads.

"Sleep, darling," Auntie Anna says. She smoothes Rosie's hair gently, then turns out the light and tiptoes out.

Mirrors, Rosie thinks. I saw myself in the mirror and thought I was Mama. She finds the string to the bedside lamp and turns on the light. On her bureau in a stand-up frame is the faded photograph of Rosie and Mama in Poland. She gets out of bed and stares at the photograph, then into the mirror. She has so much pain now, everything throbs. She couldn't have seen Mama because this is Mama and she looks nothing like the image in the bar.

When morning comes, Rosie doesn't get out of bed. "Not hungry," she tells Anna, and closes her eyes.

Auntie Anna's voice hovers over her. "You must eat, darling." Rosie hears her calling, "Nathan, Nathan."

Papa takes her pulse. "Rosie, tell Papa. What hurts you?"

She closes her eyes. Go away, she thinks. Everybody, go away.

— 32 —

Rose

1950

All along MacDougal Street, daffodils in window boxes are little golden trumpets against serious brown stone. Green baby fingers sprout from the branches of sycamores that line the street. In Clayton Lake she knows the lilacs are nestling against the side of the house, and Auntie Anna's peonies—perfume from the gods, Uncle David always said—have fat fuchsia buds. She misses the sweetness of the honeysuckle. She misses the certainty of home, that nothing has changed, that if she were to return, time would have stopped.

Rose shifts her sketch pad and the box of watercolors to her other hip. Her arm is cramping with the burden of the easel. When she comes to the letter box, she sets everything down, propping them against her legs. She pats her bulging pockets. Somewhere, in one of them, searching, she finds the envelope, only slightly bent. Smudged. She flattens it against the metal box, drops it in. Her weekly letter home.

It's three months now, and Papa is still angry. No, not angry. Papa is never angry; she has never in her life seen him angry. He's hurt. She's betrayed him.

"A car is what you need. A Ford," he had said when she graduated from high school. "Maybe a convertible?"

Rosie'd been indignant. "You're bribing me to stay home."

She'd applied to and been accepted by both Pratt and Cooper Union and had chosen Cooper Union because it was free and in Greenwich Village, where artists have gathered for years, and where the Abstract Expressionists now congregate.

Her charge hit home. Nathan looked chagrined. "You're a young girl. You can't live by yourself in the city. Tell her, Anna."

Anna smiled. "I came myself from Poland when I was not much older than Rosie, Nathan."

"That was a different time. You two are conspiring against me." Nathan glared at Anna and hunkered down in his easy chair. The pile of medical journals on his lap slipped, sliding every which way.

Rosie tried another tack. "Everything is happening in New York, Papa. Please let me go."

"It's not right. You should stay home. You'll meet a nice boy and get married."

Rosie pressed her lips together over the howl that crept up her throat; she looked at Auntie Anna, who nodded. "I'll find a nice place to live, Papa. Auntie Anna will help me. You'll see, I'll be fine. I can take classes at the Art Students League, too. It's what I want."

Nathan had grumbled, "I'll think about it," knowing he'd lost.

Auntie Anna touched Rosie's cheek. "Go, darling. I'll talk to Nathan."

Leaving the room, Rosie heard Nathan say, "You're not afraid?"

And Anna reply, "Yes, of course I'm afraid, but we must let her go. It's time."

"How can you say that? We'll lose her. Something

will happen if she goes there."

His voice had cracked, and with it, some of Rosie's resolve. She faltered in the hallway, shook it off, forced herself to keep walking.

It's really amazing, Rose thinks. For a doctor, Papa is very superstitious; he hangs onto old country ideas.

But superstitious and stubborn as he is, Rosie is proud of her papa. He was studying to be a surgeon when the war broke out and he quit and joined the Army. He went off and became a genuine war hero doctor, following the troops from Anzio, setting up field hospitals all over Italy.

Uncle David's sudden death had brought him home, this time for good. So handsome in his uniform, his ruddy hair graying at the temples. Nothing was the same, not even his little girl. Rosie at eleven, with her gangly legs and budding breasts, came as a shock.

She'd seen the disappointment on his face.

"Rose! Hey! You in a trance or something?" Crystal Cohen is a bubbling exotic stew, lugging notebooks and yellow legal pads stuffed in a Harvard book bag. Sharp dark eyes, heavily outlined in kohl, thick false lashes, her black hair cut in a pixie haircut, Crystal is her downstairs neighbor. Gypsy earrings dangle from her pierced earlobes to her shoulders and her accent gives away her Boston origins. She left Connecticut College for Women after her first year, she says, to write the Great American Novel. Rose hears her typewriter clacking way into the night, almost every night.

Rose laughs. Crystal always makes her laugh. "I just popped my head into your place. There's a strange man in your bed."

Crystal runs her tongue over ruby lips. "Oh, that's Victor." She shakes a cigarette from a pack and fits it into an elegant black holder, then lights it with a gold lighter. "He's a poet." She inhales deeply and lets her exhale stream white railroad tracks from her nostrils. Her ivory skin is accentuated by the fact that she never wears anything but black. "I met him at the San Remo last night with your boyfriend, what's-his-name, and a whole bunch of writers and poets. Or maybe it was this morning."

"My boyfriend? You mean Larry?"

"Yes."

"He's not my boyfriend. We just went to school together."

"Okay, sure, but you should have come. He said he asked you."

"I always feel uncomfortable with people like that. They're so smart, they seem to know everything and say really clever things."

"Alcohol and lies," Crystal says. "It's an acquired talent. If you don't try, you'll never learn how to do it."

"I'm not sure I want to. Besides, in my family we always made a fetish out of the truth." Rose picks up her easel. "What are you doing out this early?"

"My headshrinker changed me to eight-thirty. What a killjoy. Where are you off to at this ungodly hour, the League?"

"No." Anyone who didn't know Crystal would call her frivolous, and even trashy, but under all that flash, there is a serious writer, who lives on a tiny allowance, five dollars a week, and a part-time job at *The Daily News*. From her mouth come exquisite assessments of everyone she meets, which she generously shares with Rosie; and from her pen, what she calls exercises in stream of consciousness.

Rosie is quite convinced that Crystal is brilliant. "I'm going to Gramercy Park to do some 'scapes. Larry has a friend with a key and he's letting me borrow it. But first breakfast. Want to come?"

"No. Breakfast awaits upstairs." She gives Rosie an over-sized wink. "But I got us invited to a party tonight, so don't make other plans."

"Hell, no. I fully intend to leave my social calendar to you. What party? And what about Victor?"

"We can take him or not." Crystal grins. "Probably not. He'll cramp my style. The guest list includes Pollock, De Kooning, Clem Greenberg. Tennessee Williams, maybe. Tons of others. It's at Pinto's loft."

"Skye Pinto?" Rosie's heart does a flip. The brightest and the best. How will she ever talk to them? "You never told me you knew Skye Pinto."

"Oh, I don't. I know Clem Greenberg. He has the hots for me. My body, alas, not my work."

Pinto. Rosie sees him for the first time at the Museum of Modern Art when she is thirteen. Not Pinto the man, but the drip painting, Gone to Blue 2. *It makes her breathless. She feels a subtle madness within her respond to his. It's there; it must come out.*

He hangs with Pollock, De Kooning, Newman. And Rothko, whom Auntie Anna much prefers. But it is Pinto who seduces Rosie.

There is a small photograph of Pinto in the museum flyer on the show. A cigarette dangles from his lips, a deep frown on his face, he stands, arms folded, in front of his huge painting. Take me or leave me. I don't care one way or the other. His eyes, though shadowed by the frown, look straight into her.

★ ★ ★ ★ ★

"Pinto, I said. Your idol." Crystal teases her. "His loft on Sullivan Street. You finally get to meet the myth."

Pinto. It's years since *Gone to Blue 2* shocked her with wild possibilities. But the memory of her reaction, as if she'd been sliced open, dissected, remains as sharp. She's seen his latest work at Betty Parsons.

Pinto. The myth. Clement Greenberg describes the development of genius: Pinto's childhood in the farm country of Pennsylvania; his father, dead now, a carpenter-wood carver. No mention of his mother except to say she died young.

The great hands of a farmer, Greenberg says, are changing the face of modern art in America.

An interview in *Art News* describes how Pinto came to New York in the late thirties after years "on the bum, riding the rails." He boasts of having spent the night under the stars in every state of the union.

The interviewer comments on his distinctive speech: low, halting, curving inward, a singular way of phrasing, representing no particular section of the country. "Words," Pinto responds, "are not my art." He does not know what he will paint when he looks at the blank canvas.

"Pinto's a madman," Rose's oil painting teacher, Archibald Bradleigh tells her. Arch was in the WPA Arts Project with Pinto, Pollock, and the others. "He's a dangerous drunk. We were at the bar in the Albert and he got downright vulgar and was groping a young woman. She'd had a nice review of her mural work in the *New Yorker*. A few of us pulled him away. He went off and came back with an ax, which he held over the poor girl's head. He said that he was sorry but he was going to have to kill her. Clem grabbed his

177

arm and we distracted him long enough for her to get out of there. After she left, Pinto drove his ax into the bar and smashed every bottle in the place. They called the police. Kline and Motherwell took up a collection and bailed him out. I would have let him rot."

But that was long ago, Rose thinks. What about something more recent? A tragedy. Rose remembers the *Times'* careful coverage. Susanna Como, award-winning sculptress of singular merit, accidentally falls—or is pushed—from the sixth-floor window of a loft on Sullivan Street. Pinto's lover. Pinto's loft. Pinto is in Payne Whitney in a state of total collapse.

Pinto had stared out at her from the *Times'* photo. The same photo from the Museum of Modern Art brochure. He stands arrogant in front of *Gone to Blue 2*, cigarette dangling from his lips. Rosie still has it; it stares out at her from a corner of the same frame as the photograph of Rosie and her dead mama in Poland.

"What about the women?" Rose asks Arch.

"Women?" Arch is scornful. "Pinto has no use for women."

Rose

Rose walks east toward Second Avenue, passing the multitude of used bookshops that cluster shoulder to shoulder from Broadway and University Place to Second. At the Second Avenue Deli, she stops for a fried egg, a toasted bagel, and coffee. Special for a quarter.

The *Times* is full of stories about the Berlin Blockade, and everywhere, people are talking about it. She shivers. If war comes again, they will need doctors and Papa may have to go. It is only five years since he came home and took up Uncle David's practice.

She pushes the thought away. Obligations and responsibilities, as Auntie Anna says, will keep Papa from any new war.

After she pays the bill, Rose comes out on the avenue. The borrowed key that will let her into the private park is in her pocket. A brisk breeze is coming from the East River, warning, "Don't be fooled, spring is not yet here." Rosie tightens her scarf around her throat and pulls her beret from her pocket, setting it low on her head so it covers her ears. Her rowdy blond curls, no longer the platinum of her childhood, creep from beneath the band.

A vendor is selling hot pretzels on the corner of Fourteenth Street next to a newsstand, and the salty yeast smell tingles her nose as she passes. "Good morning," she says, liking the lilt she hears in her voice, feels in her step.

The old man in the newsstand looks up, and she wishes him the same good morning. She walks on, stops where the pavement has been smashed by some heavy object. Broken veins in the cement radiate like a spider's web from the almost perfect circle of the depression. Though she puts up her hand to ward it off, the web seems to undulate in the cement as if to draw her into its vortex.

She's seen that old man in the newsstand before, but he wasn't old then. He's the green troll man who used to follow her and stare at her when she was a little girl.

Rose makes her way back to the newsstand, and out of his line of sight, watches him. She wants to ask him why he stopped coming to Clayton Lake, but she hesitates. He just stares out from his nest with rapidly blinking eyes until a woman stops to buy a paper and blocks the view. Rose's cargo grows heavy. She turns away.

The downward slope toward the East River lures her away from her destination. A large crane and a cement mixer snarl the street, lacerate the sky. Even in the three short months she's been here, the city seems to change its landscape constantly, shedding skin and recreating itself.

The Elevated platforms have all come down, the trains buried underground, but here and there you can still see pieces of the skeleton, and the iron rails of the trolley tracks are still imbedded in many city streets, although the trolley, too, is no more.

"Ooops, sorry," someone says, bumping her. She's been waiting for the light to change. It had changed and she hadn't moved.

Once again Rose rouses herself. She feels oddly languid. Overhead, fat clouds scud in the wind, birthing smaller clouds. Her loafers seem leaden, her burden oppressive. She's been sleeping poorly, waking at intervals, frightened.

The traveling dream has returned. On a bus, going somewhere, a long trip, getting off again, waiting, never getting there. Wherever "there" is.

In her attic room she doesn't need to lie in the dark as she did at home. She can get up, make herself a cup of coffee, and read in the easy chair, wrapped in her blanket. She does this almost routinely now. Then, just before dawn as daylight hovers over her skylight, she nods off.

She passes Beth Israel, where the streets surrounding the hospital are dense with cars. Beth Israel is expanding, foundations are being dug, and workmen are everywhere carrying beams and struts. The main building of the hospital is old and its dirty stone face makes it look formidable.

The area around Gramercy Park is occupied mostly by beautiful nineteenth-century brownstones. In the front window of one of them, a cat sits and watches Rose's progress.

Gramercy Park is a lovely, private enclave—only residents in the surrounding buildings have keys—with benches and paths among the trees, flowers, and shrubs, enclosed by a tall iron fence and a locked gate, which gives a protesting creak as Rose opens it. She is immediately confronted by a small puppy, a white terrier, growling, but frisking around Rose's ankles.

"So are you the vicious guard dog that keeps watch over the park?" Rose asks.

The dog twitches his shiny black nose at her. "I'd like to think so," it says.

Has she entered a magic kingdom where dogs talk? But then, half to her disappointment, for Rose loves fantasy, she sees the man who spoke for the dog rise from a bench entirely obscured by a giant shrub.

In his nest behind the stacks of papers and magazines,

Zweikel is almost delirious. He can't believe his good fortune. He can stop searching now. No more walking the streets looking at faces. *She's* found *him*. He abandons his news-stand without another thought and follows her.

— 34 —

Ben

"Didn't mean to startle you," the man says. "Come here, Maxie." He isn't tall, but his broad frame, in khaki pants and a tweed jacket, gives him a solid look. Maxie jumps at him and with a stiff bend, he picks up the squirming creature.

Rose doesn't see the cane until she moves farther into the park. It is propped up against the bench next to a fat textbook. When the man sits down, his hand finds it, before the book, as if it is a natural part of him.

"You didn't. Startle me, I mean." Rose's smile is guarded, glad he hasn't offered to help with her art paraphernalia. "Maxie looks like a girl to me."

His eyes are burnt umber, warm. "She is. Her name is really Maxine, for Maxine Andrews." He sets the puppy down on the path.

Rose moves on into the park, Maxie trailing. She passes an old man in a wheelchair. He is reading the *Wall Street Journal*, legs covered by a woolen blanket. A nurse in a crisp white uniform sits beside him, crocheting squares of brightly colored yarn.

"Good morning," the nurse says. A starched white cap covered with sharp pleats sits atop her head like a dagger crown. Her tone of voice belies her friendly greeting and Rose decides to sit as far from the nurse as possible, though she doesn't understand why.

A sudden, violent tremor catches her, makes her drop her easel. The dog yips and scoots away. Shocked at herself, Rose picks up the easel. She feels again the strange lethargy. Her thoughts slow, sticking to each other like flies to fly paper. Her limbs grow heavier with each step.

Maybe she's been enchanted. The Gramercy Park witch has put a spell on her. She is, after all, a trespasser with a borrowed key. Come now, Rosie, she tells herself. Such an imagination.

She moves with determination and finds a spot profuse with daffodils. Around them, the earth is moistly rich and dark, giving off a fecund scent, smoldering mold. No, stop. How morbid. See how serene and clean the light is. She sets up, ignoring the clamor in her chest. She is not sick. There is nothing wrong with her. She's a doctor's daughter, for God's sake. Wouldn't she know if she were sick?

The sun inches higher and higher. The little park with its trees and plantings muffles the noise of the city around it.

Rose prepared the paper last night, soaking it, stretching it by pinning it still wet to a drawing board, and letting it dry. The surface is ready for watercolor paint, a medium they do not teach at Cooper Union. She carries a small jelly jar of water in her bag along with her colors. She'll wet the paper again before she begins.

The paper is stiff and lineny; its texture invites color.

She parks her box on the sloping surface of a bench and sets up her easel. As she straightens, her head feels weightless, as if it would float away from her body.

Maxie comes hurtling up the path and quick-brakes when she sees Rose. Her tail flaps with pleasure. The little black nose nuzzles the paint box, then Rosie's hand. Coming back to herself, Rosie stops to massage behind Maxie's ears. She takes up her brush and dips it into the jar of water. The clear sunlight begins to dictate shadow.

When Rose turns to her paper, it is already marked; bars make a vertical statement on its surface.

"No." She hears the whisper, just barely. With frantic speed she irrigates the surface, then adds blues and a pale wash of purple. Touches of pink for the spring morning. She paints over the bars with broad strokes. The bars bleed through.

A wave of fear soaks her. "Get away, get away." She slaps on more color; deeper and deeper blues spatter the paper. Abstract expression in watercolor. *Gone to Blue.* She works in a frenzy. There, she's done it. Almost safe. Then the errant branch reaches out its great claw hand for her.

She's lost her name somewhere in the endless tunnels. The light from the street seeps through the window, painting black bars on the coarse gray blanket. Bars trap her and claw branches reach for her. And although she knows it is the wind, a ghost howls, "Hoooo, hoooo, hoooo," just like Olga says, just to scare her. The black bars on her blanket hold her fast as the claw rattles against the window and reaches for her.

"Stand back."

"Give her some air."

"Get that dog away."

"Come here, Maxie."

"Get her to Beth Israel. She's had some sort of fit."

"Look, she's wet herself."

"Irene . . . I found you. Everything will be all right now."

"Get out of the way, mister. I'm a doctor. Everybody stand back. Give her air."

Rose opens her eyes. The cap of daggers bends over her.

"No! No! I couldn't help it," she cries, hiding her face. "Don't hurt me. I'll be good."

She is hot, on fire, and they take her clothes away. She stands on a table in front of the window and they look at her in the light. "A rash. See. See." The man's fingers touch her burning skin. "Poor child."

Olga picks her up again. Olga is always picking her up and hugging her, even when she doesn't want to be picked up and hugged. Every time Olga does it, the poor child's dress goes up and everyone can see her panties. Mama says not to let Olga do that. Then Olga gets the fever and dies and Papa hurts Mama and they don't want the poor child any more and give her away to a zoo. The light in the cage is so bright it hurts her eyes.

Mozart comes like a soft breath, whispers in her ears, warms her skin. A teakettle whistles. Rosie sighs. It was a dream. She's home in her bed and Auntie Anna is making tea.

Opening her eyes, she looks into the wet, inquisitive nose of the puppy, Maxie, whose thrill at her awakening is boundless.

Pipe tobacco and . . . Uncle David! No. Uncle David is dead.

She sits up—or tries to. There is the faint odor of urine and stronger one of vomit. Remembering suddenly, she presses her hands to her face. Heat and mortification. Panic. Where is she?

Think. Be logical. Stay calm. Taking stock: she is wrapped in a blanket, lying on a sofa in a strange place. A big room, rust and blue Persian rugs laid one atop the other, dark, heavy furniture. Bookcases surround an easy

chair and a fine old desk. Oil paintings, landscapes, deco-
rate the walls. Nothing here frightens her.

Reassured, she sits up, dislodging the dog. She is naked
under the blanket. What happened to her? She wraps the
blanket more firmly around her. She understands she's had
some kind of attack. A seizure. I'm very sick, she thinks.

China clinks and, "Oh, good. You're awake."

The lame man from the park is holding a tray with two
cups and a teapot. He sets it on a low table.

She sees her easel propped up near the door. Her
painting is a hideous gash of color. What has she done? She
begins to observe herself from somewhere else as she's done
often in the past. Is she going crazy? "Where am I?"

"My apartment. Across from the park." He has hair the
color of the summer sand on the beach at Seaside Heights, and
those burnt umber eyes. A cleft in his chin like Cary Grant.

"Where are my clothes?" She is pretending nonchalance.

"They were soiled." He pours a half cup of strong black
tea, dark as coffee. She watches him add three sugars. He
hands it to her.

"I don't like sugar," she snaps, her energy a surprise.

"You need the jolt." He is unmoved by her reaction, and
continues to hold the cup out to her until she takes it with
trembling hands.

She tries again. "You undressed me?" Hates the tremor
in her voice.

"I'm a doctor, Rose."

"You know my name?" She sets the cup down and holds
the blanket with her other hand.

"It was in your wallet. Rose Ebanholz." He sits in the
easy chair and stretches his injured leg. "Drink the tea."

"Oh." Reluctantly, she takes a sip of the extremely sweet
tea. Her mouth is very dry. What if he's a white slaver, she

thinks. I'll never be seen again. I'll wake up in a harem. Her eyes fill.

"I'm Ben Coopersmith."

"M.D.?"

"M.D."

"What happened to me?"

"I don't know. I'd like to get you tested, when you're up to it."

"My father's a doctor."

"Fine. Then he should get you tested. I don't want to alarm you. Do you get headaches?"

"Migraines. But I've been getting them for years. This wasn't a migraine. I don't want my father to know about this."

"Has this ever happened to you before?"

"No . . ." She is remembering the time she had an hallucination and walked into a mirror.

He notices her hesitation. "Never?"

"Never," she says.

"What do you remember—just before you screamed?"

"I screamed?" She shivers. What does she remember? "I was frightened . . . I thought . . . I don't know. I made a mess of my painting."

"You had what I believe was an episode set off by some outside event that triggered a memory."

Rose smiles. "You're a headshrinker medical doctor."

"So I am." He grins at her, and it's warm and reassuring.

"So what do you think of my messy painting?"

"Something from your subconscious, perhaps."

"A pretty ugly subconscious."

"The mind is endlessly fascinating. It can keep painful things buried for years, and then—"

"Explode?"

"Yes."

"Am I going crazy?"

"I doubt it."

"Good. Then I can have my clothes back?"

"I don't think you want them, Rose. They're a mess. But we're in luck. This is—was—my sister's place and she very conveniently got married and moved to San Diego. She left a lot of her clothes here. I'm supposed to give everything to the Salvation Army as soon as I get settled."

"You just moved here?"

He nodded. "I was in the Pacific. That's how I got this." He pointed to his leg. "After they released me, I went up to Boston to finish my residency."

The bedroom is small and filled with more of the heavy dark furniture, leaving little floor space. A double bed, a bureau, a dressing table with a huge mirror. Stacked on the bureau are the familiar framed degrees similar to those Papa has in his office. The curtained windows face out on a garden. A door leads to a small bathroom, where she finds her soiled clothes soaking in the tub.

From the walk-in closet she borrows a long black wool skirt. The bureau drawer yields sweaters. She picks out a red one. In another drawer, underwear and socks. All devised for a larger woman, but she'll make do till she gets home. She dresses, absorbed in the strange thing that's happened to her, trying to remember what she felt just before—

But it will never happen again. She'll be vigilant.

"I'd like to help you," Ben says, when she comes out of the bedroom. He's looking at her the way a man looks at a girl he likes. He loans her a navy pea jacket.

"Thank you," she says. "I mean for the clothes and everything. I'm fine now. It was just a weird thing. If you have a bag, I'll take my clothes—"

"I'll deliver them when they're clean. Where do you live?"

She flushes. Feels awkward and unsophisticated. This won't do at all. She's an artist. She lives in Greenwich Village. "Can't I just take them and get out of your life?"

"I'd like to see you again." He gives her his card, which she puts into the pocket of the pea coat without reading.

"As a patient, or . . . ?" She bends to pat the dancing dog and almost misses his response.

"Or," he says. He offers her his hand. "A friend."

She stifles a tremendous urge to laugh. Why is it taking so long for her to get out of here? She doesn't accept his hand. Instead, she unpins her drawing from the easel and writes her address and phone number on the back of it. Handing it to him, she says, "My card."

35

Pinto

A loft on Sullivan Street. Smoke; a curtain halfway to the ceiling, hides the struts and pipes Rose knows are there. Drinks come in jelly glasses, cracked and chipped. Some, soiled with dregs, sit waiting to be claimed. The floor, slick with crushed potato chips, sticky underfoot, is stained with turpentine, oils, solvents, and booze.

On a plank laid over two stacks of newsprint, Johnny Walker and Jack Daniels, gin without a name, their caps cast aside for good, sit easy with Wild Turkey. Why not?

People crowd around the drinks and don't give way, so Rose glides past. The voices mingle and rise, fiery with drink.

A guitar throbs low, aching, and deep inside her, an answer throb for throb. She presses her thighs together and leans against a column to catch her breath. The hands of the musician are large and tender. They move over the instrument as if they are attached to the guitar rather than the young woman who is playing. She strums with closed eyes, her dark hair flowing over her shoulders. Her voice is the throb. She sings, "Kisses sweeter than wine . . ." hopscotching the lyrics, returning always to the kisses.

Rose loses Crystal somewhere near the drinks. Someone offers her a cigarette, lights it for her, and moves on when she doesn't connect. The inhale burns her throat; her eyes smart. Slowly, she begins to recognize the men she has come to see: her idols, the Abstract Expressionists. Pollock, thinner than she imagined, hardly moving his lips when he speaks. Smoking and drinking. Intense. Combative. Surrounded by attractive young women. Krasner hovers, beauty nestling in her ugliness.

Rothko, massive, hulking, glaring at the lean and angular Kline who sits on the floor arguing the politics of art with the smooth and sure Motherwell, still looking more Ivy League than New York School. Newman. De Kooning. Joan Mitchell leaning to Elaine De Kooning to hear what she's saying. They are all here.

Rose stands on the edges of the various circles, humble. Someone hands her a jelly glass and pours, moves on elsewhere, pours, till everyone is drinking. She lifts the glass to her lips. Gin. De Kooning and Gottlieb argue philosophy, and Reinhardt keeps interrupting while they roundly curse him for inserting his opinion. Her tongue swims in gin. She swallows. On the perimeter, she feels detached, invisible.

The room begins to slip sideways; faces enlarge in distorted perspective. Mouths move, smoke, drink. Everywhere now she sees canvases, leaning against the walls, covered with cloths. Her cheekbones tingle, burn.

Fingers creep under her hair, caress the nape of her neck.

"I've been watching you," he says. "You are so beautiful. Your hair . . ." He wraps her hair around his hand and turns her so she faces him. "Let's go," he whispers. "It's not far." His hand rests low on her back. He gives her a firm push. She does not resist, for she sees with awe it is Skye Pinto, the finest of them all. He is not as tall as she's imagined. Up close he looks slightly foreign with his pale blue eyes, long slender nose, high cheekbones, sharp chin. His hair, red peach fuzz along his crown, hangs shaggy to his shoulders. But he is the siren and he is singing to her.

His hand scorches her skin. He is propelling her forward, past people, out the door. "So pure, Madonna," he whispers. Up a flight of stairs, then another. He stops, opens a door, draws her inside. He shoulders the light switch. Takes her empty glass from her and sets it on a wooden, paint-scarred table among the coffee cans, color dripping down their sides, jars of murky solvent, brushes, tubes of paint in various stages of use.

He wears jeans rolled up at the ankle, and suspenders over a short-sleeved white undershirt. Veins strain at the muscles in his arms. Fine lines are spokes around his eyes, deeper on his forehead, guard his mouth; he is unshaven, his stubble a contest between white and red. White wins.

A white studio, north windows, canvases on stretchers. Her eyes touch the worn palette, his palette. The sultry turpentine. Linseed oil. Everything waits on him. As she does.

This is his studio, not the other.

She watches him rummage through his atelier; "Aha," he says, finding paper and "aha" again, charcoal. Her knees tremble; she feels faint. He opens a bottle of Canadian Club and takes a long drink, watching her. Where should she put her shaking hands? She hides them behind her.

Setting the bottle on the floor, he comes for her. She closes her eyes, ready. Opens them. He sets down a high stool in front of her, takes her waist in his hands, thumbs playing her ribs. She is on the stool, then, her black ballerinas floating off the floor. His hands sting her breasts. Her body moans for him.

He stops abruptly, drops his hands to his sides. "Who are you?"

He stares into her eyes, seems to see her for the first time. Before, she was just any girl.

"Rose," she says. "Rose Ebanholz. I'm an art student at Cooper—I admire your work—" She thinks, how stupid you are, Rose. The moment skitters away.

"Of course," he says. He finds a pack of cigarettes crumpled in his shirt pocket and lights two, like Paul Henried for Bette Davis, hands one to her. Stops to take another long pull of his bottle. Then offers it. Rye whisky and Camels.

She shakes her head, holds the cigarette but doesn't want to smoke. Her wide black skirt is gray with ash. She leans over to brush a clump away, uncomfortable under his scrutiny.

He sets the bottle on the floor. The cigarette sits in the corner of his mouth. He runs his hands over her arms, shoulder to elbow, elbow to wrist, holds her hands flat in his. "I could break you bone by bone."

She gets off the stool and puts the cigarette out in a Cinzano ashtray. Cold. She is very cold and in the wrong place. His eyes tear the flesh from her body.

36

Zweikel

It is dark when Zweikel comes home. The streets are already filled with the night people, drunks and bums every one of them. Maybe except one. Though he has very little—he never thinks about money anymore—he empties his pockets as he always does for the cadaverous old man with the yarmulke and the numbers tattooed on his bony arm. The man begs only from Zweikel, it seems, waiting for him every day in front of Zweikel's building as if he knows something that Zweikel doesn't. Is the beggar someone Zweikel took money for and didn't bring over? Is he responsible for the numbers tattooed to the beggar's arm?

Dina sits in the kitchen separating the coins, putting them into their individual rolls, crying. She knows the signs. He has his mania back. That's what the doctors call it. When it comes back, he walks away from everything. Just like that. He has a bad heart and never takes his medicine. He's like a baby. One day, she's sure, he'll walk away and never come back.

He's out of breath when he opens the door, giddy with excitement. "Dina, I found her. Dina, do you hear?" He gasps and claws the air. Dina catches him as he falls. He's nothing but a bag of bones, whatever she does.

When Zweikel wakes, it is still dark outside; he knows

something wonderful has happened, but it takes him a little time to remember. He's very tired and it hurts him to breathe.

He hears Dina in the kitchen making coffee. He gets out of bed and pulls on his pants, which are hanging over the back of the chair. His slippers are next to the bed. When he sticks his feet into them, he remembers. He rushes to the kitchen and tells Dina, "It's Irene. I found her."

Dina pours him a glass of prune juice and puts toast into the toaster. She's heard this before. She's only glad he's on his feet again. He's been in a stupor for a week.

Moving the juice away from him, Zweikel takes a crumpled photograph from his pocket, lays it on the table next to the juice. He tries to flatten it. "Dina, it was Irene. I saw her. This time I'm sure."

Dina looks at the photograph. There's nothing left of the child in the picture except the barest outline. You can't even tell it's a child. But Zweikel, in his mania, sees her whole and complete. Dina knows the whole story backwards and forwards. She's the child that Nathan Ebanholz stole from Zweikel all those years ago.

He should stay home today and rest, Dina thinks, but she's afraid he won't. He'll be out wandering the streets again looking for a phantom. Harvey from the candy store's older boy has been sitting for them at the newsstand all week.

She says, "Get dressed. We have to go to work."

"But after work, you'll go with me to see her?"

Dina sighs. "Go where?"

"MacDougal Street. Not so far. We can wait outside for her."

Her patience dissolves. "Mendy, there is nobody, no Irene, don't you know that? Stella is long dead, may she rest in peace, and who knows if there even was a girl? And if there was, what would she be to you?"

"Mine," he says. "She would be mine." He pays no attention to Dina. She always argues the same thing, and lately he'd begun to think maybe she was right—until yesterday, when Irene came to him and wished him good morning. "I tried to help her, Dina," he says. "She didn't feel so good, but there was a doctor there who took care of her."

"What are you talking about?"

"She got sick in the park." He pulls on his shirt and goes to look for his shoes and socks.

"So what do you know about her?" Dina says, following him into the bedroom.

"I know where she lives and what she looks like now."

"Does she look like Stella?"

This stops him. He laces up his shoes. He has to think about it carefully. "The hair," he says. "The hair looks like Stella."

"Mendy, anyone can have blond hair. That doesn't make her Irene." He exasperates Dina when he's like this.

Still, she lets him drag her over to MacDougal Street after they close the stand for the evening. She'd rather go home and soak her swollen feet.

"You'll see," he keeps saying, "you'll see."

The narrow street is crowded with people, mostly young, artists and writers, many from the colleges, NYU and Cooper Union, that draw people to Greenwich Village. All the shops and restaurants are busy. Because they are young they play all night. Because her mama had always been sick, Dina can never remember playing at all. She thinks about that now as Zweikel stops across from a brownstone building.

"That's where she lives," he says. "She's an artist." He speaks with such pride that Dina stares hard at him. This is different.

They sit around a table, all of them, talking and smoking. Drinking. They talk about ideas and the unconscious, the psychic expression on canvas. No one is like the other. Pollock and Krasner. Rothko, sullen, speaks only to Elaine De Kooning, not the others. Why does he bother? He finally leaves.

"He hates the Cedar," Elaine says.

"Thinks he's better than we are," Pollock says. "Thinks he's the only genius."

"But we are all geniuses." Elaine smiles. "Some more than others." She looks at Bill De Kooning, who swells under her gaze.

Rose doesn't speak, she never speaks, yet they've accepted her as Skye's invention as they've accepted others before her. But she is not like the others; she is younger. Unworldly. She may be a good painter, for all they know. It's only a matter of time before he destroys her.

"We should warn her," Elaine says to Joan Mitchell when Pinto first brings Rose around.

"Would she listen?" Joan says. "Would you?"

"You have talent," Pinto says. "You need me."

They wait what seems like a long time and Dina nods off, leaning against a boarded-up storefront. Zweikel's harsh whisper, "There she is," brings her back.

Dina peers across the street. A girl has come out of the building, a girl whose face is framed with curly white-blond hair. "That's not Stella's girl," Dina says. "She's too small."

"She takes after me," Zweikel says scornfully. He starts after the girl, and Dina follows, plucking at his coat, trying to make him stop.

Dina can hear the singing from where they are, the guitars and the banjos. She follows Zweikel following the girl into the park. The music gets louder. The girl joins a group sitting on the benches and in the grass. Someone hands her a beer and she tilts her head back and drinks from the bottle. They all seem to know each other.

"Be careful," Zweikel mutters under his breath.

Dina looks at him. He isn't talking to her. He's talking to the girl, because one of the men—the one wearing the cap—has picked her up, and she's laughing with her arm around his neck, and he's running down the street with her. The girl takes the man's cap and puts it on her own head, covering the pale hair. Everyone is laughing and shouting, running after them.

Zweikel begins gasping. Dina puts a restraining hand on his shoulder, but he shakes her off and follows them to University Place. The boisterous group barrels into the Cedar Street Tavern and the street is quiet except for Zweikel's tortured breathing.

— 37 —

Rose

"So are you going to come or not?" Crystal stands, hands on hips, in Rose's doorway. Ernesto raises his tail elegantly and rubs himself against her long black skirt, leaving a trail of fur needles.

"Yes. Just let me finish this." Rose hazes the middle distance to bring the figures forward, views her work with just a tiny flicker of satisfaction, then sets the brushes in turpentine and wipes her hands on a towel.

"If you don't hurry, we'll miss him," Crystal says. "Put some lipstick on." She is talking over her shoulder, already halfway down the hall.

Rose laughs. Crystal is mad about Dylan Thomas and when he is in New York, he hangs out at the White Horse Tavern at Hudson and Eleventh Street and drinks whisky and talks a blue streak until he passes out and someone takes him home to the Chelsea Hotel.

"Okay," Rose says, "okay. Go ahead. I'll catch up." She wears dungarees and one of Papa's old shirts, both speckled with paint. She doesn't bother changing. If Auntie Anna saw her going out like this, she would have a stroke. But this is Greenwich Village not Clayton Lake.

She wraps a scarf around her hair and runs out onto the street. It had been raining earlier that evening, a drizzle that barely glanced her skylight, and now the headlights of passing cars dazzle in soft oily puddles. The

Village is a carnival of lights.

Crystal, herself, is incandescent. Rose wishes she could be like Crystal, so free and open, so of the Village. Well, she will watch, absorb, and when she's ready, the soul of the Village will open for her, too.

Only one short block away, she catches up to Crystal who has stopped to talk to someone, a man. He has his arm around her. She waves to Rose, and the man turns, drops his arm. It is Skye Pinto.

Rose swallows, tries to fight the shortness of breath, the choking sensation.

"Well, look who's here." He pushes back the cap and grins at her like a bad boy. He is standing between her and Crystal like a wall. His paint-spattered Levi's hang so low and taut on his hips it is obvious there's nothing between jeans and skin.

He wears a torn, half-buttoned flannel shirt as if he is naked. His essence is oils and turpentine, and a musky male odor.

Rose tilts toward him. The ache is deep and moist. An inexplicable ecstasy envelopes her.

"We're going to the White Horse," Crystal says, clever eyes going from Rose to Pinto and back to Rose. "Meeting someone. Come on, Rose, we'll be late." She grabs Rose's hand and pulls.

"Rosie Posie Pudding and Pie," Pinto sings in his halting sibilance. "Kissed the boys and made them cry." He laughs and steps back, making a sweeping motion with his hands. He makes no pretense of following. Rose falters.

In Pinto's sibilance, Crystal hears the thin overlay of another language. "He's got a thing for you," she tells Rose, clutching Rose's icy hand.

Rose looks back at Pinto, who waits, arms folded. "I'll

see you later," she tells Crystal.

"Be careful."

San Remo drinking beer. Their shabby group includes Rose and Larry, her friend from high school, Crystal, someone named Cassady. Ginsberg is here, a hairy bear with an incredible sweetness about him, and others whose names Rose doesn't even try to remember. It's late and she's tired, and she is smoking to keep awake. They talk writing, all of them, and she nods off on Larry's arm.

"Let me take you home," he says.

"No, stay here. You're having a good time. It's not that far, and it's beautiful tonight." She slips away before he can insist.

On her steps, someone sits smoking, the dot ember of the cigarette like a solitary firefly in the darkness. The street light is out. Not an unusual occurrence.

"I've been waiting for you." He doesn't get up. Inhales, exhales. He holds out his hand to her, and she sits beside him. He fingers her hair almost as if he's afraid. "Why don't you say something?"

She shakes her head, unable to take her eyes from his. They flame in the dark like the ember.

"Come along then," he says.

She goes with him, no will of her own, drawn by his magic, the voodoo of turpentine. Her hand tight in his, he begins to run.

Candles burn in ashtrays and jars. The street lamps blear through huge windows. And everywhere the paintings that thrill her. He turns up the lights.

"They are wonderful," she says, "wonderful." She's never seen so many Pintos all at once.

"Ah, she can speak," he says. "And so well."

She looks at him. He's making fun of her, of her awkwardness and inexperience. Does he want to sleep with her? If so, what will she do? She moves on to the painting on the easel, and before she can stop herself, cries out. The paint is troweled on with a violence that shakes her, and everywhere among the fierce spatterings are sections of her face cut up, tiny green eyes outlined in black. Pinto and not Pinto.

"What do you think?" he says.

She is mute, hand over mouth.

He laughs and picks a bottle from the floor and takes a swig. Offers it to her. Still stunned by the painting, she shakes her head. "She doesn't like it." He taunts her in a sing-song voice. "She doesn't like it." Laughing, he grabs her, begins to shake her, harder, harder. Her teeth slam together, her head flaps.

"Please." She doesn't struggle, can't struggle. Out of time, she's in a separate place.

He lets go, and she staggers, unbalanced, to her knees, palms to paint-streaked floor, up again.

"Who sent you?" he shouts. The bottle smashes against a window; glass shatters glass.

Awareness comes slowly. No one knows where she is, that she is alone with him. The door is a brilliant blue. *Gone to Blue.* Never coming back. She ignites, throwing herself forward.

The blow staggers her. His hands twist her hair, force her head back, loosening her grip on the knob. "Please."

He stares into her eyes, lets go, almost shoving her away from him. Her hands fly out to stop her fall.

He catches her throat, squeezing. Tears spill slowly at first. "Please."

Fire roars from his mouth. "Who are you?"

Her sobs come from someone else. Her hands tear at his shirt, dig into his flesh.

He screams obscenities at her, but his hands leave her throat. He lifts her to her feet and props her up against the wall. She fights him, tries to wriggle away. His fist finds her cheek. Displaced, head thundering, pain sears her. The floor is no solace. She draws her knees up under her chin and hides her face in her arms.

He bends over her, peels her arms from her face. "Open your eyes! Open those goddam eyes!" His voice comes through as an echo. Her eyes burn, won't open all the way, and the side of her face is numb. He twists her hair in his hands, forcing her. "Look at me!" She tries, but he's a blur. "Who are you?" he screams again, and the blows come. "Who are you? Who are you?"

She floats over them. Why does he keep asking her? She's told him who she . . . she's . . .

"Who are you?" His voice pierces her eardrums. "Who?" Like a wolf, all teeth, foaming at the mouth.

She is slipping away, losing herself. She's . . .

"Who are you?" His shriek is a wail. Her wail.

She hears the blows from way off, thunk, thunk, thunk.

"Who are you?"

Tell him who you are, Jenny.

— 38 —

Crystal

Crystal leaves the San Remo and runs into a raucous group of artists, Pinto among them, moving like a scourge through the Village. Pinto is ranting. They are all drunk, heading for the relative quiet of the Cedar Tavern on University, where a journalist for *Life* has offered food and wine in exchange for pictures and a story.

She has a fleeting, guilty thought of Rose, but banishes it. Rose is timid, socially backward. She's not good at repartee and doesn't know how to flirt. Crystal is always fixing her up, but the boys complain she doesn't talk. Rose has probably been home for hours. It's very late. Or very early.

Pinto unzips and pees a geyser into a tub of morning glories on the steps of a brownstone.

"Pipe down out there," someone yells.

The group roars and moves on.

No, she won't worry about Rose. Pinto's playing with her. Cat and mouse. He'll tire of the game, if he hasn't already.

The night is cool, and Crystal shivers in her thin dress. Pinto drapes his arm around her shoulders, nips from a pocket flask, his arm across her throat. She's had too much to drink and nothing to eat. He walks her along as if she is his property and has no mind of her own.

Skye Pinto makes Crystal wary. He's an ugly drunk. She saw him slash one of his own paintings at a gallery show. Three years ago the woman he lived with, another artist, threw herself out of the sixth-floor window of their loft. It was ruled a suicide but almost everyone thinks Pinto pushed her, or at the least, drove her to it.

Right now he begins to shout at Motherwell. "God damn pinko!" Curses violate the otherwise quiet street. With each shout Pinto tightens Crystal's throat in the crook of his arm. She is being dragged along and she's angry, clawing at iron sinews.

Motherwell answers Pinto in kind and Pollock turns on him as well, both heaping abuse on some betrayal of Pinto, something Pinto has been awarded. A grant, or a fellowship. Fists begin flying and in the ensuing melee, Crystal escapes.

She stands still, breathing hard, and watches the contingent straggle off, arms flailing, a comic strip of snarls and growls exploding into the night. For once she has had enough, and it comes to her that she much prefers the company of writers.

On the corner near her apartment, a group of college kids are all crouching down around something on the sidewalk. Playing craps? Unlikely. But that's what it looks like. Closer, she hears a girl with long blond hair say, "Do you think we should get a cop?"

"Maybe a doctor?"

Crystal skirts the group. A child cries. Has someone found a baby? Only last week there was a story in the paper about a baby abandoned at Grace Church. If it happened to her, she would go to Cuba and have an abortion. Imagine going through an entire pregnancy, hiding it, and then leaving the baby on the church steps.

Stopping, Crystal peers over their shoulders to get a look at the baby, but what she sees is small, pale haired, and female curled on the curb, rocking and whimpering, bloodied. Help is being offered, hands out, but there is no response.

My God. "Move away, move away. I know her." They clear a space and Crystal drops down beside Rose. "Rose, Rose? What happened?" She says again to no one in particular, "I know her." She puts her arms around Rose and feels the flinch. "What happened?" she asks the others.

"We don't know," the blond says. "This is how we found her."

"Is she a friend of yours?" a boy asks. He's wearing a black sweater with a large red "R" sewn to the front. "Do you want us to get the police? Or—"

"I don't think—" Crystal holds Rose's battered face gently in her hands. The street is dimly lit. Rose moans. "Rosie, what happened? Who did this to you?"

"Why do you call her Rosie? She keeps saying she's Jenny."

"Jenny? No. You must have heard wrong. Her name is Rose."

"Jenny," Rosie murmurs.

"Rosie, can you stand? Don't worry, I'll get you home. You'll be okay." Crystal looks around at the college kids. "Can you help me get her on her feet? I think she's just had too much to drink." But Crystal has seen the bruises, the blood, the torn dress.

Crystal says, "I didn't know what to do. I didn't want to call her family—they're in New Jersey. She keeps saying she's Jenny. I found your card on her easel."

Ben Coopersmith stands at the top of the stairs, his hand on the wall, waiting for the pain in his leg to subside. He carries a black bag. "Let me see her."

"It's pretty bad, Dr. Coopersmith." Crystal is frightened.

She doesn't notice her own tears.

He steps into a studio. The space is almost a triangle. A large skylight slashes the high ceiling as it slopes down the side of the triangle. A stepladder stands open under a ceiling light fixture.

In the brick hearth a weak fire barely takes the chill out of the air. Photographs and drawings are tacked to every bit of wall surface.

A mostly Siamese cat rubs up against his trousers. He is Ernesto, Crystal's cat named for Ernest Hemingway, who wanders from apartment to apartment in the building, a restless spirit.

Rose's painting materials are on the other side of the room, a distance from the fireplace. A closet without a door holds a tiny kitchen. Ben follows Crystal into a small bedroom, spare as a monk's cell.

On the chest of drawers are framed photographs. The man in uniform must be her father, the couple, her aunt and uncle. A photo of a young Rosie, her hair in pigtails, sitting on the back steps of a white clapboard house. And there's a faded old photograph of a mother and baby daughter. And among these, the small clipping photo of Skye Pinto in front of *Gone to Blue 2*.

Rose lies fetal on the narrow bed. Ben turns down the blanket. Her clothes are torn. The purple swelling on her face has doubled its size, her eyes swollen shut. She moans in a child's voice, rocking her head from side to side. "Jenny hurt, Jenny hurt."

She is cold, then hot, then cold again. She's in a closet with four beds attached to the walls. A boy says, "They're going to cut you. I heard them."

"No," she cries. "No. No. No."

208

*But they take her away and she wakes with bandages
on her neck.*

*She hears the echoes of their laughter over and over,
like the waves on Orchard Beach, and she covers her ears.
But the claw scratches at the window trying to get in,
trying to get her because she was a bad girl and let Olga
pick her up and her panties showed and Olga died.*

She is sweating and cold to his touch. She's gone into
shock, he thinks. He paws through his case, finds the syringe,
fills it from the vial of adrenalin. He wipes an unbruised spot
on her arm with alcohol and gives her an injection.

"I want to get her cleaned up," he says. "See if she has
any broken bones. Can you boil some water for me? And
bring me a large bowl."

"She must have fallen, don't you think?" Crystal says.
When he doesn't answer, she does what he asked.

Crystal returns with a kettle of steaming water and a
bowl, finds Ben Coopersmith examining Rose, listening to
her heart.

"She doesn't appear to have any broken bones," he says.
He begins cleaning Rose's cuts and bruises with pieces of
cotton soaked in hot water. As he finishes, he paints them
with iodine. Although Rose has stopped moaning, he knows
she is conscious.

Crystal watches him work. "Will she be all right?"

"I think so."

"Why does she keep saying she's Jenny?"

"I don't know. A middle name? A nickname?"

"No. She told me she doesn't have a middle name. How
did she have your card? I didn't even know she had a doctor
in New York. Her father's a doctor." Crystal is so nervous
she's blathering.

Ben shakes his head. He wets a cotton pad with hot water and cleanses Rosie's face. "Rose," he says. "Who did this to you?"

Rose's sob is sudden; she hides her face in her pillow. "No more, Papa. Papa, please, no more."

— 39 —

Ben

He hadn't meant to get involved. Emotionally involved. He isn't ready. His patients are something else entirely. His mind is clear on his work. He's a disciple of the master, and even the master had let his guard slip—albeit with his sister-in-law.

He's drawn to Rose's fragility. It is his job to understand himself first, and he does. Man has primal instincts. They appear when you least expect them.

Rose's tests after her spell in Gramercy Park had come back negative. Except for mild anemia, nothing unusual in the blood, no evidence of tumor. He can't rule out schizophrenia, yet instinct tells him no. And perhaps, his feelings for her won't let him admit the signs are there.

The internal dialectic begins at once, and Ben debates it for days. Is it ethical? Technically, she isn't one of his patients, but then again, she is. And he is already incapable of keeping himself aloof. He recognizes the signs, and he's afraid for her. But what if it's something else? Repressed childhood memory returning? Yet she owns to no childhood trauma, remembers no illness other than the normal, chicken pox and measles. And she speaks of her aunt, uncle, her father with unqualified love. So what is it? In the episode he witnessed she'd regressed, talked like a young child. Something buried deep, wanting to surface.

Then this. Someone—she's refused to say who—beat her

badly. When Ben saw her like that, he'd wanted to kill the man who'd done it. *Papa* she'd called him. Yet her father is at home, not in New York.

Ben had tried to get her to talk to him about the event in Gramercy Park and what she remembered when she woke in his apartment, but she shut him out, walked away from him, wouldn't respond to his calls until he promised he'd drop it.

At a loss, he tries to deal with his fear for her.

He's still debating with himself as he picks up the phone and asks information for the number in Clayton Lake, New Jersey, of a Dr. Nathan Ebanholz, then dials the number.

A woman answers, "Dr. Ebanholz's office."

"This is Dr. Ben Coopersmith," Ben says. "May I speak with Dr. Ebanholz?"

"He is out seeing patients. I can have him call you back." The woman is friendly, but professional.

Is this Auntie Anna, he wonders? "I am calling about his daughter."

He hears the sharp intake of breath and the professionalism disappears. "Is something wrong with our Rosie? You are speaking to Anna Blackwell, Rosie's aunt."

"She's all right now. The tests were all negative, but I'm concerned about her. She had a fainting spell and afterward was unusually disoriented, with memory loss."

"Dear God," Anna says. Dear God, she thinks, and she's afraid. Like last time. Like the time with the mirror.

"I'm a psychiatrist. I happened to be present when the episode occurred, and I was able to help her. She didn't want me to tell you."

Anna calms herself. "She's had them before. One." After a moment's hesitation, she continues, "She may not have told you about the fire."

"The fire?"

"She almost died in a fire in Poland before the war, before she came here. Her mother died. Her father, her uncle, and I brought her up."

There it is. The early childhood trauma. It explains everything, he thinks. He hangs up with the promise that he will keep them informed. He says nothing of the beating.

Anna's tears wait until she replaces the receiver. How did they lose their way? For they have. She is consumed by the torment that she's been able to keep down deep in the recesses of her being. Now it gnaws at her very core.

They'd been such a strong family. Rosie, their joy. Then David had died, and sorrow, instead of drawing them together, had left them each isolated from the other. She'd abandoned both Rosie and Nathan in her grief.

Mistakes. Missteps. Sooner or later, there is payment due.

She goes into the kitchen and puts on the kettle. They took the wrong path, she and Nathan, like Robert Frost's poem about the two paths in the wood that diverge. They stole a child, telling themselves it was for the child's benefit. But how much was for the child and how much was for them?

Yet how could she have left that motherless baby with Topinski? He was a monster. She'd done what was right. She'd done what was wrong.

They've come too far to turn back, and David, who had loved them all so much, who had cared for Rosie as his own child, is no longer here to guide their spirits.

She'll talk with Nathan about Dr. Coopersmith. He can treat Rosie's mind, but she and Nathan must heal her soul, even if it means . . . it terrifies her to consider it . . . even if it means telling the truth.

Rose

Her fingers end in bloody pulp. It is easier to hold a paint brush than a pen, but her wounds burn and puff up from the chemicals. She uses the pen, for there is something odd in the way she sees color.

Miss Malone looks over Rosie's shoulder. "Of course, in reality, there's no such animal as a green horse."

"I know that." Irritated, Rosie gives her horse a proud, abundant tail. Does Miss Malone think she's stupid?

"Then why are you painting a green horse?"

"It's not green, it's brown." Rosie admires her horse. He's a beautiful brown. What is Miss Malone talking about?

Rosie takes her picture of the beautiful brown horse home and shows it to Auntie Anna, who is sterilizing Uncle David's instruments.

Auntie Anna says, "That's beautiful, Rosie." Auntie Anna never fails her.

She gives Auntie Anna a test. "What color is my horse?"

"Don't you know, darling?" Anna stops what she is doing and looks at Rosie.

"It's brown, isn't it, Auntie Anna?" Rosie talks so fast that her tongue runs over her words. "That's what I said

it was and Miss Malone said it was green . . . and horses aren't green. Why would I draw a green horse?"

Uncle David comes home and shows Rosie a book of pictures all made with colored dots. One page after another. He asks her to look carefully at the dots and tell him what she sees.

Sometimes forms materialize, like a rabbit. She sees his ears. Other times, she sees nothing. Just colored dots.

"Color blind," Uncle David says, closing the book.

Rosie is stunned. "But blind means you can't see. I see colors."

"But you don't see what we see, Rosie." Uncle David smiles. "Which makes you very special. The Army Air Corps uses color blind people to see through camouflage. Spotters see camouflage others don't. The conclusion is that something is hidden. You are special because you don't have an ordinary eye."

She thinks about that and decides she likes not having an ordinary eye.

"Is Nathan color blind?" Uncle David asks. He looks very tired and the lines around his mouth are deep grooves. "Is there any more coffee?"

"About Nathan, I don't know," Auntie Anna says. She fills Uncle David's cup half-way and sets the empty percolator in the sink.

"How will I know what colors to use?" The thought strikes panic. Rosie sees a whole world of horses mistakenly painted green. They will laugh at her. She hears them laughing now and claps her hands over her ears, but it does no good.

Auntie Anna has a solution. "Labels," she says. "Everything in a tube already has a label. And we will make labels for the paint box." She smiles at Rosie. "Don't worry."

"But people will see them and find out."

"Then we must look for a way to do it so they see but don't notice."

"Like camouflage," Uncle David says.

Like camouflage, Rosie thinks.

Her oil painting teacher at Cooper Union is Archibald Bradleigh, who is known for his land and seascapes of the Massachusetts coast. His paintings have a distinctive character and are much imitated by lesser artists. As a young man he painted murals for the city through the WPA Federal Arts Project.

He calls Rosie his jewel, for her color sense is exquisite, he says, and he takes her to a city event that honors the Arts Project murals and those who created them. After the reception, they go to the Cedar Tavern for martinis.

Arch Bradleigh is a Victorian dandy. He smokes brown Schimmelpfennig cigarettes in a Dunhill holder and wears a velvet jacket and a red paisley cravat with a moonstone stickpin. His voice drones on and on and she nods and eats the olive from her martini. She chews slowly, leeching out the gin.

Eyes rake her back and she's compelled to turn. Skye Pinto stares at her from where he sits with Barnett Newman and Ad Reinhardt, two painters of the New York School she knows by sight and the quality of their work.

As Arch Bradleigh talks about the horrors of the artistic temperament squeezed into a confining marriage, Rosie shrinks in her chair. She wants nothing more than to run, but her feet have sprung roots into the sloping wood floor.

"Arch." Pinto's slap on Bradleigh's back is more punch than slap. "Long time no see." He is drunk, his words slurred. His hand holding the cigarette hovers close to

Rosie's hair, so close she feels the heat.

Arch's nostrils flare; the hairs on Rosie's nape shiver.

"Pinto." Arch's voice is delicate with the hostility of a gentleman.

"Aren't you going to introduce me to your little friend?"

"Rose Ebanholz. Skye Pinto."

Skye laughs, a boisterous, triumphant laugh. He drops the cigarette and grinds it into the wood floor. "We've met, haven't we, Rose of my dreams?" His hand burrows under her hair, then travels slowly down her spine.

The small amount of gin that Rosie swallowed chugs back up her esophagus, strangling her. Her eyes plead with Arch. He stands. He does nothing. She is sweating. She breaks away from the proprietary hand, runs into the street, mad, and throws up in the gutter.

When she hears Arch call, "Rose," she straightens and runs, fear flaying her hair. The pavement moves under her feet like a flat escalator, urging her on.

In Washington Square Park she searches for a private bench, void of lovers or squatters, and finds one near the fountain. Her knees are no longer trustworthy. She's a marionette on a madman's strings.

Leaning over the back of the bench, she has nothing left but dry heaves. She holds tightly to the bench to keep from falling. When the trembling eases, she dries her eyes and wipes her mouth with a tissue from her pocket.

"Are you all right, Miss?"

A policeman stands over her. He is big and blue, with a nightstick protruding from beneath his coat.

She looks up at him shivering, and he steps back, a surprised look on his face, as if she's said or done something shocking. Her teeth chatter so loud she thinks he must hear the clicking. She wilts in his gaze.

"Miss, do you need help getting home?" the policeman asks. "Where do you live?"

He is squatting so he can see her face, and he is staring. Staring at her the way . . .

"Where do you live?" he asks again.

If you get lost, Mama says, be sure to tell a policeman your name and where you live. That's why it's very important to learn your address.

She wipes her tears with her fists and whispers to the nice policeman, "My name is Jenny. I live on Barker Avenue. Can you take me home now?"

— 41 —

Rose

The cop, Eddie Dolan, looks around for a cab. Barker Avenue is in the Bronx. These kids come down to the Village at night looking for thrills. The innocent ones always get messed up.

"Rose!"

A crazy man is running toward them, waving his arms. He is carrying a small leather purse. His silk scarf flies behind him.

"Rose!" He stops in front of them. "What's the matter, officer?" His face glistens with sweat. "Rose? Are you all right?"

"Rose?" the cop says. "Miss? Didn't you say your name was Jenny?"

"Jenny?" The crazy man is starting to catch his breath. "You've got it wrong, officer."

Dolan thinks the man is a queer. He looks weird even for the Village, with white hair down to his shoulders and carrying a purse. "Oh, yeah?" Dolan says.

"See here, officer. My name is Archibald Bradleigh. I teach at Cooper Union. This is my student, Rose Ebanholz. We were having a drink and she got upset about something." Arch thrusts the purse at her. "You left your purse—"

"Do you have any identification with you, Miss?"

She offers him the purse. He unsnaps it and they all look

inside. There is a red wallet, a key chain with keys, a hand-kerchief, a lipstick, and a comb. In the wallet is a library card made out to Rose Ebanholz at an address on MacDougal Street.

Dolan thinks, Christ, another crazy. "Didn't you tell me you live on Barker Avenue?" He hands the purse back to her.

"Barker Avenue?" Rosie is confused. "No. I live on MacDougal Street. Where is Barker Avenue?"

"In the Bronx."

"I've never been to the Bronx." She is so tired she can hardly keep her eyes open. Her head droops.

"I'll see her home, officer. Thank you." Arch has his hand on her elbow.

"Thank you," Rosie tells Dolan, though he's beginning to blur in front of her eyes.

She smiles at him and once more Dolan gets this weird feeling he's seen her before. Well, what the hell, his beat is the Village and she lives here and goes to college here. So maybe he's caught a glimpse of her before.

But he's not so sure. He watches them go off through the park, then follows. The Village beat is anything but boring.

Costello's is crowded, smoke-filled and dark as a cave, as it always is, especially at the end of a shift. Dolan and Riccardi edge their way through to the bar, greeting and being greeted. There's corned beef and cabbage on the steam tray and rye bread and hard boileds on the counter. Beer and butts. And cop talk. About the drunk and disorderly, the hold-up of the Brink's wagon in Chelsea, two prosts who cut each other up over a foot of space on Second Avenue.

"Eddie?" Costello slaps the bottle down in front of Dolan. The foam rides up the long neck. Dolan finger-skims it off and takes an extended swig. He coats a hard boiled with a layer of salt and pops it in his mouth.

Riccardi and him have a routine. A couple of beers at Costello's, some schmoozing, then home. Because the women talk to each other. See, it doesn't always pay to introduce them and have them start comparing notes, but Dolan married Mary Salerno from the neighborhood and Mary was already friends with Frannie Riccardi from school, so there's nothing for it. He wiggles the empty bottle at Costello. Costello takes it and hands him a fresh one.

Dolan looks around. He lights his cigarette from his smoked-down butt.

"Hey, Eddie. How are you, kid?" Jack Kelly pounds him on the back. The old guy grins at him bleary-eyed, feeling no pain.

"Hey, Jack. What's up?"

"Put my papers in today. Drinks on me. Hear that, Costello?"

"The whole joint, Jack?" Costello smiles, wipes his hands on a towel, tucks the tip of the towel in the back of his pants where he used to keep his gun.

"Why not?"

Costello picks up a bullhorn and announces, "The next round's on Kelly. He put his papers in today."

A cheer goes up. Kelly grins again, raises his bottle.

Costello sets a shot glass down in front of Kelly and fills it with Schenley. Kelly chases the whisky with the beer. "Fill 'er up," he tells Costello.

"I can't see you sitting around, hoisting a few and tending your garden, Kelly," Eddie says.

"Well, I won't be. I got me a job as head of security at Macy's, at a hell of a lot more than I make around here."

"Not bad."

"Yeah, and decent hours. Hit me again, Costello. Yeah. Twenty-five years I gave the job. Trained a lot of kids. Partnered more detectives than you see in this room." He begins to rattle them off, squinting and grimacing. "Let's see, let's see. Rogers, he's a sergeant at the One Nine. Lawrence, he's in the Commissioner's office. Natale's in ballistics. Gottfried, he's a lu and so is Morrisey. I did all right, I did."

"You did all right, Jack," Eddie agrees. "But you forgot Dolan." Jack Kelly was one of his instructors at the Academy. Kelly knew the street and he was a good cop in his day.

Dolan is rewarded with a bleary grin. Kelly's on a roll. "Morrisey, yeah," Kelly says, continuing his monologue. "Now there's a good guy, wife died young and left him with a boy to raise, married that girl—what's her name, whose kid got stolen . . ." He downs the whisky in one swallow. "Yeah. He done all right for himself. His boy is at the Thirteen now."

Riccardi turns up. "You ready?"

"Yeah. Let's hit the road."

"Thanks for the drink, Kelly," Riccardi says. "And have a good retirement."

"You know my partner, Vinnie Riccardi, Jack?"

They shake hands.

"Jack's going to head up security at Macy's. Thanks for the drink, buddy."

"I'll be around. I'll be around." Kelly belches and smirks. "Yeah. Go on, go on." His eyes water; the corners of his mouth turn down.

"Hey, Kelly, boyo," someone shouts, and four cops push into the space at the bar that Dolan vacates.

It's Riccardi's car tonight. They settle in and get the Yankee game. They don't talk much. Smoke, listen to the game. But Dolan is distracted. Morrisey sticks in his brain. Something about Morrisey he should know. Then Tommy Hendricks hits one right out of the park, and he remembers.

Yeah. That's who she looked like—the girl in the park tonight. Morrisey's wife. She'd come to the Academy with their kid for some special award Morrisey was getting . . .

Brakes squeal and Dolan's body lurches forward. He's half asleep, so relaxed. His head stops just shy of the windshield. Riccardi leans on the steering wheel cursing. Some asshole drunk sideswiped them and sped on. He and Riccardi look at each other and nod. Riccardi gives chase.

— 42 —

Rose

When she changes her position, the woman's pendulous breasts swing free and slide down her chest to her distended belly. Her thighs are a thicket of small puckers that bag over the dimpled knees. Shapely calves slim to surprisingly delicate ankles and beautiful feet with long, straight toes.

Rosie's sliver of charcoal lingers too long on the ankles, and the woman changes her position again. Several sketchers groan. The model drapes the white sheet around her, reclines, pushes back the sheet, and gives the final minutes of "Drawing the Nude Model" class a prodigious rump view.

Shouting. Papa's come to take her home. She gets out of bed. It's very dark but the light through the small window in the door shows her the way. The shouting is louder when she passes through the door into a long, dim hallway. She presses her hot forehead against the cold metal.

He's yelling at Mama again. Another door, open just a crack.

"Papa," she whispers, pushing the door. She picks up Papa's cap and holds it to her face. The smell makes her dizzy.

The mean nurse is undressed, lying on her white dress. The man is not Papa, but he is yelling, yelling. The nurse laughs as her huge breasts swing free. She sticks her tongue out at Jenny. The man makes the bad nurse stop laughing.

Jenny can go home now.

Flipping the newsprint over the back of her sketch pad, Rosie starts a fresh page, sketches faster, finds the substance of the model in short, almost brazen lines. Suggest. Distill.

"Interesting," Miss Neal says, her breath like stale peppermint.

When Miss Neal moves on, Rosie signs her sketch, printing boldly across the page, obliterating the drawing. *Jenny.* Then, *Barker Avenue.*

She packs up her sketch pad and charcoal and leaves the room. Takes her coat from the rack, ties a scarf around her hair. Her legs are like soft noodles. She's forsaken food.

Someone else inhabits her skin. A stranger. Someone she doesn't recognize. Her heart beats with an irregular, foreign beat. She has not answered her telephone all week. Night after night she lies in bed listening to the branches of the sycamore tree scratch at the skylight. Afraid to sleep. Afraid to move.

When she leaves the building, Pinto is there.

She sits cross-legged on the floor, a bottle of beer in her hand, watching him. He is performing for her, manic, spilling his paint like an ejaculation on a huge canvas spread across the floor. She has no idea how she got here.

He wears paint-spattered overalls with no shirt, and the hair on his chest and shoulders is reddish gold in the light streaming through the windows.

Near her on the floor is a tin Cinzano ashtray with a

lighted cigarette burning its way to ash. She sets the bottle down next to the ashtray and stands, begins to move. Get away, for if she stays, he will kill her, the way he kills everything he touches. She knows that now. She watches the muscles on his back ripple. So absorbed he won't see her leave.

He catches her at the door, where her bag of materials is hooked over the knob. Lifts her like a doll, sets her down in front of his canvas. Stands behind her, his hands press her thighs into his rolling hips. She whimpers as the room convulses. He sweats turpentine.

The painting is madness in intersecting lines, reds like blood. His hands slide under her shirt, find her breasts. Breath hot on her neck, he wrenches through the cotton fabric of her bra, and tears her shirt from its buttons. Her hands flap useless against his grip.

Somewhere close comes the sound of the elevator. It stops and the sliding door creaks. Voices approach. His teeth break through the skin on the back of her neck, sucking, rough fingers probe her wetness. As if she's his to do with what he wants. She has so little left. "I'm going to paint you," he says. He strips her more than naked.

"Pinto? I've brought the Elsworths." It is Clement Greenberg, the essayist, the critic, the philosopher.

"Son of a bitch," Pinto growls, shoving her from him. She stumbles to the floor, crawling, clutching the remnants of her clothing around her. When the door opens, she is behind it, raw, disgraced.

Hiding her face, Rose, poor mouse, scurries away.

She goes to Ben. He is teaching at Columbia three afternoons a week and sees patients in the mornings. She's put herself together so that a quick glance will confirm for a stranger her status as a Village bohemian. She shivers on the steps of his brownstone, waiting until it's too dark to see. Pinto recedes from view, first a gray memory, then an erotic dream. That's all.

Ben finds her curled on his doormat and makes her hot, sweetened tea while she borrows again from his sister's wardrobe.

"Do you want to talk?" He thinks she's been with this man Pinto again, but she's never spoken once about what happened to her. What Ben knows about Pinto is from Crystal.

Maxie licks tears from Rosie's cheeks. She is silent, and he does not ask her again. He picks up her empty cup and puts it in the sink.

She fumbles with her sketch pad. The sketch on which she's written the strange name and street. The name the policeman said she'd told him. She shows Ben the drawing, tells him what happened with the policeman.

"Your subconscious is working overtime," Ben says. At least she's talking, he thinks. The rest will come eventually. It's part of the process. "Relax and let it happen."

"You're shrinking me again." She is testy. "You don't give me fifty minutes and I don't pay you to listen to me." Doesn't he understand how frightened she is?

She's right. But he's walking a fine line between his training and his feelings. "I want to help—"

She puts her palm up and ends it.

Ben has a patient coming, someone who can't come in the morning. His practice is growing. She cannot stay.

"I'll come to you afterward and take you to dinner," he says.

She shakes her head.

"If you like, tomorrow we can see if we can find—" he

227

looks at the address she has slashed on her drawing "—Barker Avenue."

"Okay," she says. *If I'm still here tomorrow.* Shimmering in the front of her eyes is Skye Pinto. Oh, God, she thinks. Oh, God. He crooks his finger and she follows him though he terrifies her. Crystal says she's Trilby to his Svengali, that she must stay away from him. There's no happy ending.

"Such a sad face." He touches her cheek. She flinches and he drops his hands.

"Please," she says. "I'm sorry."

He longs to make love to her, but he doesn't. She is so young. So confused. It's more than Pinto, but Pinto is enough.

Rosie thinks, Ben is a good man, like Papa. But not like Papa. She could never tell Papa about Pinto. Ben is a shrink. He would listen, yes, but if she tells him about Pinto, he will want to protect her by taking charge. Like Papa. So she will not tell.

Yet this she knows: To erase Pinto from her consciousness, she needs Ben. She must not flinch the next time he touches her. Crystal will help.

She recognizes the car at once and slows down. It's parked in front of her building, flaunting its New Jersey plates. The Garden State, it says. M.D., it says.

Three bags of groceries sit on the sidewalk. Papa, holding a fourth bag, closes the trunk. He looks weary, thinner.

Auntie Anna, beautiful in her black fitted coat with the fur collar, comes out of Rosie's building. "She's not home."

When Rosie has her fill, she waves, calls to them. She's excited to see them, although she continues to make excuses for not coming home.

"Oh, darling," Auntie Anna says. "There you are."

"Rosie." Papa puts the bag of groceries down and folds her into his arms. "Why don't you call us? We worry about you. You're never home when we call."

"Papa . . ." Her love for him keeps her mute. He has never hurt her. Did he hurt Mama? Is that what she's buried? No. No, that is a false memory. She's known nothing but love from him. She begins to cry.

"Now don't do that, baby," he says, holding her. "We miss you. Don't we, Anna?"

Anna sees bruises on Rose's neck though the scarf she wears almost hides them. "We want you to be happy, darling," she says. Her eyes are wet. "Come inside. We are making a spectacle of ourselves."

"What's the matter with your lip?" Papa asks. He touches the small ridge she's had since the cut healed.

She wants to say, take me home. Hide me. I'm afraid all the time. But she can't say the words. She tosses her response away. "Paper cut. It took forever to heal."

Auntie Anna puts the groceries away in the scant space. "I don't think you're eating properly. You look very thin, doesn't she, Nathan?"

"You would think I live on a desert island. I'll never eat all this food." Maybe this is the time, she thinks, to ask about the fire.

"We can't stay too long. Nathan has been working so hard . . ." Anna looks at her brother. Nathan's face is drawn. "The headache is back?"

He nods. He sits in Rose's big easy chair from the Salvation Army smoking, his eyes closed. "How are your classes?"

"Wonderful. The teachers are really good. I'm learning so much . . ." This is it, she thinks. "I have to do

229

an autobiography in pictures," she says. "Will you tell me about Mama and the fire?"

"Do you see Larry?" Anna asks, as if Rose has not spoken.

"Sometimes." She is cautious. Everyone hopes she and Larry will marry. Everyone except Larry and Rose. "He's working hard, but he came down a couple of weeks ago with some friends."

Auntie Anna brings Papa a cold cloth for his forehead and a glass of water. He swallows a pill.

Migraines run in the family.

"Are you meeting people?" Auntie Anna picks up her sketch pad where Rose dropped it and begins to leaf through it.

"I have a date tomorrow," Rose says. She feels shy about telling them. She stands near Papa, watching.

"Who with?" Anna asks.

Papa catches her hand and places it on his cheek. His cheek is cold. Rosie kneels beside him. "He's a doctor, Papa. His name is Ben Coopersmith."

Auntie Anna looks up. She is holding the sketch pad as if it's dirty. Her face reddens. "Rosie darling—"

"It's a class, Auntie Anna. Drawing the Nude Model."

"A doctor?" Papa has opened his eyes.

"He just finished his studies at Harvard." She doesn't tell them more. Ben is twelve years older. They would say he's too old for her. They have their hearts set on Larry.

Papa gets to his feet and holds Rose's shoulders. "You are our life," he says. "Don't cut us off. Call us. Come home and see us once in a while." He smiles. "I know we're boring now that you live in the big city."

"Oh, Papa, I'm sorry. I promise—"

Behind her she hears Anna's quick intake of breath, the

thud of her sketch pad hitting the floor, turns. Anna is pale as death.

"What's the matter, Anna?" Nathan asks.

"Nothing. Nothing." She picks up the pad and straightens it. "I can't remember if I put gas in the car."

"We stopped on the road. Don't you remember? You're getting as bad as I am."

"Rosie," Anna says, kissing her, brushing the hair back from her face. "The printing on that drawing—"

"Come on, Anna, let's go before we get caught in traffic."

Rose is apprehensive. "Do you know what it means?" Now the answers will come.

"Anna!" Nathan is already on the stairs.

Anna's eyes meet Rose's, skid away. "No. No, darling. Why should I?"

"Anna!"

"Coming, Nathan." She kisses Rose's cheek. "Not this way," she murmurs. "Not this way."

— 43 —

Rose

They get out of the car and go their separate ways, agreeing to meet. Rosie is very busy. She has so many things to do.

"If I'm not back," Mama says, "don't follow me." Mama crosses the street and walks away.

Rosie finishes her errands and returns to the place they've agreed to meet. Mama is not there. She waits and waits. Then she tries to find her.

She asks everyone if they've seen Mama, but no one has or admits to. She is on a dark street full of deserted warehouses.

"Jenny! Here!"

She opens the door and falls down a long tunnel.

"Mama, Mama, Mama!"

She is falling, falling. Then she gets wedged in tight, unable to move.

The rain slams against the French doors that lead to Ben's garden. They sit on his couch, her feet in his lap as he towels them dry. She's rushed over without an umbrella and the rain soaked her.

"Ben, I feel so strange, as if someone else has gotten under my skin and is taking over my life. Someone named Jenny who lives on Barker Avenue."

"What else are you feeling, Rose?"

She does not tell him about Skye Pinto. It is a sickness in her blood. "Nothing else, Herr Dr. Coopersmith." She watches Maxie sneak up and pounce on one of her saddle shoes and carry it off. "Maxie, come back here."

"Barker Avenue is in the Bronx." Ben's hands caress her instep. So gentle.

"Ben." She pulls her feet away and tucks them under her. "I don't know anyone in the Bronx. I've never even been there."

"Rose, sometimes repressed memories are triggered by a smell or a sound or an event."

"How about a dybbuk?" she asks, making light of it. Or perhaps she's serious.

"I don't think so."

"The nurse I saw in Gramercy Park." Her eyes burn, feel as if they're sinking in her skull. Her sleep is erratic.

"Yes. Or possibly a reflection on the canvas—something that you felt compelled to paint over, to hide."

"I don't remember. I don't want to talk about it anymore, Ben." She is very tired.

"We should go back to the park and re-enact the scene."

Rose shudders. "No. I'd rather go to the Bronx."

"Okay. I still think you should ask, if not your father, then your aunt."

"She saw the address. I know she did. I'd forgotten it was on my pad. She saw the name Jenny. She was very upset. And Papa had one of his migraines. I asked about the fire, but they acted as if they didn't hear me. They were so distracted."

"Because of what you asked?"

She thinks this over. "No. They were upset when I got there." She presses her lips together. She will not cry. "Something was wrong. It almost seemed that . . . they were afraid of me."

"You could be distancing yourself from them to keep from getting hurt."

"You don't know them, Ben. They would never hurt me." If only the rain would let up. She feels trapped, immobile.

"Come on." He offers his hand. "Let's take a ride up to the Bronx and have a look at Barker Avenue."

He's humoring her, she feels. Irritation dissolves her lethargy. "Never mind, I'll go myself." She swings her feet to the floor, but is without socks and one shoe.

Ben's Studebaker is parked just around the corner. They drive to the Bronx. Rain pounds the windshield, the roof. The windows keep fogging up until Ben opens his a crack. The wipers jerk back and forth, kathump, kathump. One-two, one-two. Jen-neee. Jen-neee.

She says, "Please don't be mad."

Ben cleans the windshield with the side of his hand. "I'm not mad."

She sighs. "I'm sorry to be such a baby."

He smiles at her. "Rose, you are going to be a magnificent woman."

Squinting her eyes, she studies his profile. He has a strong chin and jaw line, a large straight nose that suits him. She resents the implication that she's not yet a woman. "What will we do when we get there?"

"If it stops raining, we can walk in the park."

"The park?"

"Bronx Park."

"You know the Bronx, Ben? I thought you said you were from Forest Hills."

"We lived off Allerton Avenue—that's in the Bronx—until I was ten. Then we moved to Queens."

She is breathless, squeezing her chest. "You know who Jenny is! Say it."

"No, Rose." It's raining so hard it is impossible to see. Ben pulls the car over under the El. "Rose, listen to me. I am twelve years older than you are. You weren't even born when my family left the Bronx."

Maybe, she thinks, Jenny is a dead girl who has come back in my body to avenge her death, just like in that Robert Montgomery movie, *Here Comes Mr. Jordan*. She watches the rain stab the windows, over and over again. Each droplet is a wound.

Rose

Thousands of lights, gaudy against a navy velvet sky. Colors explode into tiny fragments, initiated by whistles and pops, drowning out the cicadas' song. The air is scented with boxwood.

Although well into the evening, it is still hot. She sits at the bottom of a long flight of stairs scratching her mosquito bites above her lolling socks. She is waiting for Papa and Uncle David and Auntie Anna. It has something to do with Mr. Layton's sickness. She hears Mrs. Layton crying, and she climbs to the top of the stairs. The voices rise and fall. They are taking so long and she's getting very sleepy. Finally she doesn't hear the voices any more. They have gone away and left her. Left her. Gone away and left her.

Whistle. Pop. Another burst of colors breaks over the sky. She rests her head on her knees, closes her eyes. Then she is flying through the air, tumbling.

Screams roll over her, but they aren't hers. She sits up, surprised, confused. She is at the bottom of the stairs. Papa holds her tight, rocks her, "Rosie, Rosie," he says. His tears are salty on her lips.

Hadn't they told her to wait at the bottom?

Rosie doesn't cry. She's a big girl now. She has six candles on her birthday cake, and Mr. Layton dies of Rocky Mountain Fever, and everyone says how young he was—the same age as Papa. What will happen to her if Papa dies?

★ ★ ★ ★ ★

The rain has settled into a fine mist.

"Come on," Ben says. He's walked around to her side of the car and opened the door.

She stares at his hand, then at the soft fog floating low over the park. Above the fog, streaks of light try to break through. Shadow edges, the light behind the dark.

"Come on, Rose," he says again. "Isn't this what you wanted?"

Is it? She takes his hand and emerges. Standing here, she knows the El hulking against the afternoon sky. The screech and thunder of the train do not surprise her. Behind the scrim there is soft light.

Mama holds her hand. They are standing on the corner where there's an open yard, waiting for Papa. The train roars into the station. Here he comes. Here he comes. Down the stairs with all the other people. Not like the other people . . .

Sunlight, so pure and clear, it hurts the eyes. Two little girls scream, coursing up the sidewalk on roller skates.

Skinned knees, she thinks. My fault. Please don't hurt Mama.

She shivers, so terrified she's losing whole sections of time.

"Rose?" He has his arm around her. "Do you want to go home?" He sounds uncertain.

She shakes her head, shrugs out of his hold. "Not yet." This is her only chance. She knows she will never come back here.

Baby carriages and strollers. Children's shrill voices

grate. In the street a stick-ball game is in progress on the wet pavement. Boink, boink. She knows the sound.

They pass one building after another. This one? No. That one across the street? No. Does anything look familiar?

Yes. The smell is like no other. A smell of sun and grass and chicken soup. And children.

Then she sees it. A sound catches in her throat, strains to emerge. The apartment building is like the others: stone facade, five floors. The entrance is through a courtyard. Shouldn't it be wider, she thinks. It seemed wider . . .

Three little girls are playing potsie, blocking the way, hopping from chalk square to chalk square. She drifts forward. Stops. Around the entrance, mothers are sitting in chairs, talking. Rocking babies in carriages.

"Ma!" The shout comes from a girl with long curly hair who is standing in front of the building, looking up. The girl shouts again. Louder. She wears purple lipstick and exudes over-ripe fruit. The girl waves her hand at a grubby boy of about sixteen, who hides in the vestibule.

Rosie looks upward. She feels Ben's hand on her shoulder.

A window opens on the third floor, and a woman sticks out a head covered with curlers. "What?"

"I need money for ice cream."

"I gave you money already. What do you think, it grows on trees?" The woman leans halfway out of the window. "Who is that with you?"

"I'm not with nobody." The girl signals to the boy in the vestibule to stay back. "What's a lousy nickel?"

"I'm coming down." The window shuts with a slam.

"Shit!" The girl stamps her foot. "I'll meet you there." The boy in the vestibule takes off, dodging the potsie girls.

"Excuse me," Rose says. The girl stands in her way.

"Beatie!" The woman from the window, her backless shoes clapping on the stone floor, has come down the stairs. A kerchief barely covers her curlers. Her short, fleshy body is wearing a chenille housecoat. She stares at Rose.

"Aw, Ma."

"Here's a quarter. Don't bother me. Just be home in time for dinner."

Beatie looks quickly from her mother to Rose, grabs the quarter, and doesn't stick around.

"Laura?" The woman comes close. She gives off a cloying scent that smothers Rose, makes her weak.

She shrinks back. "Ben?" He holds her hand. Get me out of here, she thinks.

Ben says as they move away, "Soothe the child, Rose. Tell her it will be all right."

"It *is* Laura," the woman says, following them. "No, it can't be. You're too young. Excuse me, I made a mistake." She turns away. "For a minute I thought—"

"Wait," Ben says. "Who is Laura? We are trying to trace a family. Maybe you can help us."

Rose tugs on his arm. "Please, Ben, let's go."

The woman looks at Ben, then Rose. "Funny, you look just like her." She shakes her head, and a curler loosens under the kerchief, hangs precariously. "Of course, it's been so many years already, but you never forget a thing like that." She purses her lips. "Let's see, Beatie was a baby, not walking yet even. So it has to be fourteen years."

"Maybe you can help us," Ben says smoothly. "We're writing a book about it."

Rose looks at Ben aghast. Where is this coming from?

"Ah, of course," the woman says. She snatches up the tilting curler just as it begins to fall and rolls it back up in her hair without missing a beat. "I'm Esther Apter," she says. "I have a pot roast on the stove. You want to come up and have a glass of tea? I'm the only one left in the building from that time." She is in the vestibule and motions for them to follow her. "Another month and I wouldn't be here neither. We're moving to Flushing." She says this proudly; Flushing is a special place. She motions to them again. "Come on up. I'll tell you all about it."

Rose

Esther Apter leads them up three flights. The landing is grimy; the walls, chipped and gouged, reveal layers of paint. They reek of burnt onions and sweat.

"It was a nice building once," Esther says.

Inside the apartment are boxes and cartons. And ghosts. Rose hears them.

"Sit. Sit." Esther shows them into a small kitchen. The windows here look into the kitchen of another apartment in an adjacent building, where a woman in a house dress and curlers in her hair stirs a pot. She looks over at them. Esther waves and pulls the shade down. "That's Yetta Kaplan. She always has to know everything."

Rose is mute. She hovers above her body, watching.

When the kettle boils, Esther pours water into the glasses. The Lipton tea bags float. Ben puts four lumps of sugar into Rosie's glass. "Drink," he says.

"You're not the first, you know," Esther says. "Right after it happened a woman came—a relative from Hartford." She looks questioningly at Ben and Rosie. When there is no response, she shrugs. "A few years later someone else came. A crazy old man who didn't make sense to me. And the detective, he also came many times; then he stopped, finally."

"What year was this?" Ben asks. He writes notes on a little pad.

"Let's see." Esther wrinkles her face, makes zooping sounds over her tea. "Beatie wasn't even walking yet. And it was very cold. We had a lot of snow. Nineteen thirty-six, it had to be. Maybe January, February."

"Drink, Rose," Ben says. He holds the glass to her lips and she swallows once, turns her head away. Setting the glass back on the chipped porcelain tabletop, he asks Esther, "What do you remember?"

"What do I know about any of it? I can only tell you he was a monster, a drunk. He beat that poor girl—you remind me so much of her—" She tries to catch Rose's eye, but Rose looks down into the tea. "He beat her all the time, screaming, I never heard such screaming. Her you never heard a complaint from. Laura. Such a nice girl, she was. That last time he almost killed her. I called the police. I couldn't stand it no more. An ambulance came and took her away. I never saw her again."

"She never came back to the apartment?"

"No one ever heard from her again. I think he must have killed her because he disappeared also. Afterward, the landlord had to fumigate the apartment." She waved her hand. "This is it. We were across the hall before. When we moved in, you could still smell the turpentine. He was a painter, you know."

Rose slips back into her body with a soft sigh. *He was a painter, you know.*

Ben pats her hand. He asks, "How old would you guess Laura was?"

"I know for a fact. My age. We had the same birthday. Twenty-two. A pretty girl. So much like your daughter—"

Rose starts to laugh, then finds she can't stop. Ben squeezes her hand. He says, "Rose is not my daughter."

"Oh, I'm so sorry," Esther says. Rose's laughter makes

her uneasy. "I didn't mean—"

"Their last name—what was it?"

Rose's laugh catches in her throat. No, don't say it, don't say it.

"Let's see, let's see." Esther gets up and pours hot water into the glasses without asking if they want more. "Taminksi. No, Topowski, I think. Something like that. It was in the papers for months. They looked everywhere for her."

"Maybe she just wanted to change her life," Ben says.

"A child that age wants to change her life?"

"Excuse me? I thought you said Laura was twenty-two."

"Not Laura. I'm talking about their little girl. She was very sick and in the hospital. If you ask me, I always thought he killed that nurse and stole the girl away from the hospital."

The window shade rolls up with a loud snap. Sitting in the neighboring kitchen is the woman Yetta and two children.

She's in her high chair in the kitchen. They're having dinner. Suddenly, the window shade growls and rolls up like a thunder clap, and there is another family—a father, a mother, and a child sitting in a high chair—looking back at them from another window, where they're also eating dinner.

Look, she wants to say, just like us. But Papa is angry. He yells at Mama to pull down the shade. Pull down the shade!

When she gets up from the table, Papa knocks over the table and throws all the dishes on the floor. He drags Mama out of the kitchen.

"Please, Papa, no, Papa!"

The other family is framed in the window, no longer a mirror image.

Mama cries in the next room.

★ ★ ★ ★

"Ben!" Rose rises out of her body and floats on the ceiling.

"The child. Do you remember the name of the child?" Ben's voice is distilled, fragmented.

As from a long tunnel someone calls, "Jenny. Jenny. Jenny."

Rose

*Sunlight dazzles the grass, the trees, the eyes. It makes
everything yellow. Mama says God makes parks and sunlight and the grass green and the yellow and black butterfly that flutters round her head.*

So God is a painter like Papa.

*She wears soft, white leather shoes and white socks and
a new dress. She runs through the tall grass until she
comes to the pond.*

Olga calls, "Where are you? Jenny! Where are you?"

*The pond is like a mirror. So still. It's her fault that
Papa hurts Mama. Maybe if she went away . . . she
stares at her reflection. Her hair is wild around her face,
white, like cotton candy from the boardwalk. She leans
into the pond.*

*"Oh, there you are, you bad girl," Olga cries and
grabs her roughly by the arm. "If you fall in they will
blame me. Why are you such a bad girl, Jenny? Do you
hear me, Jenny? Why don't you answer me, Jenny?"*

"Excuse me," a woman says.

Rose sits up with a jerk.

"You wanted the *Times* from January and February,
nineteen thirty-six." The woman holds a small cardboard
box. "They're on microfilm. Do you know how to use it?"

"No." She follows the woman to a long, narrow room,

separate from the reading room. She's doing this without Ben. This is not about Ben. Or Jenny, whoever she may be. It's about Rose, who has lost her way.

Repentances. That's what the director of the Philadelphia Museum called it. A drawing, painted over, begins to reappear because as paint ages, it becomes more transparent. She is the portrait of Rose becoming more and more transparent.

It is dark here save for the light from the big machines. The machines have their own voices, somewhere between a hum and a whine.

The librarian finds her a machine, the last one in the line, and turns on the light. At once the machine begins to talk, sigh. "Do you want to begin with the January spool?"

"Yes."

The woman threads the microfilm for January 1936 through loops and crannies. "Just move this to center. This knob sharpens the image. Then you turn this knob to move the pages."

The room has the musty smell of an attic, where the past lies mildewed in an old trunk. She listens to the monotonous shung, shung from the machine as it waits for her to make her first move.

Her promise to Ben that she won't act alone, that they will search together, lies crumpled like the tissues in the pocket of her coat. He's gone to Chicago for a conference, gone away and left her.

The fine design here—her art—becomes how she turns the knob that slips her into 1936, the year she came to America from Poland. The year Mama died.

Slowly, Rose guides the pages across the viewer. Looking for Jenny. Come out, come out, wherever you are. Someone coughs. Catarrh. Was the ship like this, she wonders. She stops turning the knob. What was it like? Searches her memory for a shard of the past. Why has she no memory of the voyage? No memory of the fire, or how she came here.

She rolls the knob again. Reads of a cold spell on January 16th, and a big snowstorm on the 19th. An ad for Doubleday, Doran announces Sinclair Lewis's *It Can't Happen Here* for $2.50.

On the 30th and 31st, there is a thaw, and two people are sentenced to die for a poison murder. The Nazis celebrate three years in power. And they are looking for accomplices of Bruno Richard Hauptmann in the Lindbergh kidnapping murder.

The Ziegfeld Follies with Fannie Brice and Bob Hope is at the Winter Garden and *The Children's Hour* is at Maxine Elliott's Theatre.

She rewinds January. Nothing. Replaces the January spool with February and begins again.

There is no break in the sub-freezing temperatures and Huey Long's widow is named to fill his seat in the Senate. Ezio Pinza is singing *Carmen* on the radio and Jeanette MacDonald is in *Rose Marie* at the Capitol.

There is no Laura. No Jenny. No Taminski or Topowski. There is war in Ethiopia and the Winter Olympics in Garmisch-Partenkirchen. Long skirts are in and Chanel's daytime fashions reveal a determined boyish air.

On February 4th, a headline stops her:

NURSE FOUND SLAIN
IN CHILDREN'S HOSPITAL

It's a short piece about a murder. Still . . . hadn't Esther Apter mentioned the murder of a nurse?

The partially clothed body of a nurse at the Willard Parker

Hospital for Contagious Diseases was found in an anteroom this morning by another nurse who came to relieve her. Although she appeared to have been strangled, the cause of death of the nurse, Mrs. Stella Zweikel, 28 years old, has not been determined. The Medical Examiner's Office had not completed an autopsy yesterday.

The police are investigating the circumstances under which Mrs. Zweikel died. Mrs. Zweikel lived with her husband Marvin at 401 East Third Street in Manhattan.

Nothing about a missing child. Too bad. Rose's eyes shift to the blurry photographs. The dead woman at a happier time in a Jean Harlow pose, her hand on the shoulder of a smaller, obviously older, man.

Rose turns the knob, moving on. Wait. The husband. She rolls the film back. It can't be, she thinks. She stares at the photograph.

It is the odd little man who followed her around in Clayton Lake. The one Auntie Anna sent away. The one Rose thought she recognized in the newsstand near the Second Avenue Deli.

— 47 —

Rose

"You musta been 'dopted," Bobby Larson says, " 'cause you don't look like your father."

"Was not." Bobby Larson is a know-it-all, who's been left back twice, so Rosie doesn't believe anything he says. But he makes her think of the photograph of Mama and Rosie in Europe before Mama died. "Was not," she repeats emphatically.

"Oh, yeah? So where's your mother?"

"She died. I look like her."

"Well, I think you're 'dopted, just like me." Bobby Larson rides off on his bike, but Rosie is confused. She begins to look closer at parents and children and she sees resemblances. All except with Bobby Larson and his parents because Bobby was 'dopted, and Rosie, because her Mama is dead and Rosie looks nothing like Papa. She stares at the photograph. Mama has dark hair. Rosie's hair is pale gold. Papa has red hair. The photograph is not colored, so maybe it makes blond hair look dark.

Although he's home now, Papa is going away again, into the Army. He's a doctor like Uncle David, but Uncle David is too old for the Army. He and Papa talk about it all the time. Uncle David would like to go, too.

When Rosie comes home from school, Papa and Auntie Anna are in the kitchen talking while Auntie Anna makes dinner. Papa hugs her. "How's my best girl?" He brushes

249

her hair back from her face. "Let's have a look at your beautiful face."

Rosie pulls back, blurts it all out. "Am I 'dopted, Papa?"

"What makes you say that?" Papa's voice is harsh. His hands are heavy on her shoulders.

Auntie Anna puts down her paring knife and looks at Nathan. "Nathan—"

He crushes Rosie to him so hard she bleats. "Never. I am your Papa."

"Always and forever?" she whispers into his neck.

Holding her at arm's length, Papa kisses her forehead. "Always and forever."

"Then why don't I look anything like you?"

"You look like your Mama, Rosie darling. Don't you see from the picture?"

No, she doesn't see. She keeps trying to find herself in the child, in the woman, in the somber faces, in the strange clothing, but she can't.

"Nathan—" Auntie Anna says suddenly.

"Don't cry, Papa," Rosie says. She cradles his head against her child's breast.

She's lost all sense of time. She closes her eyes to 1950 and opens them again. It is February, 1936.

HUSBAND ARRESTED IN NURSE'S SLAYING

A distraught and incoherent Marvin Zweikel, 41 years old, was arrested Thursday night for the murder of his wife, Stella Zweikel. The superintendent, John Sokolnicz, of 401 East Third Street, where the murdered woman and her husband lived, said that Mrs. Zweikel, who worked the night shift at the Willard Parker Hospital, frequently entertained gentlemen while Mr. Zweikel, a clerk in a pharmacy, was at work. Sokolnicz said that Mrs. Zweikel had told him her husband was a violent man. Samuel Evergood, Mr. Zweikel's lawyer, said that his client denies the charge.

There is nothing more. She rolled into the next day, and there it is.

CHILD MISSING IN NURSE'S SLAYING

A desperately sick child, Jenny Topinski, age three years one month, was discovered missing from the ward at the Willard Parker Hospital supervised by Stella Zweikel, the slain nurse. The child's disappearance escaped the notice of hospital authorities and was reported to the police late yesterday by Dr. Edgar Eldridge, Acting Administrator. It has come to the attention of this newspaper that the missing child's father, Carl Topinski, an unemployed house painter, attempted to break into the hospital to see his daughter the night Nurse Zweikel was murdered. Topinski had to be forcibly ejected. Topinski, who lives at 2431 Barker Avenue in the Bronx, was out on bail for assaulting his wife, Laura, age 22, who is in critical condition in Bronx Hospital after what neighbors called "another bitter argument."

Rose stares at the photograph of the child with the wild mass of pale hair. She has a sweet, almost anxious smile. The caption reads: *Jenny Topinski, missing child, possible witness to murder.*

Hands over eyes, Rose's tears seep through her fingers.

She turns the dial into another day.

MISSING CHILD LINKED TO NURSE'S MURDER
FATHER DISAPPEARS
SUSPECT RELEASED IN NURSE'S MURDER

The husband of slain nurse, Stella Zweikel, was released late yesterday afternoon when the superintendent of the apartment building where he resides corroborated his statement that he had been at home when his wife was slain. The detectives of the Ninth Precinct who are assigned to the case said that the police are looking for Carl Topinski, who has not been seen since the night of the killing. It is believed that Topinski returned to the hospital later that evening after he was ejected and took his daughter.

The newsstand. She's found her way here somehow from the library, half-blind. Her vision swims in a herringbone arc. She sees nothing clearly. Only the other self.

"Why do you stand there? Go away!" The woman sitting in the newsstand shrieks at her. Why is she shrieking like that?

Passersby pause, ogle.

Rose comes out of her trance with a violent start—which makes the woman shriek louder and swat at her with a rolled newspaper. "Leave us alone." Swat, swat. "You only make things worse." Swat. The newspaper sings as it slices the air.

The change bowl rocks, coins joining the complaint.

"Please," Rose says, removing herself to a safer distance. "Where is he?"

"He's sick. You make him sick. Don't think I don't know

who you are." The woman shakes the newspaper at Rose.

Rose edges closer, eyes on the weapon, and thinks, the news rolled. That's what. The news rolled all over her, flattened her into one dimension. "I just want to ask him if he knows me."

"He knows you all right, you bloodsucker."

A man in overalls slides up to the stand and eyes Rosie warily. He sets his tool box on the sidewalk and looks at the woman, a sort of Humpty Dumpty's wife concoction. "Is there something wrong, Dina? You want I should get a cop?"

"No!" Rose answers before Humpty Dumpty's wife can. "I was looking for the man who usually works here."

"Zweikel is not himself," the woman says. Her face puckers up and to Rose's horror, fat gobs of tears drip like paint from scrunched up eyes. "It's all right, Solly. Go on. Go on." She waves him away.

"Okay, if you're sure." Solly picks up his tools and walks down Second Avenue. He looks back once, nods, goes on.

They watch him until they don't see him.

Coins jingle in the bowl as people stop for a paper, a magazine, and hurry on.

"He's sick," the woman says. She wipes her nose with a napkin. "He saw you on the street and he went crazy. Why do you want to hurt him? He didn't kill your mama."

"My mama?" Rose staggers backward, barely misses an approaching customer. "Excuse me." She steadies herself against a tall stack of *Journal American*s.

"That kurveh Stella. She was his first wife." The woman blows her nose into the napkin with a loud snort. "I lived next door. I know what went on with her. Men all the time. All the time." Her voice drops to a mutter.

"Wait, please. Who do you think I am?"

"I know who you are. Zweikel too knows. He's been

looking for you for fourteen, fifteen years. Why did you come back now? He's old, he's sick. His heart can't take this."

"But why is he looking for me?" Rose is in a parallel world, a mad kingdom. All the sounds are gathering forces against her, like a funnel tunnel. She's in the eye of the storm. Car horns, the conversations of people attack her, children's shrill voices, dog's barking, whining, the squeal of a bicycle tire, a motorcycle, a siren. "Why? Why?"

"She gave you away to keep you from him, that Stella, and wouldn't tell him where. Then one of her fine boyfriends killed her. I know it. And Zweikel looked for you all over and ended up in the crazy hospital. I'm begging you, Irene, on my hands and knees, please go away and leave us alone."

Chingle go the coins. Chingle. Clunk.

Ching, chung, go the coins. Irene? Irene? The sidewalk moves under Rose's feet. She puts her hands up to touch her face and feels nothing but air.

No, no, not Irene.

The faded photograph of the mother and child sits in its frame. She holds it in her hand, then pulls the back off and tears it from the frame. The clipping of Pinto floats to the floor unnoticed.

Look at me, flat, dead eyes that lie.

She feels no sorrow, not even pity.

Holding mother and child over the sink, she puts a match to them and watches the flame catch, brown into black, shrivel and char, then the relentless creep to ash. She watches the faces grimace and fold into each other. Ashes to ashes. When the heat bites her fingers, she drops the burnt remnants into the sink and turns on the faucet.

— 48 —

Anna

Furry cat tails of fog waft around the Buick as Anna grips the steering wheel and peers into the sickly yellow light. She knows Route 9, though it's growing less and less familiar as the fog thickens.

Nathan groans softly, and she adjusts her rear view mirror so that she can see him. He lies slumped in the back seat, a towel of ice against his forehead, his pain dulled now by the morphine. The migraines follow a pattern. Soon he'll sleep, and when he wakes, the pain will be gone entirely. And he will radiate the nervous energy that makes her uneasy.

She sits forward over the wheel, concentrating on the road. But her mind wanders, as it must, collecting the detritus of fourteen years. Fog knits a cocoon around the car, closing her off from the world. Her aloneness mingles with despair. Her teeth crunch her lower lip.

So many lies from Nathan's one terrible act. No, two. He had killed someone. It is still hard for her to conceive. Her brother had killed that evil nurse—yes, she was evil—and kidnapped a child. Rosie was a precious gift and they'd tried to give her a happy life.

But what about her mother? They'd never tried to trace her. Though from what Anna'd read, her recovery was unlikely, what if she recovered and has been looking for her child all these years? And what about the nurse's family? The husband, that crazy little man in the green suit.

Anna slows to a crawl for nothing is visible except the faint red tail lights of a car just ahead. Nathan sleeps now, deeply.

But she sees with stark clarity. The mistakes. David had allowed for Nathan not wanting the practice. They should have sold the practice and Nathan should have become the surgeon he wanted to be. She herself is to blame. She had wanted to hold on to what was left, which meant Nathan would take over David's practice.

Why hadn't Nathan fought her? Because of Rosie. Rosie, Anna told him, Rosie needs a stable life with her father. Would you uproot her and take her to a strange place where you would never see her because you'd be in the hospital all the time?

"But you'll come with us," he'd said.

"Why would I leave my home? I have a life here." Oh, she'd been hard, unmoving. What life without David? Rosie needed Anna as much as Anna needed Rosie. Of course she would have come with them.

There could have been compromise, if only he'd fought her.

The tail lights of the car she's following turn off the road and disappear. She sees only inches ahead. She glances at her watch. Almost three hours since they left the city. For a drive that normally takes less than two hours. They must be close to Clayton Lake.

When Rosie went off to school, Anna signed up for a class at Georgian Court College, even though it is a Catholic school. Nathan poo-poos her, but she wants to get an education. It is a class in psychology. There are a lot of statistics. Not very interesting. What is interesting is what she is learning about the history of psychology. She's discovered Freud.

She drives tight to the right side of the road, no idea

where she is. This is not good. She edges the car off the
blacktop onto dirt and grass and bumps something gently.
Putting the car in neutral, she slides across the seat and
opens the passenger door with care. She's bumped a sign.
Gets out. She is practically on top of the sign before she
sees the words: Entering Clayton Lake, population 3125.
She leans on the open door.

Memory is a funny thing. You cannot control it. It belongs to the subconscious. Smells, sounds, lights, anything
can spin it back into your consciousness. Rosie looks at herself in the long mirror and sees her mother. Dr. Freud
didn't have to tell Anna this.

Anna is afraid. Rosie is her child, not of her loins, but
her soul. Loved and protected. But not Nathan nor Anna
can protect her from her past now. What they can do is help
heal the damage they've done. They must tell her the truth
and accept the possibility that she will not forgive them.

Washington Street is drenched with fog but Anna knows
the way, or maybe, as David used to say, the Buick knows
the way home.

"Anna?" Nathan is sitting up. "Where are we?"

"Almost home. How do you feel?"

"Better."

She sighs with relief when her headlights pick up the sign
on the front lawn: Nathan Ebanholz, M.D. She drives into
the garage and shuts down the engine, the headlights. Rests
her shaking hands on the wheel.

Nathan touches her shoulder. "Are you all right?"

"It was very foggy. And I'm not all right."

He gets out of the car. "So everything's fine. We're
home now."

He's halfway to the back door, as if he's running away
from her. "Nathan!"

Holding the door for her to precede him, he says, "What's the matter with you?"

"Me? Not me, Nathan. Everything is not fine. We have to tell Rosie the truth. It can't wait any more. She's suffering and doesn't understand what's happening to her."

"Nothing's happening to her. She should have stayed home with us. The city is too much for her." He leaves her in the kitchen and goes upstairs.

Anna checks the answering service, finds only requests for appointments, which she'll take care of in a little while. She puts water in the kettle for tea. Anger stiffens her back, makes her neck ache. What is she to do? Upstairs, she hears Nathan moving around. When the kettle begins whistling, she hears his step on the stairs. She prays he's not going to that whore in Island Heights.

"Do you want some tea?"

"No."

"Nathan!" He's shaved, dressed. It's always the same with him. She sets the kettle down or she might throw it at him.

He picks the car keys from the table. "I'll see you in the morning."

49

Rose

Turpentine is her scent; she inhales it like the vanilla Auntie Anna uses for baking. It permeates her skin. The canvas waits. Her brush attacks her palette. The broken Madonna lies bleeding, child peering from beneath the Madonna's skirts.

She lays on color, luminous reds and yellows, for a golden Madonna, cowering. Then with the brush, rough ribbons of blood like marionette strings, gathered in grotesque hands. His face is the problem; she works and scrapes and works again, throws the brush down and with her fingers as palette knife, finishes in triumph, for hasn't she known it all along? His laughter surrounds her, flails her, crushes her.

God is Skye Pinto.

The little cowboys on the blanket twirl their lassos over her. The telephone rings and rings and rings. Rain slams the skylight like fistfuls of pebbles, branches claw the glass to get in. The storm is personal. It crowds out the telephone.

She has no interest in answering it, for it is not for Rose Ebanholz. There is no such person. She is oddly serene. She has stopped eating; soon everything will go away.

From time to time, when the wind takes a breather, she hears the tap, tap, tap of Crystal's typewriter. It swirls in and out of the storm, lulling her as she drifts on the warm cloud.

"Rose!"

Reluctantly, she is drawn from her euphoria, opens her lids partway. No strength to go farther.

"Rose! What's the matter with you?" Crystal sounds frightened, and Rose wants to reassure her. She is pleasantly calm. Her lids close. She is drifting backward.

"No! Rose, sit up!" Crystal props the pillows up, then Rose. "My God, you're all bone. Are you eating?"

"Don't remember." She can't feel her lips. "Not hungry. Feel wonderful." She tries to slip back under the covers, but Crystal is holding her up. Crystal smells of cigarettes and coffee. Rose smiles at her. "How is the novel coming?"

"Great. It's coming great. It's almost finished. But don't change the subject. Stay here." She rushes off and Rose hears cupboard doors banging, the tea kettle being filled.

The phone rings again, and Crystal answers it. That's good. Crystal is a real person. She has an identity, parents, and a history. So she should answer the phone. Rose sinks down under the covers and goes away.

"Rose! Wake up, damn it! Did you take something? Did you take Miltown?"

"Go away." Rose's lids flutter. She rolls on her side, back to Crystal. Ernesto jumps on the bed and sniffs around her face, a hair's breath, with his soft nose, purring loudly.

"Rose! God! Sit up! Drink this." Cup rattles against saucer.

Slowly, butterfly wings of honey—dark and nutty—take precedence over the wind and rain. She feels a faint nausea, then an overlay of hunger. Rose sighs and slides back into her skin.

Hunger, she thinks, has a curious texture. She can subdue it by not eating. But eating anything at all leads back to hunger and more eating. She sips the honeyed tea from the cup Crystal holds to her lips with one hand, propping her up with her other arm.

"What have you done to your hand?" Crystal asks. "Finger painting?"

The fingers of Rose's right hand are crusty with paint, her fingernails grubby with color. Where has she been? Has it happened again? It offends her, as if it were someone else's hand attached to her wrist. She can't bear to look at it. She must get up at once and cleanse herself, but she is too weak.

Wheatena follows next with slices of ripe banana, ever ripening as she lay dreaming.

Tears roll down Rose's cheeks. Ernesto purrs, puts his pink tongue into the cereal bowl, and licks up what Rose leaves.

Crystal says, "Your parents are worried about you."

"I don't have any parents," Rose says.

"You know what I mean. Your father and your aunt."

"Nathan is not my father and Anna is not my aunt. They lied to me."

Crystal stares at her. There's a black smudge on Crystal's cheek and her fingertips are stained black. She's been struggling with a typewriter ribbon, which is probably what made her stop working and look for Rose. Rose always changes Crystal's ribbons. Black-eyed, black-haired Crystal in her long black skirt, her black sweater, black stockings, and black ballerinas. Rose feels a surge of love for Crystal like a pale red wash rushing over watercolor paper. The storm is subsiding. She leans back against the pillows.

"Tell me," Crystal says.

Rose's voice is pale. She starts and stops. Waits for the words to force themselves free. Crystal does not hurry her.

"Not far from here, fourteen years ago, a nurse was murdered in a hospital for contagious diseases. At the same

261

time, a three-year-old girl named Jenny, sick with scarlet fever, disappeared from the hospital."

Crystal listens, not taking her eyes from Rose.

"Jenny's mother was in another hospital dying from a beating by Jenny's father. Jenny's father had threatened the nurse in Jenny's hospital—the one that was murdered. But the nurse's husband was arrested for the murder. And no one looked for Jenny." Rose's voice thins, breaks. "No one looked for me, Crystal. I just disappeared. They forgot all about me." She can't hold back the tears.

Shock freezes Crystal's pliant features. Disbelief. "Are you telling me that you're Jenny, that your father—I mean, Nathan, killed a nurse and kidnapped you? How do you even know he was there? It doesn't sound possible."

"Not Nathan, Crystal, my real father. His name was Carl Topinski. I keep remembering things. My name. Jenny. I remember a street in the Bronx. Ben and I went up there and walked around. I recognized a building. I lived there. And someone in the building recognized me. But it's my mother she recognized."

"It all seems too farfetched. I couldn't get away with a story like that if I wrote it."

Rose smiles. "I read all about it on microfilm from the *New York Times*. At the library. I look like my mother. My real mother—her name was Laura—not that woman in the picture—Nathan's wife." She sighs, remembers coming home after looking for Zweikel and burning the old photograph, watching the lie disintegrate in her hands.

". . . she die?" She catches up to Crystal in mid-question.

"Who?"

"Your real mother."

"I don't know."

"And your real father?"

"I don't know. But there has to be a way to find out what actually happened."

"Ask him, I mean Nathan."

"I could never—"

"But you must. Or Anna. She'll tell you."

Rose shakes her head. "They won't. I asked them for my birth certificate, but they hedge."

"They love you. That was Anna on the phone. I told her you went on a museum trip and would be home tomorrow. You have to talk to them."

"I hate them. They lied to me." Rose's anger scalds, harsh and burning. "Crystal, do you think my mother gave me away?"

"You said she was dying. Maybe she died. Maybe Nathan and Anna don't know very much." Crystal wrinkles her brow. "I wonder if the morgue has anything—"

"The morgue?"

"The library at the *News*. They have all the back issues. The *News* is trashier than the *Times*. I'll bet it'll tell us more."

"Us?"

"Of course, us. I'm your friend. You don't think I'm going to let you solve this puzzle all by yourself, do you? I'm a writer and this is a wonderful story. We can be Mr. Kean, tracer of lost persons, or Hercule Poirot, take your pick."

"Crystal, I'm afraid. I can't—"

"Yes, you can, Rose. I'll help you. This will come out right. Too many people love you." Crystal begins bustling around the room, laying out clothes for Rose, running a tub. "Come on." She stops in front of the painting on the easel. "What's this? It looks like . . . Pinto—"

Rose stares, then looks down at her paint-scarred hand. She doesn't remember painting it. The face is the child in the newspaper, shadow-edged. She is crawling from beneath bleeding vines that form a woman's skirt. The laying on of color is Pinto-esque, abetted by the suggestion of Pinto himself, a grotesque malevolence in the upper right of the painting.

But it is the raw violence that compels.

And the palpable terror in the child's eyes.

50

Rose

It's evening and no one is in the morgue. The man who oversees it during the day is long gone, Crystal confides. This is where Crystal works part-time. She knows how to find information about anything in the whole world.

A cleaning woman, her swollen feet in slippers, is washing the floor with a wet mop, sliding the bucket with the wringer behind her.

"Wait here," Crystal tells Rose.

The music comes from the organ grinder and they hear it before they see the tent or even the merry-go-round, which plays its own melody. Papa lifts her to his shoulders and, riding high, she sees a whole little village camped on Maguire's field.

Rosie's nose is sunburned and her cheeks feel hot. Papa buys her cotton candy and they sit on a wooden pony and go round and round three times. The cotton candy gets in her hair. Rosie smiles and smiles and smiles. She sees other children with mamas and papas but no papa like hers. She snuggles into his lap on the ride home.

"Did you tell her?" Auntie Anna whispers when they get home and Papa carries her to bed.

Nathan shakes his head. "I can't. You tell her."

"Oh, Nathan, it's not for me to do it. You must tell her."

Tell who, Rosie wonders. Tell what? She is asleep before she can ask.

In the morning Auntie Anna wakes her early. Papa is wearing a suit and he smells nice. His face is very smooth and soft. He sits on the bed and holds her.

"Rosie, darling," Auntie Anna says. "Nathan has to go away."

"No!" Rosie breaks from his embrace, looks at him.

"He's going to medical school to be a doctor like Uncle David."

"Then I will go to medical school, too," Rosie says.

"No, Rosie, you can't. Children don't go to medical school." Nathan gets his voice back. "I have a small room near the hospital and I will be working hard all the time. I won't have time to take care of you. Besides, you start school in September so you have to stay with Auntie Anna and Uncle David. They love you very much. And I won't be so far—only Philadelphia—you'll see, I'll come home often."

She clings to him. "No. No. You're going away. You'll never come back. Don't go away, Papa. Please don't leave me alone."

"But you won't be alone. Anna and David are here. You can keep them from being lonely. Give me a kiss like a good girl."

She turns her face away.

The air is stuffy, stale with cigarettes, pungent with ammonia. Rose sits on a table, her feet dangling, while the woman cleans around her.

Crystal reappears with two cups of coffee black, thick as tempera paint. And very bitter. She breaks a Milky Way in two pieces and offers one to Rose. "The old papers are filed by year, then month. "Let's hope 1936 hasn't gone out to be microfilmed," Crystal says.

Rose bites into the candy, and the chocolate and caramel are a sweet paste in her mouth.

Mama slices the Milky Way into thin slices with a small, sharp knife. Jenny holds out her hand, then Mama is on the floor and Papa has the knife. Mama is crying, "She's such a good baby. It was only a treat." Mama's nose is squirting blood. Papa kicks Mama hard over and over. Jenny doesn't get any Milky Way. It's her fault Papa hurts Mama and makes her cry.

"Here we go, here we go. 1936. February," Crystal says. She wheels in a cart of newspapers. "Finish that before we start."

The Milky Way has melted in Rose's hand. She licks the chocolate off and wipes her sticky hand with a tissue.

Crystal begins turning pages. Stops. "Oh, boy," she says. "Look at this."

Rose peers over Crystal's shoulder. *The Daily News.* A huge headline proclaims: **WHERE IS LITTLE JENNY?** And underneath is a photograph.

"She looks so frightened," Rose whispers.

Crystal looks up at her and back to the photograph. "She does look something like you, but—"

Rose pushes Crystal's elbow. "Turn the page."

"Oh, my God," Crystal says. "It's you. I can't believe it. Laura Topinski. Near death, it says."

Rose reaches out and touches Laura's face on the yellowing page. "You gave me away," she says. She holds herself tightly but her hands quiver.

"Read this, Rose," Crystal says urgently. "If she did give you away, she probably saved your life."

The headline here says: **THE PIECES OF THE PUZZLE**.

There is a picture of Stella Zweikel, labeled: MURDERED NURSE.

Another of Zweikel: IS THIS MAN A MURDERER?

A photograph of Carl Topinski is so grainy and blurred it is impossible to decipher features. The man is bearded. He wears a cap low on his forehead. IS THIS MAN A MURDERER? is written underneath his photo.

"He looks like Tolstoy," Crystal says, screwing her eyes to the photograph. Giving up, she turns the pages. Two days later there are more photos. Then:

SUSPECT IN NURSE SLAYING MISSING
No Trace of Child

Rose sits and dries her eyes. "How did I get to Nathan Ebanholz then?"

"You'll have to ask him. He's the only one who can tell you. Nathan or your aunt."

"What about my mother? Do you see anything about her? Did she die?"

Crystal turns pages, one after another. Day succeeds day. Nothing. "Doesn't say."

"They just forgot all about me."

"Wait." Crystal sits up suddenly. "Look here," she says.

PAINTER SOUGHT IN NURSE MURDER

"Read it to me," Rose says. "I can't—"
Crystal reads:

Sergeant John Kelly of the Ninth Precinct detectives
squad, who with Detective Brian Morrisey has been investigating the case of the murder of Nurse Stella Zweikel
and the disappearance of three-year-old Jenny Topinski at
the Willard Parker Hospital, said that police are looking
for Carl Topinski, the missing child's father, who has not
been seen since the night of the murder. Sources in the police department confirm that Topinski's cap was found
near the body of the slain nurse.

"Oh, God." Rose puts her head in her hands. "No more,
please, Crystal. That's enough. I don't want to hear any
more."

"Rose, listen—"

"What am I going to do? My real mother is probably
dead, and my real father is probably a murderer. We already know he was a wife beater." She sops up her tears
with a tissue, blows her nose. "I just wish I knew what happened to my mother."

"That's what I'm trying to tell you. The article mentions
two detectives by name. See here. Sergeant John Kelly and
Detective Brian Morrisey. That's a real lead. They'll know.
All we have to do is find them."

51

Rose

Rosie sits on SOPHIA RANDOLPH, 1892–1898, Age 6, Go With the Angels. On her sketch pad she draws the gnarled sinews of the ancient oak tree. It is August hot. A fine heat haze vibrates low over all. The sun smells like the ocean on her skin. Sand and sweat and salt water.

Larry leans on AMOS APPLEGATE, Father, Brother, Grandfather, Great Grandfather. 1865–1940. Barefoot, his sneakers are tied to the handlebars of his Schwinn. Both bikes lie on the grass near the tree. He is reading her a poem he's written. "Hiroshima," he says. "We have lost our innocence."

A large mushroom rises from the top of Rosie's penciled oak tree.

Larry's lips touch hers like a dry feather. Nothing happens. "Will you always be my friend?" he says. "No matter what?"

"They lied to me." Rose hurls the accusation at Ben, as if he's in the conspiracy with Anna and Nathan. She paces back and forth, fist hitting palm, fist hitting palm.

"Perhaps . . ."

"What do you mean, perhaps?" Her anger is potent. She wants to hit him, to draw blood. Is she, then, like her real father?

Stop. Think. Why is she turning against Ben? For not

being on her side? But how can she think that? He is, isn't
he?

She stops pacing. Ben lights his pipe and makes her
wait until the whole pretentious process is finished.
Finally, he says, after drawing in and drawing in, "Do you
think it's time you confronted them, asked them about all
of this?"

The rich aroma of tobacco tricks a memory so fleeting it
almost gets away from her.

*Papa pulls the car up to the roadside tavern. He is
looking for someone, a house painter, and has spotted his
car. It is still daylight. Rosie wears a blue and white pin-
afore with a short skirt, white socks, and white lace-up
shoes. Papa sits her on a high stool and slides a bowl of
little pretzels in front of her. He lights his pipe. The
leather seat of the stool clings to the back of her thighs as
the men begin to talk. She strokes the warm scarred wood
of the counter, leans her elbows on it, lays her cheek on it.
It is cool and has a dull gleam. She runs her fingers over
it. The salt of the pretzels lies sweet on her tongue. Legs
wrapped around the barstool, she is transported up and
over the low rumble of their voices by the mix of smells,
beer, alcohol and wood and leather, cigarettes, tobacco,
and . . . paint.*

"Rose? Where are you? What are you thinking?"

Hot resentment jolts her. "I've found out enough to
know they lied. My whole life is a lie. My name isn't even
Rose, it's Jenny. Topinski. My real mother is dead and my
real father probably killed her and ran away."

"You're not thinking straight, Rose. Put your emotions
aside for a minute. What if you were legally adopted? Just

271

because there's nothing in the newspapers doesn't make it so."

She sits, holds her head in her hands. She remembers something for a quick second; then it is gone. Something about Ben. Don't trust him, she tells herself. He's a doctor, like Nathan. Whining, Maxie tries to worm her way onto Rose's lap, but Rose is already on her feet, up and away. "Ben, I'm sorry. I have to do this. I was wrong to involve you."

He catches her hand, upset. "Don't go. Where are you going?" As she pulls away, the dog begins to bark. She's glad he's upset. He's always so together, so detached. "I'll be back," she says. Maybe, she thinks.

In her portfolio are her sketch pad and soft pencils, but they stay there. She doesn't want Crystal or Ben. Running, the numbness seeps outward and downward from her head to her feet. She clenches her toes in her loafers, can barely feel them.

The copper pennies beam up at her. It is all a joke.

Who is Rose Ebanholz? Who is Jenny Topinski? What difference does it make anyway? She could even be Irene— what was that name again?—Zweikel. She could be nobody.

Nathan and Anna rise up before her, arms out to her, "Rosie, Rosie." She pushes them away. How could the two people she's loved most in the whole world, who had taught her to honor truth, have built her whole life—and theirs— on a lie?

The sidewalk slopes downward. She is nearing the river. It is harder to run here because cars are parked askew, some even on the sidewalk. Black and white police cars and others. From across the street she watches men, some older, with big bellies, others young and muscular, like the one who'd helped her in Washington Square Park. Some wear uniforms. Ninth Precinct is carved in the grimy stone over tall doors.

Sergeant Kelly, she thinks. *He* had looked for her. He'd cared what happened to her. She sees him as a kindly man, a bit like Santa Claus, round, ruddy-cheeked, jolly. He draws her across the street clogged with the fellowship of men, the bustle of activity.

She climbs the stone steps behind an old woman in black carrying a cloth-covered basket. Rose focuses on the steel gray of the bun showing under the black straw hat.

A tall man with dark hair, just leaving, holds the door for them. Rose doesn't look at him. If she had, she would have seen his sharp glance, the puzzled pause.

The old woman's basket holds cookies and shortbread. "For all you nice boys," she says. Her voice is sweet with Polish flavor, almost like Anna's. And Nathan's. Rose's teeth hold tight to her lower lip.

"Help you, Miss?" She cranes her neck up to the high desk, to see the sign that says, HAMISH LOGAN, DESK SERGEANT. Butter and sugar aromas slather over her. Sweat and tobacco. Hamish Logan has old eyes and a vein-splattered face. He wears cookie crumbs on thick pink lips. "Miss?" He puts another cookie in his mouth. Rose sees teeth chomping and watches bubbles of saliva in his open mouth. If he stood up, she wonders, would she see into him? Would she see bones and sinews, muscles and tendons? Would she see blood coursing through his veins and arteries?

"Sergeant Kelly," she says. "Is he here?"

"He's out on patrol. Are you Ellen?"

Ellen? "Who's Ellen?"

"Chris's girlfriend. You're not Ellen then?"

"No. John Kelly is who I'm looking for. He was a detective here before the war."

"Kelly? Oh, you want Jack Kelly then, 'cause Chris has only been on the job two years." He stops chewing and wipes his mouth with the back of his hand.

"Yes, Jack Kelly."

"He retired—"

"But I have to talk to him." She's panicked, feels invisible as men pass through. They don't seem to see her.

"Excuse me, Miss." A broad man in a suit nods at her, gives her a cursory look. "Logan, whatcha got for me?"

She turns away.

"Hold on there, Miss." Logan looks down over the desk at her. "Why dontcha leave a number and I'll tell him to get in touch with ya."

She shakes her head. No. It must be now while she still has the fragile need to know. In its absence she will finish her walk to the river. What was the other detective's name? She reaches into her bag and pulls out a scrap of paper. "Morrisey," she says. She raises her voice to reach Sergeant Logan. "What about Detective Morrisey?"

"Now you're talkin'." The desk sergeant leans over the massive desk. "You missed him by a hair. He musta just walked outa here when you came in. Maybe you can catch him. He's—"

She rushes for the doors. "Excuse me, excuse me," under arms, dodging, broken field running. "Morrisey," she mutters. Morrisey, she thinks. Out the door, on the steps. "Morrisey," she says. "Morrisey?" As if he could hear her. She begins calling, "Morrisey, Morrisey."

People are staring at her. The man who had held the door for her not ten minutes earlier is standing on the street, his back to her, leaning over, arm on the roof of a police car talking to the cop inside. He looks up and around, surprised.

He stares at her with fierce blue eyes, puzzled again, makes up his mind. He walks toward her, up the steps, his blue sport coat open. Damp brown curls cluster on his forehead. He stops short. Not fierce-eyed. Gentle. Squinting at her in the sunlight.

She reaches out her hand and touches the soft wool of his jacket.

"I'm Morrisey," he says.

52

Rose

Papa measures one inch of black coffee into her cup, then fills the rest with milk. She is afraid at first, but he holds the cup for her and she sips. It is wonderful. "Thank you, Papa. Thank you, thank you."

"You're spoiling her, Nathan. Children shouldn't drink coffee," Auntie Anna says, clucking her tongue. "You tell him, David. He never listens to me."

Uncle David beams at Rosie. "If that's the only way she'll drink milk . . ."

"Oh, you men," Auntie Anna says, throwing up her hands. But she laughs, too, so Rosie, who is holding her breath, knows it's all right. "She has you both wrapped around her little finger."

Rosie looks at her pinkie, perplexed, and they all laugh.

Sometimes, when she sips the coffee-flavored milk, Rosie catches the edge of the dream where she is in another place with other people who call her by a different name. But their faces are not clear and she doesn't stay long. She is going somewhere all by herself and she is frightened.

Auntie Anna holds her and kisses her and says it's from losing Mama in the fire. But there is never any fire in her dreams.

They know him here. He is a cop and they treat him with deference. The woman gives them the booth he requests in the back of the shop, and brings them coffee without asking. Black and dense, the coffee is almost alien in heavy white mugs.

"It's uncanny," he says, studying her face with intense eyes.

He can't be the right Morrisey, she thinks suddenly. He is far too young. "How old are you?"

"Twenty-three," he says. He smiles at her and a dimple appears on one side of his mouth. "How old are you?"

"Almost eighteen."

"Are you in school around here?"

"Cooper Union. What's uncanny?"

"Why were you looking for me?"

"I wasn't. Not you. You're too young."

"Too young?" He laughs then. "I don't think so."

He is making her self-conscious, staring. She takes a sip of coffee, but her hand shakes and she misses her mouth. Coffee dribbles down her chin. She's going to cry. Setting the mug down, she blots up the dribble with the paper napkin. "The Morrisey I'm looking for was a detective at the Ninth Precinct, fourteen years ago."

He nods as if he's known all along. "That would be my father. I'm Bill Morrisey. He's Brian. He works downtown now."

"Brian Morrisey. Yes." She speaks the name, then feels her skin absorb it. "His partner was a man named Kelly?" Her hands flee to her lap and hold each other.

"Yes. Uncle Jack." He stirs sugar and cream into his coffee and takes a big swallow, pushes the mug aside. "Tell me your name," he says. Patting his pockets, he pulls out a brown leather wallet and a pack of cigarettes. He offers her one and when she shakes her head, puts it in his mouth, lights up, and takes a long inhale. Exhaling, he waits.

"Rose," she whispers. "My name is Rose Ebanholz. At least, that's what I thought it was until a few days ago. Now I don't know." He squints at her through the smoke and stubs the cigarette out in the glass ashtray. If she could have stood safely, she would have left in that moment, but her limbs are filled with lead.

He's opened his wallet and is looking for something, turning the plastic picture holders. "Here," he says. He slides the wallet across the table.

It's a snapshot. A man, a woman and a teenage boy stand on the front steps of a house. "That's me," he says, pointing to the boy.

The photograph begins to undulate. Her hands knead her face. She doesn't hear the sound she makes.

"Rose? What's the matter? Rose?" He reaches across the table and touches her hand.

"Who is she?"

"That's my mother. See what I mean? You look just like her. You even have the same green eyes."

She covers the photo with her free hand but can feel it moving. "You look like your father."

"Yes," he says. "But Laura is my stepmother. My real mother died when I was nine."

"Laura? Oh, God. Her name is Laura?" She closes her eyes, swallows, chokes.

"Yes. Why were you looking for my father?"

Eyes wide, she says, "He was the detective on a case fourteen years ago where a nurse was murdered and a child was stolen from the hospital."

"Yes. I know all about that." He speaks very carefully. "She was Laura's little girl—"

"Jenny."

"Jenny. She would be almost eighteen now." He is

gaping at her. It can't be, he thinks. After all this time.

"I know," she says.

He fishes a dollar from his wallet and leaves it on the table. "Come on," he says, pulling her to her feet. "Let's get out of here."

She has to run to keep up with him and finally, she stops. He goes on down Second Avenue with long strides.

Zweikel sits in his newsstand eating a fried egg and onion sandwich on a pretzel. He sees her coming toward him, running, crying. "Irene!" She needs him; he can tell. Dropping everything, he fumbles with the door to the ramshackle stand, cursing his twisted fingers, gets it open at last. "Irene!" he screams as she runs by, but she gives no sign of having seen or heard him.

— 53 —

Rose

Robert Frost reads his poetry at Columbia and Larry invites her, although he thinks Robert Frost is old hat. He says Allen Ginsburg is a genius. Rose thinks maybe, but she still likes Robert Frost.

Afterward, they get on the subway to the Village, and she gives him back the key to Gramercy Park that belongs to his friend.

"You don't want it anymore?"

She shakes her head. The train reels, driven by a madman on mad tracks, throws her against him.

He takes her to a bar on Tenth Street. Julius's.

The smoke is thick as winter fog. They find a table and order beer. He says, "I don't want to have secrets from you. This is who I am."

Everyone has secrets from me, Rose thinks. She looks around, sodden-eyed from the smoke. She is the only girl here. Well, almost. There is an odd-looking woman with a beak nose and lots of red hair and the stubble of a beard behind the bar.

"Oh," Rose says.

"Are you surprised?"

"No."

"Do you hate me?"

"Hate you? Never, Larry. Never. I'll always be your friend."

★ ★ ★ ★ ★

"He's afraid she might hurt herself," Nathan says, hanging up the phone. "What are we going to do?" He speaks in a low voice so his patient, sitting on the examining table in the next room, naked under the short cotton robe, can't hear.

Rose in her gray cap and gown from high school graduation smiles down at them from the framed photograph over Nathan's desk.

"I knew we would have to pay one day," Anna says. "It wasn't right what we did. We took someone else's child."

Nathan shakes his head. "She was mine. She came to me. We gave her a life. What kind of life would she have had with that father? Even if the mother had lived."

"We don't know for sure that she died. And if she didn't, could she ever forgive us?"

"How many left in the waiting room?"

"Only Mrs. McKelvey."

"We'll go into the city, then."

"But you have house calls. The Kosta boy has whooping cough."

"We'll stop on the way."

"And old Mrs. Fried."

"She can wait till tomorrow. Call her. Say I have an emergency."

"Nathan, we'll have to tell Rosie everything."

"She'll never forgive us."

Anna sighs. "She'll never forgive us if we don't."

All afternoon they sit in Washington Square Park listening to the folk singers on their guitars. Kisses sweeter than wine. He holds her hand.

"In the beginning she never talked about you," he says.

281

"She never talked at all. Topinski almost killed her. Dad brought her home for us to take care of, but she ended up taking care of us."

She didn't die. Rose's heart rattles in her chest. She didn't die. "She never looked for me."

"They looked. Dad used to go back to the Bronx all the time and talk to people. He kept hoping your father would show up somewhere. He even hired a private cop to try to find him. Everyone thought your father killed the nurse and took you away with him."

"She didn't die," Rose says.

"This man Ebanholz and his sister. Who are they?"

"It's not what you're thinking. Nathan is not Topinski. He couldn't be my real father. His wife and daughter died in a fire in Poland around the time he adopted me. Maybe Topinski gave, or sold, me to them."

"And they just took you without asking questions? Not likely."

"It's not possible." She has terrible clarity in this instant. "No, you're wrong. They are good people, Bill. They care about me. I love them." Ben is right. She must talk to them. There is an explanation. Topinski, it always comes back to him. He sold her to them and they can't face telling her the truth.

"Rose? Jenny? What shall I call you?"

She thinks for a few minutes. "Rose, I think. I am more Rose than Jenny." Jenny is that frightened little girl inside her, the lost girl.

"I'm not sure how to handle this," Bill says. "I'll talk to Dad. It's going to be a shock for her."

"You mean I have to meet her? Meet Laura? I'm not sure. I need more time." She jumps up and stands in front of him, pleading, ready to flee.

"Rose, listen. It's all right. She might not be ready either. That's why I want to talk to Dad. He's a good man. He'll know what to do."

Rose

She is on the bus again with her package. The bus rides over country roads, pulls into deserted stops, where she gets off each time and waits for another bus. There is no way out. She is always the child with the long skinny legs who doesn't speak. She is always searching, for what she doesn't know, but the search continues. She worries, will she know it when she finds it? Will she ever find it?

From the dark of the vestibule she watches him stand for a moment, then leave. Before she turns away she sees him hesitate at the phone booth on the corner, go in, and close the door.

Rose climbs the stairs in utter darkness, for the hall lights are out as they often are. Bill Morrisey will tell his father, and maybe Laura, or maybe not Laura.

She has a living mother. Lightheaded, her fingers follow the molding to Crystal's door. She knocks. "Crystal?" There is no answer and no warm slit of light from under the door.

Ernesto's whining meow makes the darkness quiver.

She has not been to classes today, or yesterday, yet the elixir of turpentine cleaves to her.

Again, Ernesto's cry comes, this time from the direction of her own apartment. Has Crystal gone off and left him with her? Rose fumbles with her key, stabbing at the lock in search of the hole, hitting the brass plate in the spongy darkness.

She is going to be sick. Everything is coming loose, crashing down, wanting out.

The door opens, but not because she finds the keyhole and turns the key in the lock. It is already open, waiting for her. Cat eyes glow, then a smudge of fur tears past her and is swallowed by the dark hollow of the stairs, leaving the faint odor of something burnt.

"Ernesto." Rose's spontaneous call trips into the chasm, but Ernesto is gone. She closes her door, leaning back against it to calm the dry heaves that ride her, again and again, until whipped, she slides to the floor, back against the door.

Turpentine and whisky. She sits on the bar stool, the salt of the pretzels dissolving on her tongue, waiting for Papa. Turpentine and whisky. Cool gleaming wood. Turpentine and whisky. She is so cold . . . cold . . . sliding down the tunnel . . . wait, wait, no . . . No.

"Rosie, darling!"

"Rosie?"

They are knocking, calling her name, pushing on the door. She stirs, comes slowly to her feet and opens the door.

"Rosie, darling." They fall on her as if she is their long lost child. As if she is their . . . what?

"Why are you sitting in the dark?"

"What happened to the lights on the stairs?"

"It's a good thing Nathan had a flashlight in the car."

Of course, Nathan would. He is always prepared. Until now.

Rose presses the light switch. The light is not welcome.

"Darling, are you all right?" Anna sniffs the air, puzzled.

"Don't you see she's all right, Anna? Don't fuss."

They just keep talking, talking, filling the room with words. Words bound from the walls, shoot from the skylight, cry from the kettle, but not the words she wants to hear.

"Stop!" She's crying. "You must tell me the truth. No more lies."

"Lies?" Anna looks dumbstruck. She moves to comfort Rose, who stands firm behind folded arms. "Lies. Of course. That's why we're here, isn't it, Nathan? It's finished. Tell her, Nathan."

Nathan avoids her eyes. He wanders the room hunched, like a tiger in a cage. "Ei-y," he says. "Ei-y."

"Nathan," Anna says. "Oh, Nathan. Rosie darling, Nathan—we have something to tell you."

Nathan collapses in the overstuffed chair. Head in his hands, he says nothing at first. Then, "We love you, Rosie. You wanted to come with me. You held out your hand to me, as if you were Rayzela herself. I tried to be a good father." Terrible, painful sounds come squeezing out of him. Rose has never heard anything like it.

But she is angry. She hardens her heart against him. "Don't do this to me, Pap—Nathan—Dr. Ebanholz."

Anna says, "Oh, Rosie, don't you see how miserable he is? We never meant to cause you unhappiness. In the beginning we didn't even know who you were, and you were so sick. We would have given you back, but that man, that animal, would have killed you like he killed your mother."

"My mother didn't die. She's still alive."

Anna's heart clenches. "You know this?"

"Her name is Laura Morrisey."

"God forgive us, we gave you love and a life without fear." She stands behind Nathan.

"You did," Rose says, forcing back her own tears. "But why did you keep me after you knew who I was? Why didn't you bring me back?"

"There was nothing for you to go back to, Rosie darling. Believe me. I saw that for myself. Topinski was a monster."

"I'm trying to understand. You lied, both of you. Uncle David, too."

Anna's pain is palpable. "Not David. We didn't tell him. He loved you so much. He wanted a family."

Uncle David sits in the car, his hands on the steering wheel, staring straight ahead. On the seat beside him is his black bag.

Rosie taps on the window, calls, "Uncle David." She knows he will turn to her, his eyes full of love. "Rosie darling," he will say. But this time he doesn't move.

Ernesto slinks into the apartment, watchful, then rubs himself on Rose's shins, purring. His tail fur is singed.

Nathan lowers his hands and looks up at her. "We had only love for you. That's all we had—me, Anna, and David. You made our life a joy."

"Oh, Papa." Rose falls to her knees in front of him. He is her papa. Her arms reach out to him. "I always felt loved, but separate. Not really part of anything. I didn't look like anyone. You should have told me. How could you have let me find out this way?"

He folds her hands between his. "I was afraid you would hate me." He looks up at Anna. "Hate us."

"It's all too new. You have to tell me now. Where did you find me?"

Nathan tilts his head to Anna, his face a ghastly gray. She doesn't know everything, his eyes say. How can I tell her the rest? To Rose he says, "Give me time."

"No! No! No!" Rosie screams at him. "You've already had too much time."

He sighs heavily, begins to speak. "I was at the hospital to have it out with her—"

"You were at the hospital? The Willard Parker Hospital, you mean? Where I was?"

"Yes. I worked there as an orderly." Nathan waits for her to push him forward with his story, but she does not. Anna's hands prod him.

"Oh." Rose has not even considered this direction. "Then you knew the nurse who was murdered . . ."

Nathan looks at Anna, then back at Rose. "I knew her," he says. "Stella and her husband Zweikel had a business bringing people over from the old country—"

"Wait. Zweikel?" Where had she heard that name before? Yes. That strange little man from the newsstand on Second Avenue. The newspaper article about the murder. Marvin Zweikel. The murdered nurse's husband. Rosie's eyes meet Anna's. "He's the man who came to Clayton Lake and watched me?"

Neither Anna nor Nathan responds. Anna, her hand over her eyes, moves away from them, stops at the painting on Rose's easel, stares.

"Zweikel and Stella, they knew Miri and Rayzela had died in the fire, but they took money from me anyway, and told me they were on the ship already."

"Did you see my father kill her?"

Nathan laughs, a short derisive laugh. "Oh, yes," he says bitterly. "Oh, yes. I listened to her laugh about it and put my hands on her throat and squeezed. And when I was finished, she was dead. Then I turned around and saw you standing there with your hand out to me, and I took you away."

"I don't understand. You, Papa? You killed her?"

"She killed me and I killed her."

Rose presses her forehead against his knees, and he strokes her hair. "You are everything to me, Rosie. More than my own Rayzela. If not for you I wouldn't be alive."

Rose murmurs a memory fragment into his woolen trouser leg. "She hurt me. I was so scared. She kept screaming at me all the time: crybaby, crybaby."

Nathan isn't listening. He says, "I was crazy. Everything died that day. I didn't know what I was doing. Then you reached out your hand to me and I took you to Clayton Lake and Anna and David."

"Come home with us, Rosie darling," Anna says suddenly. Under the easel is an empty whisky bottle. She nudges it with the toe of her shoe.

"Home?" Nathan repeats. "Yes, Anna is right. We must all go home now. Come, Rosie."

Rose lifts her head. He thinks he strangled that nurse, but he doesn't remember. All he remembers is his hands on her throat. Someone else could have done it. Topinski. Must she choose? She looks at Nathan as if she would never see him again. Nathan sighs. He kisses her forehead, rises, and offers his hand to her. "Yes, it's time to go home," he says.

She gets to her feet. "I have things to do here first." Lots of things, she thinks. Everything, she thinks. She will not run away anymore.

"David will be doing double work," Nathan says.

Anna gasps. Softly, she says, "David is dead, Nathan. You know that."

"It's not right he should have so much to do. Where are my keys?"

"David died four years ago. Give me the keys. I'll drive."

"Not David, too?" Nathan says. He takes the keys from his pocket and hands them to her. "It's a terrible thing."

A silent exchange floats between Rose and Anna.

"Let me take your arm, Nathan," Anna says.

"No, I will," Rose kisses his cheek. "I love you, Papa."

"Yes, of course," he says.

The electricity is still out on the stairs so Rose leaves her door open to light their path down to the street.

After Rose and Anna settle Nathan into the front passenger seat of the old Buick, Anna straightens and turns to her.

"He'll be all right. It wasn't easy for us to tell you."

"I know."

"I ask you to forgive us. We would never have kept you, but I saw what you would go back to and I couldn't—"

"I know." Rose throws her arms around Anna. "I know."

"Rosie, darling." Anna holds her at arm's length. "The painting upstairs. Why did you cut it to pieces?"

"What?"

"Hey, blondie. There you are." The voice is lush with booze. "I've been waiting for you."

Pinto is sitting on the steps of the brownstone next door, a cigarette dangling from his lips. His threadbare overalls are streaked with paint and he wears no shirt.

Fear is a hot coal rising from the pit of her stomach to her throat.

The hair on the back of Anna's neck shivers. "Who is that man?" she asks.

Rose opens her mouth but her throat closes on the words. She squeezes out, "Skye Pinto."

"That's Skye Pinto? The painter? He looks a little crazy. Maybe we shouldn't go—"

"No, you must." Quickly, or Rose will jump into the car with them. "Go on. Take Papa home. I'm all right."

Anna kisses her and goes around to the driver's side, gets in. She casts one final worried glance at Pinto before starting the car.

Nathan sits up, stares out the window, a strange look on his face, as Anna drives off. He doesn't wave.

— 55 —

Nathan

She wets the paper, and stretching it gently with a firm hand, as she has seen Auntie Anna make lokshen, tacks it to the drawing board. Although she's only a freshman, Miss Bogart has given her advanced lessons.

The paper feels vital under her fingers as it dries, stiffens, comes alive. Here in the art room, she doesn't have to talk. The images will talk for her.

The first strokes of color on the newly wet surface bleed; they are supposed to.

Rose watches the car drive off, Papa's face ghostly and unfocused in the passenger side window. Faint, cottony fuzz—prologue to migraine—obscures her vision.

"Very touching." Pinto raises the whisky bottle in a salute, then drinks.

He sits with a kind of drunken arrogance, mocking her with his scent. Turpentine and whisky. His cap pulled low over his forehead. He kindles a primal fear, a longing. The air around him crackles and burns.

She thinks, Kill me. Kill me. Papa.

He laughs. "You think I don't know who you are?"

She turns and runs. She is not Jenny, she is Rose Ebanholz, running up the stairs in the darkness to her apartment. She slams the door shut, locks it. Pulls the easy chair over to the door. Panting, she dials the operator and it rings and rings and rings.

Footsteps thump on the stairs. The sharp meow of the cat spirals upward.

Anna's hands are rigid on the steering wheel. She doesn't like driving in the city. Cabs shoot out in front of you. You have to watch everywhere, have eyes in the back of your head. But Nathan is in no condition to drive.

She wonders nervously, looking over at him, if he has had a small stroke. He hasn't moved since they pulled away from the curb in front of Rosie's building, his eyes staring out the side window.

Miraculously, she finds a parking place on Gramercy Park East. She lines up the car with the one in front, and as David taught her, parallel parks. The loss of him comes on her with such intensity that, powerless, she leans her head on the steering wheel.

"Anna?" Nathan touches her shoulder.

"I'm all right," she whispers. "Come."

They've been here once before—the house on Gramercy Park, not long after his first phone call. Anna's finger on the bell next to his name brings no response. Then they hear the dog bark, and a moment later the door opens.

"Ben," Anna says. "Thank God."

"Come in, come in. Did you find her? Is she all right?" He stops. "Nathan? What's the matter?" The puppy gets underfoot and Ben picks him up.

"We talked to her," Anna says. "She knows everything now."

"How did she take it? I cancelled my appointments and waited in front of her building for hours and she didn't come. Where was she?"

"I don't know. Walking maybe."

Nathan moans. They sit in Ben's living room, questions flying on different tracks, at different speeds. They are deflated. Wrung out.

Anna says, "I'm sorry we dragged you into this, Ben. You've been a good friend to all of us."

Nathan's face is white and drawn. Ben takes his pulse, looks in his eyes. No sign of stroke, steady pulse. He hands Nathan a jigger of Scotch, which Nathan drinks down in one shot.

Nathan stares into the distance. Their voices come to him, but he's trying to salvage some scrap of memory. Then it drops on him, an avalanche of horror. He jumps up. "No. No. Wait. No."

"Nathan." Anna rushes to him. Is he having a seizure?

"Nathan, what is it?" Ben catches his arm, for Nathan has started to move. He's in a great hurry now.

"Don't you see? We have to go back," Nathan cries.

"Go back where?"

"Rosie!" Nathan tries to get past them. "Let me go—" But between them, they hold him back.

"My God," Anna says, loosening her grip on Nathan. "The painting on Rosie's easel. It was cut to ribbons. The knife was still in it."

Nathan howls, breaks free. "It's him. Topinski. I saw him. He'll kill her."

56

Nathan

People walk and talk on Rosie's street, as if nothing is wrong. What's the matter with them, Nathan thinks. He rushes from the cab, Anna following, as Ben pays the driver.

"Dr. Ebanholz, Mrs. Blackwell—" Crystal comes down the block toward them, swathed in her usual black, her hair in a fringed turban. Their fear is palpable. "Is Rose okay?" She sees Ben as he steps away from the cab. So Rose has finally confronted them.

"Let me go first, Nathan," Ben says. "Anna, you wait for the police."

"The police?" Crystal says. "Where's Rosie? What's wrong?"

"Stay here with Anna, Crystal," Ben tells her. He watches Nathan, uneasy. A siren rises over the background noises of the Village street.

They stumble in the pitch darkness as they climb the stairs enveloped by the tortured meowing of a cat. On the second floor landing, someone opens the door, lets loose a flash of light, then closes it, leaving oily smells of fried fish.

Once he gets the feel of the stairs, Nathan sprints like the young man he'd been, faster than Ben, who still favors one leg and takes each step in two movements. He hears the void before her scream. He can't let it happen again. Not again.

Topinski shouting, like that night at the hospital.

He hears his baby's cries, her terror mixing with the howling of the cat.

"Nathan, wait," Ben calls.

But Nathan has waited all his life with more patience than a man should have.

Her door is off its hinges.

He hears the blows. The screaming is done. On the easel is the painting cut to shreds with the knife still caught in the canvas. His hand closes around the handle. It feels good, as a scalpel. As if he is born to it.

"Bitch," Pinto screams, his fists thump, thump, thump against her flesh. "Bitch. Bitch. Who told you to come back?"

Jenny on the floor, crawling, crawling, get away from him, trying to squeeze under her bed, flat as paper. Flatter. Flatter. "Papa!"

"Rosie!" Nathan's voice shrieks in her head like a distant memory.

Pinto yowls, a crazed animal sound.

Repentance comes with the full force of his body.

57

Rose

"Nathan, let me—" Ben tugs at Nathan's arm.

Nathan's pulled the monster from his child and, crouching, holds her close, rocking back and forth. "They've killed my baby," he mutters. "They've killed her."

Rose lies limp in his arms. She is soaked with blood. Ben takes her pulse, holding the thin wrist. He feels faint but steady life. There is so much blood—on Nathan, on Topinski, on Rose. Artery blood.

Bending over Nathan, he says, "Nathan, she's alive. Get her on the bed while I call an ambulance." He stands back.

"She's alive?" Nathan stares up at him. Blood stains his face like a red beard.

Lear and Cordelia. Ben dials the operator.

Rose whimpers when Nathan lays her gently on the crumpled blanket with the cowboys twirling their lariats. "I'm here, Rosie darling. Everything will be all right now." He is frightened by her fragility, by the blood, yet as he examines her, he sees no fresh blood, only swelling, bruises, a broken nose and jaw. He cradles her in his arms. How close he came to losing her.

"I've called the police," Ben says. "St. Vincent's is sending an ambulance."

The building trembles with the upward traffic of the law. Two young cops, Anna and Crystal in their wake.

"Rosie?" Anna cries. Everywhere she looks is blood.

Ben says, "She took a terrible beating, but I think she'll be okay. Physically at least. Nathan saved her life. Topinski is dead. Nathan was right. He was Pinto."

"Oh, dear God," Anna says.

"Lady?" One of the cops calls. "Stay with your daughter while we talk to your husband."

"Not my husband, my brother."

The cops pick through the dead man's pockets. No I.D.

"I killed him," Nathan says. "And I would do it again to save her."

A cop writes in his notebook and another phones the precinct. Homicide. Detectives.

Ben blots blood from Rose's swollen face with a damp washcloth while Anna tries to brush the tangles from the pale blond hair. The smell of death permeates.

"Rose?" A tall young man, another cop, stands in the door. The call for help gave Rose's address. He notes the body on the floor and bends to check the pulse. Rises. "Rose?" he says again. The emotion in his voice informs Ben.

"She'll be all right, I think," Ben says. "Do you know her?"

"Who are you? What happened here?"

"I'm Dr. Benjamin Coopersmith. This is her aunt. Her father, Dr. Nathan Ebanholz. That man on the floor attacked her." Ben's leg gives out on him and he sits on the bed. "I called for an ambulance," he says.

"Who is he?"

"Topinski," Anna says. "He went by the name Topinski years ago. Now he calls himself Skye Pinto."

"The painter?"

Anna nods. She hears Nathan's voice and others in the next room. "Do you know our Rosie?"

"Yes," he says.

"Morrisey—" A cop sticks his head into the room. "Ambulance is here."

The bus takes her over winding country roads on the long ride. Remember this, she tells herself. Remember all of this, for you'll have to find your way back. But then, while she's peering out the window, the bus runs head on into something, and she begins to come apart. Pieces of her fly like Pick-up-Sticks, and without warning, the tunnel swallows her and she is falling. Falling.

"Mama," she cries. "Mama. Mama."

The touch on Rose's hand is so soft she almost thinks she's imagined it. She tries to open her eyes, but cannot. The voice that speaks to her is softer than the hand.

The door to the bus opens for her to get on. "Get on, Jenny," Olga says.

But Jenny doesn't get on because she doesn't have to. The door closes and the bus goes on without her.

And Rose sleeps.

— EPILOGUE —

Zweikel lies on a gurney surrounded by a cotton curtain. Excruciating spasms squeeze his chest like a tight fist over a spaldeen. But he is not afraid. He smells Stella all around him.

He has no recollection of getting here. He remembers only the shadow of someone in front of the newsstand, and then his old mother, of blessed memory, standing there as clear as day. She smiled at him and said his name. "Mendilla," she said, "Zeesilla," and motioned to him. He stood up to go to her and that was all until now.

Pain thunders through him, stampeding his heart, followed by waves of nausea. He should never have eaten the knubblewurst sandwich.

Someone comes with a cold stethoscope and tells him to breathe deep, but it hurts too much so he gives up. Why don't they leave him be?

He wants to be alone again with the smell. Stella's smell.

"Mr. Zeekal," Stella says. "Can you hear me?"

Why does she call him Mr. Zeekal? He tries to correct her but can't say the words. He opens his eyes. A nurse is looking down at him. She has blond hair under her ruffled cap. She speaks to him in Stella's voice, but he knows. Joy suffuses him. He reaches up to touch her face. "Irene," he says.

Another nurse comes into the room.

"Irene," he repeats, with a big sigh, like air slowly let from a balloon.

He is smiling when his heart stops.

The nurse closes his eyes and folds one hand over the other on his thin chest. She takes the sheet the student hands her and covers him head to foot.

"Did you know him?" the trainee whispers. It is her first dead patient and she is anxious.

"No," the nurse says.

"Then how did he know your name?"

Irene shrugs. She has another emergency to deal with in the next cubicle. "It doesn't matter anymore," she says.

— ABOUT THE AUTHOR —

ANNETTE MEYERS has a long history on both Broadway and Wall Street. On Wall Street, she spent sixteen years as an executive search consultant, and since 1996, has been an arbitrator with the National Association of Securities Dealers (NASD). On Broadway, she was assistant to Broadway director-producer Hal Prince for sixteen years, working with him on such productions as: *A Funny Thing Happened on the Way to the Forum, Fiddler on the Roof, Cabaret, A Little Night Music, Company,* and *Follies.*

Murder Me Now, Meyers' latest novel, is the second book in a new series set in Greenwich Village, in 1920, featuring Olivia Brown, a young woman poet based loosely on Edna St. Vincent Millay.

Meyers is also the author of seven published Smith and Wetzon mysteries, *The Big Killing Tender Death, The Deadliest Option, Blood on the Street, Murder: The Musical, These Bones Were Made For Dancin',* and *The Groaning Board.*

Meyers' short stories have appeared in the anthologies *Murder for Mother, Malice Domestic 4, Lethal Ladies, Vengeance Is Hers,* in the German anthology, *Skrupellose Fische.* Her story "You Don't Know Me," which appeared in *Flesh & Blood,* (Mysterious Press, 2001), was chosen by guest editor James Ellroy as one of the twenty American mystery stories of the year and has been reprinted in Houghton Mifflin's annual anthology, *The Best American Mystery Stories 2002.* Her books have been published in

German and Spanish.

She is a former president of Sisters in Crime and is current president of the International Association of Crime Writers, North America. Other organization memberships include: Mystery Writers of America, The Authors Guild, Private Eye Writers of America.

Her Web site address is: www.meyersmysteries.com.